Rescue
the Lonely

R. A. Milner

Cover Art by Olivia Milner

Dedication

To my siblings: Olivia and Matthew.

The ones who have taught me to be nothing less than extraordinary and for having my back every step in the way in everything that I do. I am proud to call both of you my siblings and cannot wait to share more adventures with you too.

Episode Selection (Table of Contents)

Prologue

This is my first time attempting to write anything, let alone a novel. I assume that it is not very hard because there are millions of people out there who have written books. All it appears to be is getting thoughts or ideas from your brain and transmitting them to paper. When I think of transmitting intel, I immediately pull up data on Morse code. Morse code is a method of transmitting text information through a series of on-off tones, lights, or clicks. Morse code is not as popular as it used to be back in World War 1 through the use of telegraphs. Nowadays though the invention of the radio, Morse code is only used in various professions, including piloting and air traffic control. If everything the teachers in school taught me was correct, then the captain of the Titanic sent out an SOS through a telegraph the night it sank. Soldiers in World War 1 used Morse code to send artillery coordinates to base from the battlefield to bomb the enemy.

My mother has to use Morse code every time before entering my room. It is her train ticket, if you will, to board the train. It is a sequence of knocks and extensive pounds at the door. If she does not do the secret knock, I become very upset and tell her to get out until she does it correctly. The only time that she did not do it was on the night of June 17th. She did not even bother to do the knocking. She was so upset with me that day. I do not know why she made a big deal out of nothing. I was sitting in class one day being my normal self, but for some reason, I was attracting a lot of attention that day. Mother continuously tries to explain to me why I got escorted to the office that day, but I refuse to listen, because in my mind; I know I was acting perfectly normal that day.

What is normal? What is average? There is no precise meaning for these words. But the way everybody explains it is that these two words coincide with each other. Meaning that they have the same meaning as the other. From what people tell me, being normal/average is being with society. It is the act of not walking in the other direction, if you will, acting, talking, and thinking like everybody else does in society. I do not like society for one big reason: *change.* Society continues to change daily with upgraded technology and ridiculous phrases. I want to walk the other way from society. I do not to be completely excluded from it, but rather walk the other way that people are not traveling. The road untraveled.

The only person who will travel with me on this road does not fall into the category of friends or family. No. They believe that it is "absurd." That the only way that I can succeed is to fall in line with society and follow their tracks. But I object and will not believe any of that nonsense! And Amadeus: my personal sidekick, will assist me in my travels. He always tells me that I am destined to do anything once I put my mind to it. I ask him how far I can go on my journey, but he always seems to respond the same. "Do not travel far enough that you lose your sense of direction." I have had the pleasure of meeting Amadeus on the 11th of March 2007, three months and six days prior to the incident in class. Mother had taken me to visit Amadeus for my troubles. His office was located about 45 minutes away from my place of residency. It was a very small building with circular windows, each 12 diameters apart from each other. The door was painted to a red complexion, and to this very day, I continue to not like the color red for superstitious reasons. I suggested that the building would change the color of the door to blue rather than red. They do not seem to care about the customer's complaints, so in my book, they have the worst customer service. The first time I met this man, there seemed to be something very off-putting about him. He smelled very strange and looked extremely silly, almost unprofessional. I was very afraid. I begged Mother to turn around in her tracks and walk out the door with me just so I did not have to see this strange man. She did not listen and pushed me on through the automatic sliding doors.

Amadeus led me to a very colorful room, one with various shades of blues and yellows. All different kinds of animals from the safari were painted on the walls. Just to name a few: lions, hippos, and giraffes. There was a bean bag, which was the first one that I had ever sat on. I liked it, not only because it was blue. But also, because it was very comfortable. Amadeus reentered the room with a clipboard; what was on that clipboard, I did not know. He pushed his glasses back up on the ridge of his nose then proceeded to stare at the clipboard. All I could focus on was that bright red building across the street. It was driving me mad; there has to be a way to eliminate that color from my vision.

Amadeus cleared his throat. "Sophia, right? Tell me, do you know why you are meeting with me today?" I sat there very quiet and very nervous because this was one of the few instances where I did not know what to expect. Whenever I get nervous or anxious, I begin to spell out my name with my hands. I did not confirm or deny my identity. I purposely made it a guessing game for him. But I believe that he is telepathic, I never have to say anything, and he already knows what I am thinking. This happens every single time I come to see him now!

He said, "You are here because your mother is very worried about you. Your condition is becoming more severe and I can help you with that. I am positive that I can help you with your disability because I am trained to help kids like you."

While continuously looking at that obnoxious building from across the way, I finally gave in and spoke to him. I was bound to do it sometime. I looked at him very sternly. "Do not call it that, I despise people who use words like-" It hurts me to the bone just thinking about it, let alone speaking it. "disability or illness. I also do not like literary contractions. So, if you follow those two rules of mine, we will get along just fine."

His eyes opened and he fell back in his seat, surprised that I had finally spoken after 20 minutes of me being there. "Thank you for correcting me; I appreciate that. I won't -will not- use any more contractions from this day forward. Now.... we need a new name to identify the illness. Sorry, thing that you possess."

I saw him ponder that word for a while. His face lit up and asked if I was interested in superheroes. I shrugged my shoulders. I was not interested in them, but I was not opposed to them. I guess I am neutral on the subject. Then Amadeus suggested *"Superpower."* I was unsure of that term, but later, he explained the importance. He said, not everyone has superpowers, only the selected few; prophecy states that they are destined for greatness. When he put it that way, it sounded quite alright.

Before Amadeus could say another word, I stood up from the bean bag and rotated the mirror. The mirror was the type of mirror that was very long and could see your entire body. He started to question my actions, but he soon caught on. He asked why I did not like the color red. I explained that whenever I see red, I seem to have a bad day and because of it, my superpower worsens.

It is strange how we meet people for the first time, and the initial thoughts consist of lividness or judgment. Though after time, the views of those people are now replaced by pleasant views. Have you ever had a friend… or even a family member that you totally despised and wanted to get away from at all costs, then after being with them for a fair amount of time, you realized that you were a fool to judge them on-site without knowing a thing about them? The problem with humans is that we tend to place ourselves upon the pedestal without realizing; I fall short of this too. The only way that I can fix my problem is to clear my brain and listen to the other person. I believe that this can be very difficult at first, but after doing it a few times, it comes naturally to me. Then I can become the best person I can be.

Why is change so constant? Why is it a part of our daily lives? Why can we not shine the light on the conservatives for a second? I am very opposed to change, I would not admit that I have Obsessive Compulsive Disorder, but I have an odd obsession with keeping things on repeat. Why do I do this and not branch out more? Is it the very same reason why I am here today? I know every part, every second, and moment of every day because nothing will go out of line for as long as I am present.

How does the viewer perceive me? Do they think I am bound to a wheelchair or hooked up to a ventilator, thus having severe medical problems? Is it because I go and visit Amadeus that I am broken? Answer me that! I will not reveal what I look like underneath. The thought of imagining what I look like is so much more exciting. The only way that the reader can "see" me, is through my actions depicted right here in the novel. I will make it simple, so you do not have to think so hard, just picture yourself. That is all that you have to do, whatever I am doing, replace me with you.

Why am I just now starting to write a novel and in hopes someday to start a revolution? First off, it is just me in this lone, sad world of mine. No one takes the time to dissect me. To pick up a scalpel and dig into my brain to see what makes me tick. Secondly, there is something about putting pen to paper that I can get with no other activity. The entire aspect of you being the author and making it up as you go; there are no things to memorize, no formulas, no dates. The reason that I enjoy it so much is because I am talking to myself. It is very similar to taking Tylenol on a sick day. But imagine that feeling all the time. The feeling of a burst of energy rippling down the spine and up again to the brain, giving it loads of ideas and thoughts. I talk to myself more than usual, sometimes I catch myself doing it aloud. But I do not retreat to normalcy. Having a conversation with yourself is the best form of entertainment. Things, facts, thoughts that were buried down deep inside now get washed up onto the surface. Studies have proven to show that people who generally talk to themselves are more capable of doing more with their minds than others. For entertainment reasons and intellectual reasons, that is why I talk to myself.

The title is not said and done; I still have a lot more revisions I have to attend too. But for now, the title is okay with me. *Rescue the Lonely*; what does that mean? *Exactly* mean? I do not have an isolated answer for you. I am deeply sorry, but I will explain what it means to *me*. Hypothetically speaking, the *Lonely* are the ones who are more advanced than everyone else, more superior if you will. Every *Lonely* person on this earth lacks heavily in at least one major area, whether that be mind, body, or soul. For the slow readers, I struggle deep in the soul and mind. I know I have a case that people like to identify as awkwardness. I reply that I am not awkward; I am just internally insecure.

Episode IV:
The Shackles That Hold

What is it about getting a new puppy that is so exhilarating and exciting? Is it the thought that you can afford to feed one more at the table? Or the concept of responsibility? "Oh daddy, please, please, pleeeeease, may we get a puppy?" That is how every conversation starts. Is it not? The aspect of taking care of a pet is more excruciating than the child thinks. In the end, the father takes care of the dog. The dog is actually the one giving orders to the humans. They do one of two things to get their point across: sit and begin to stare or they can bark until you give in to their demands. The thing that always baffles me is that dogs are watched more than humans are. Some of the people out there in the world are exponentially dumber than dogs. Dogs are those types of animals in which humans love or hate. But the ones who hate dogs have not had the full experiences of life yet.

Thus welcoming Mr. Parker into the world, August Parker, to be precise. August Parker was born five years prior to my existence, the year that Bill Clinton got elected for the second term, the year that jazz singer Ella Fitzgerald died, the same year of the birth of archaeologist and tomb raider, Lara Croft. He lives across the country from where I am now, 2,437 miles away to be exact. It is roughly a six-hour plane ride from my place of residency to his. Mr. Parker was put on the earth for a purpose. For what reason? He does not know yet, but he will, when the situation presents itself.

Every good story starts in a place of origin, and mine will be no different. 5:45 pm on October the fourth occupied this wonder of a person, yet nobody knew it yet. He was born in the same city that used to be the capital of California but is now home to both the hockey team "Sharks" and the soccer team "Earthquakes." He is very lucky to be born in such a marvel of a city, compared to me on the other side of the spectrum. I am confined to a city that contains ten letters in its name, the very same city that established *Graeter's Ice Cream* and *Skyline Chili*.

August was born substantially smaller than all of the other babies, one of the tiniest humans I have ever seen in my life. When the doctors weighed him, he was only one pound one ounce. Doctors and nurses rushed in to save the boy's life. They immediately operated on him so he could breathe correctly. I do not know how someone has a hard time breathing. It is only the movement of your diaphragm in and out. I can do it without thinking sometimes. If he needs help breathing, I would be more than happy to be his tutor. Do you know that scene in *Star Wars: A New Hope* when Luke and the gang are in the garbage chute on the

Death Star? His birth was like that, but 1000 times more real, with actual people.

I know what some of you are thinking, why did I pick this character to be so far away from where I am? Why does he have to live halfway across the United States? California is one place that I want to visit more than anything. Everything is perfect there, from the weather to the people. Mother says I cannot travel to California ever because of my superpower. She informs me to avoid flying all around. I have never been on an airplane before, let alone seen one in motion. Although I truly want to visit California one day, I do not want to travel by airplane. The chances of dying in a plane crash are 1 in 9.2 million. I do not feel comfortable with those odds.

I have discussed traveling to California with Amadeus at times, but he seems to think it is a foolish decision. Why is it that everybody has the freedom to reign except for me? I have devised of a game plan and ran it by him multiple times but to no avail. I am not sure if I will ever get a chance to visit my desired destination. Sometimes when I have writer's block like I am experiencing right now, fantasies of California flood my mind. I will do anything for these thoughts to disappear and try and get back on track. I usually end up doing extensive amounts of research to know everything there is to know about it. A couple of days ago, while I was surfing the web, San Francisco appeared and caught my eye. Of course, I have heard of San Francisco before, but no knowledge of it whatsoever. Whatever day that was, change was occurring.

Now that I reflect on that day, it was going to be a bad one from the beginning. When I awoke from my slumber, I witnessed abundant dark shades of red slithering down the side of my bed. I have never been so worried in my life. I for sure thought I was going to enter the afterlife that day. I examined all of the possible ways of entry. C3PO was covered in blotches of *it* that exploded from an unknown point of entry. As I arose from the upper level in a panic, my head slammed against the ceiling. More of this liquid now ran from my head onto *me*! But surprisingly, I did not make any commotion in all of this pandemonium. Locking the door after a slam, I went to work. To avoid any confusion about the size of him, C3PO is roughly one foot give or take, or 12 inches if you want to get technical. It took me 53 minutes to pristine him. I have to keep track of the time in order to make room for my daily challenges. Challenges help me become productive throughout the day; for instance, today's was to adjust the lighting in my room. He had it all over, in his gold miraculous eyes, the wiring at his abdomen, but the worst part was on his left arm. All of it eventually washed up EXCEPT for the arm. I am upset about this, very much to this day.

The sinkhole that is San Francisco attracts people for one reason: profit. Residency seems unbearable over there. There are massive amounts of people. I do not do well in crowds; I could barely attend having guests over at the house. People make me so anxious, with all of their stupid chit chat. They come up to me and ask how I am doing and what I have been doing lately. My answers will always remain the same, no matter the circumstance. "I am doing the same as you, surviving through life." People are interesting creatures; they need to have a sense of community or importance to feel like they are of any self-worth. Obviously, every living organism in the universe survives on food and water, but humans are most dependable upon acceptability. If somebody is not accepted by the race in power, it can turn undeniably evil.

Acceptance is the factor that gets humans up in the morning. People go to work, go to school, go volunteer their time, go out in public, knowing 100% they are accepted by society. However, there are also those who exist within the margins. People who are either rejected or are unsure where they lie. I know so much about this because I fall into this category of misfits: *"The Lonely."* People are like turtles, especially the "privileged" or "accommodated" like me. Hiding in shells waiting for somebody, anybody, to pear in. My people are built on victims of any kind, have gone through any trauma, and, most importantly, have a remarkable *superpower*.

No human is born with acceptance. They have to earn it the way August Parker did. Although evil factors did play into his early childhood, he never let that define him. You can imagine someone being born this small, had some life-defining issues. Such as every mother would, August's mother wanted to hold her newborn, but fate had something else in store. He was immediately these doctors' main priority. They put him on the operating table and began to work. Remember how he was born with a breathing deformity? Well, they pro-longed that issue by installing something called a tracheostomy. From what I have discovered, it is a tube that is inserted at the base of the neck, and he can breathe like that. The inhale of oxygen and exhale of carbon dioxide come out of the neck rather than the nose or mouth like everybody else. Although that was one major problem dealt with, it was not the only one. In addition to the apparatus equipped in his neck, he also had to get a feeding tube in the upper left level of his large intestine and a fundoplication to halt reflux from entering his fragile throat. My August was not going to be a beacon to the world, and I will address that even more as the story progresses.

Now that he has to deal with that contraption in his throat, that also means that he is unable to speak. In that case, he uses sign language in order to communicate. Since sign language has never been a primary form of communication in any country, it is only applicable to acknowledge that nobody can understand him. It is such a foreign and underused form of communication that it is almost as outdated as Egyptian hieroglyphics. I have never seen anybody discuss this form of communication, let alone seen it on television at all! The only people that I could imagine that benefit from it are the hearing impaired.

Finally, at age 1, August was able to enter the "world." No more of being constantly monitored *in* the hospital. Nothing changed much once August finally came home. It was the same routine of constant eyes on him at all times, but now at least he has a new environment. If I were in August's situation, I would not mind it too much. We are like the same person. He likes the indoors, and so do I. Some would say that we were made for each other.

Like a dog on a leash, he could only go as far as the wires would let him—no running around the house like an ordinary child. But August did not need or want to be ordinary. Deep down, all he wanted was for him to be himself. That is exactly what he did, too, when he met his first companion. Mr. and Mrs. Parker purchased a dog for their son, and immediately it changed his life. I am not good with dogs because I have never had one, and I do not think there are any nice dogs out there. All of the ones that I have encountered are frightening and intimidating. August's dog was different, though. This one never barked and never complained. He was loyal and empathetic towards his owners.

Once August was old enough to process the world around him, he recognized that he does not have to walk the tightrope of life alone. His mother was holding his baby brother in her stomach. August Parker has some gigantic shoes to fill, being a role model? How can he do that when the only things he has ever known from this point are oxygen tanks and a language so difficult it might as well be Morse code?

Mother enters my room through the same series of knocks she does every time, to warn me that we are leaving for Amadeus' in 10 minutes. I acknowledge her warning then proceed to finish up the remaining paragraph. From previous encounters, she usually leaves the door open a crack then is on a wild goose chase for her keys, but today was different. She saw something she was not supposed too.

"Sophia! What is that you have there? It is right there under your pillow. Don't let me repeat myself!" Mother seems livid today; might be something she had for breakfast.

"I cannot do it!! Stop! Stop! Stop! Stop! All of you. Disappear!" I quickly say to myself. There is no sympathy when I am in control. Why did she say that word?! Is she trying to torture me? I tell her to get out and to ignore it. It is none of her business, this is my room, and everything in it belongs to me.

That only get her angrier too, then shuffles around my room for more of a reason to get me in trouble. She does the worst thing ever, grabs Threepio, and hides him from me. I get very upset when someone touches Threepio, let alone kidnaps him. Everything is very accurate and precise when it comes to my arena. Next to the door is my bed; it is an AT-AT bunk bed. You know, the giant walkers in *The Empire Strikes Back*. When I lay in my bed, I have to pull the hatch for the capsule to close. I made this all by myself with no help at all. It looks phenomenal! At least that is what I tell myself to feel superior. Mother did the majority of the work. But Mother is not as big of a fan of it as I am. A big clunky waste of space is what she says. I just turn the other cheek and do not let it get the best me. A capsule was always the necessary plan for the bed. Since it can never be an exact replica, it might as well be 95% accurate with my distinct touch. Confined spaces have opposed as a threat to me. Cramped with barely any wiggle room is where my revolutionary ideas manifest. I have yet to devise a plausible reason as to why people fear tight places with restricted movement. On ground level, we have the desk where August Parker and I go to "spend time together." That is also where C3PO was. Even See-Threepio gets lonely on that elevated plank of wood, I know because I ask him. I need something else to make my blank space more alive.

It is overwhelmingly impossible for me to obtain any outcome of a friendship. Everybody at school is convinced that I have some sort of plague and avoids me in the halls. The only respectable people on campus are the staff. How come grown-ups are exponentially nicer than children? Is it because all grown-ups know what kids are going through? At break and lunchtime, I invariably return to my second-period history course to accompany my professor. There, nobody can make fun of me. Nobody has a clue where I am during these 20- and 30-minute increments of time. I have no friends, except for Amadeus. He is the one person who understands me and is always eager to see me every week. I must be his best friend too, because he keeps scheduling me to come back every week.

"High and mighty." This phrase has always puzzled me ...until now. Now I know what it means when people say it. I only wish I had the upper hand here. Why do parents get to be the king and queens over their worthless peasant children? Yes, I do understand; but it is not fair. I cannot wait until I have kids of my own one day so I can be in authority and be a role model for someone. If I had the authority, I would recapture C3PO and get back what was abruptly stolen from me. Mother did not see much of the orange bottle; I made sure of it. This is one thing she can never find out. The one and only exception is if I tell her from beyond the grave....

Episode V:
Friend or Foe

There are no instructions for life. Jump right into a world full of locked doors. Novels are supposed to consist of chapters. Correct? But how long are the chapters supposed to be? Two pages, five, thirteen, sixteen, thirty-three, forty-four?!?! How is one to write a novel with no set direction? I am fully aware that the previous chapters were not long at all; it was more of a test run if you will. My end goal for this novel, created by me, Sophia Collins, is to be a century defining masterpiece with an appropriate page quantity. Page quantity is hard enough, but defining an entire chapter based upon the content within is another level. We give proper objects a title as a way of identifying something. But this is more complex when speaking in the realm of literature. Before reading a single word, the chapter is there to let the reader know how far they are into the story and to set the tone with a subtitle.

Every Tuesday is usually the same routine, but today is different. Mother did not blow me a kiss or say, "I love you" before dropping me off at Amadeus'. I exit the vehicle, then she drives off. There is nothing in the world that I would have done to make Mother fumigate. I am a good little girl; I never get anybody agitated. Just ask C3PO, he will tell you. I walk in as scheduled, not a moment too early or nor too late. Always before the seriousness starts, I always observe the fish and hermit crabs over by the window. The red building across the street can never divert my attention from marine life. I can comprehend the importance and value of the red building holding the red trucks inside, but can their color please be something else other than the color of blood coming in contact with oxygen? When blood is in a closed system like a mammal, the blood is dark red or as I like to think, blue. But when it rises to the surface, oxygen latches onto it and turns it from a dark red to bright red. Amadeus has all sorts of life in the tank. For starters, he has every kind of fish possible: Angelfish, Blue Tang, Clownfish, various species of Betta fish and guppies. But nothing can compare to the racoon butterfly. For those uneducated, the Raccoon Butterfly is a passive Hawaiian originated fish which also resembles Threepio in an astonishing way. The fish is similar in color and is very intelligent like him, but the two now have two major distinctions. C3PO has a red arm, and Raccoon Butterflies wear a mask. Though I do not actually believe it is a mask, it surely mirrors one.

Common knowledge on fish is effortless for me; I can open the fish file in my brain and instantly read off any facts. However, hermit crabs are a different story. In order to understand these sand creatures, I had to fish out some facts. The brain works identical to a personal computer; files are stored then accessed in the brain. Whenever a topic is brought up, the brain explores all locations for that specific file. However, the time it takes is instantaneous. Then all the information on the topic of discussion is at the click of a button. Fish facts have always come naturally to me. It must be because of my wide obsession with them. Thus, fish would, without a doubt, top on my list of which animals I would choose to own.

Hermit crabs used to be despicable, boring little rebel scums! However, my initial view on these shallow, diffident creatures has changed throughout the days of our sessions. The word hermit is essential to the crab's name because of its action to venture from one living quarter to another. The shell on its back is used as protection in addition to regulating body fluids. It seems like the shell is not useless after all and not used as just decoration. In similar tastes to humans, crabs get unsatisfied with their place of residency, too; when this goes on, they pack up their things in search of a new shell. My house is all that I have ever known. I have never moved locations at all; I do not want to. Although, I am quite curious, about what it is like to leave your old life behind with previous memories never being able to be replayed again; I doubt it will ever happen to me. After digging in the sand for an appropriate amount of time, the hermit crab's life expectancy can be anywhere from 15-40 years! That is almost as old as Mother! For being such minuscule creatures, they sure do live considerably longer.

Though I do think it is very peculiar that the trucks never leave this red building. Is that not what they are supposed to do whenever somebody calls in? Maybe nobody knows their phone number? Who would not know their phone number, though, it is the easiest one out there? For an abundance of trucks, never have I ever seen a soul enter or exit the building. It must be currently vacant for the time being. Dalmatians are a key part of that occupation, not to mention the mascot of the profession. Dalmatians are fascinating rescue animals; they are one of the few if not only, dogs layered in spots. They are one of the *"Lonely,"* which by itself is a very intriguing fact.

Amadeus finally enters the room with the clipboard and sits in his normal spot as he always does, the far right end of the interestingly shaped sofa, while I make myself comfortable in that blue bean bag that I told you about last time. Like I said before, I do all of my observations before the man in charge walks in, then the session really begins. I have learned to become more confident and comfortable around Amadeus from the first initial time. Before, I was very angry and scared of him, but now the opposite effect is happening. The man first starts off by asking me how my days and weeks are going. This is a loaded question by my definition; it could have a multitude of possibilities. I should be cautious at what comes out of my mouth next; I do not want to unload on him right away.

"You want to know about my day. Well then, this Tuesday has been extremely confusing, and I am uncertain that it will get any better. As for the total seven days that we have not seen each other: Tuesday to Tuesday, let me admit there is no escape from the labyrinth." I wait and watch as he perplexes my loaded answer. Dying to see how he would respond and what advice he will give me.

He is taking an uncomfortably extended pause; I must have stumped him to the core on this one. By first adjusting his glasses following a glance at the plank of wood, he calls a clipboard. The sounds that form into words are not what I am expecting at all. "Where is your companion? Did he take an arrow to the knee? R2D2 cannot survive long without his sidekick." Sneaking a half-smile, my anger begins to dwindle some. We have this running joke. I am R2 while Threepio is...well himself. I dislike being R2; I would like to remain as Sophia. Thank you very much.

It is still very difficult for me to discuss; I have to make a conscious effort to remind myself that I was conscious, and this was reality now. Explaining it to Amadeus was not an easy task at all, catching myself choking up more than anticipated. Shedding some light on mine and Mothers confrontation, he finally understands why my little friend is missing in action (MIA). I know what he is going to ask next, but I will not reveal that just yet. Stay firm, and hopefully, he will abandon the topic.

Exceedingly agitated and concerned now, he asks the dreadful question. Staring into my eyes the exact same way I do at August Parker, but with the intent of different emotional feelings, he urges me to admit to what my protocol droid is hiding. I tell him I cannot fully release all the details because I do not know what it is exactly either. The only thing I reveal is that it is stolen property, and the owner does not need them as badly as I do. No one knows the details of the medication except the patient and me, who shall remain nameless for now.

Appall is a poor word choice when it comes to the expression I witness. I can tell he wants to continue this discussion, to finally be able to play 20 questions with someone. I most certainly would accompany him, but I am not feeling up to it. This is classified information that cannot get exposed. Exposure cannot be the end product of the day. Distractions cloud the mind to a point where I once again, possess control. While still being baffled at the earlier conversation probably, I tell my best friend about my latest creation.

Containment of the supernatural ability which I possess has proven to be more of a challenge than anything. Amadeus is providing me with tips and pointers on what to do when it acts up again. Maybe tips and pointers are the incorrect phrases to use, rather, suggestions. He gives me an acronym which 1 enjoy; B.L.U.E.

1)<u>B</u>ANISH *the rage*
2)<u>L</u>EAVE *the area*
3)<u>U</u>PHOLD *one's own foundation*
4)<u>E</u>XHALE

Never thought of using an acronym before, most likely because I could never think of one. The only concern that I have with this helpful tool is with the letter U. What sense of the word "uphold" is he using? I will never know for sure, but it may allude to what my values are and what I cherish in this short life we have together. We; being identified as Amadeus and me or everybody who has interacted with me, including the reader.

As I proceed to share my novel, he seems extremely intrigued or flabbergasted. I am not good with expressions of the face; it might as well be one of my many weaknesses. If it is intriguing, then I am pleasantly pleased. Glad to be showing off my true potential. However, if flabbergasted is the verb he is referring to, then I am deeply concerned. Has no autistic girl done anything achievable in their lifetime? Am I another broken member of society?! No. I am extraordinary; I am beautiful. I am unique. I have not been placed on this planet to change the world. No. I am unsure of my destiny, but I am certain that I am not going to waste it away with the expectation that "mutants" are disgusting misfits.

From our first encounter, Amadeus gave my condition the title; *superpower*. None of my interests remotely consist of superpowers, but I began to do some investigating of my own after that. I found the only universal topic that I enjoy out of all comics superheroes are mutants with the addition of the X-Men. Mutants live among ordinary humans in the Marvel Universe who possess extraordinary abilities that can be used on either side of the karma spectrum. Mutants look human for the most part, though there are some exceptions. Mutants have lived among the humans for as long as man has existed, and they are not going away anytime soon. In other words, a mutant can be another term used as *"Lonely."*

Our 45 minutes are almost up, and I refuse to answer any more of his questions for now. I have to wait for his dismissal, and then I am free to look at the fish again. In conclusion to our intimate conversations, I bring up the red building one last time. I want answers to ease my mind but only silence filters through the air. Where did Amadeus say he bought this bean bag again? It is one of my ultimate favorites. If I can recall correctly, he purchased it a few years back in a warehouse store in which I forgot the name.

Numerous times I have searched for a blue bean bag like this, made of cotton, though none to my avail. Leather is the only texture the online stores have in stock. I must be searching for something in the search engine incorrectly, or either bean bags of that particular style are not in demand. From the bag's angle, I have the necessities of the room in my vision. Though at this particular moment in time, the fish call me over to them, especially the racoon butterfly. These guys are so gorgeous and beautiful; I cannot seem to ever get enough of them. The routine they have is surprisingly simple and looks like it requires almost no effort. First, traveling through the castle structure Amadeus and I installed the previous time I visited, then through the spewing bubbling treasure chest, next up to the filter in search for who knows what, and finally plays as the pay troll under the castle bridge. Tensions began to boil as Mother retrieves me. Mother has to call me at least five times before eventually looking up. With only mouthing, "Hurry it up." I know that it is time to depart. Compact schedules are one of many activities where procrastination is a viable option. However, I do not want to push my luck any more today than I already have. Running to him with arms wide open, embracing him banishes the rage and worries of my world. It will not be long until I see Amadeus again, another seven-day wait to be precise.

This concept of waiting reminds me of the tragic event to occur on Cloud City on the planet Bespin in *The Empire Strikes Back*, though there are many instances depicted in that episode. For starters, Luke gets his arm severed from his body. Next, Darth Vader reveals that he is

Luke Skywalker's father. Then, Solo is encased in carbonite, Lando betrayed Han. I am sure the reader gets the idea. However, the instance I am referring to is when C3PO aimlessly wanders into the junk room infested with Ugnaughts. Referencing the timeline, Luke is still in the mists of his Jedi training with Grand Master Yoda on Dagobah. While Han and the others land on Bespin in search of his long-time friend, Lando Calrissian. Lando Calrissian then leads the clan minus C3PO into a trap with Luke and Leia's father, though unbeknownst to them at this time. As curious as this protocol droid is, he sure does have a reputation of getting into trouble. He gets spotted by the worker Ugnaughts, dressed in their blue overalls. Screaming and frantically disassembling my dear friend in hopes of incineration. It is hilarious how they thought they could triumph, taking in all the factors, the probability of success is 4:15, or more appropriately displayed 26.7%. The Ugnaughts are not victorious. Chewbacca then storms into the incinerator room with the intention of a daring rescue. Retrieving all parts then attaches C3PO's fully functioning head with torso to Chewbacca's back in order to reunite with the then prisoner Han Solo.

There is no precise date telling how long aliens have been living among the humans, but one thing is quite certain, something drives them in order to stay. Motives can range from any sort of desire from a loved one or an thought that is in the works. For most war stories, motives rely on family members and the dream of reuniting with them once again. War can accumulate an abundance of thoughts and motives to get soldiers through the next day. Comprehending all the information given, humans are also similar to aliens in retrospect to motives. Humans need something to look forward to in order to rise from their deep sleep every day. My reason for waking from a cavernous slumber every day has been viciously stolen from me. I have had access to the capsule prior to writing this novel. It has gotten me through everything from my episodes to homing in on my thoughts. It works best when I am writing, of course.

Extremely accessible is an understatement; it comes easy for some people, however. I watch them as they approach the pharmacist and sign papers in exchange for the very one thing I so desperately need. Recalling the name is harder than I thought. Glancing at the bottle from time to time again to recognize the name of whatever I am ingesting would have been an intelligent decision. Though I cannot remember the name, I do, however, remember everything else about it. Split down the half forms a two-tone orange and clear side. The orange is not a dark orange either, more like the color of a grapefruit. Inscriptions are visible on both ends of the pill; orange reads 30 milligrams while the clear side contains the name with an XR symbol.

Seeing what is inside of the capsule is both interesting with conflicting feelings of terror. I have only peered into it, never have I stared at it for more than 5 seconds. Usually gripping it from the clear side, then to only look at the orange milligram end. Ingestion is the most exciting part because I know what is going to occur. However, the first time was anything but exciting. I took it by accident. Activation starts from anywhere to 30 minutes to one hour. From what is apparent, my effects are drastically longer than in other cases. I began to focus extremely well with the added benefit of cat-like reflexes. Severe cases include degradation of the muscle, in addition to the mind entering a state of consistent delusions and hallucinations. Nothing terrible can and will happen to me; I am the new hope, restoring the world from its brokenness. I will never reach the point of no return.

Unlike my uneventful day, August had something to look forward to, at least. A messenger from above or below has never been at my disposal. What is it like to have an older or younger sibling? From what I can fathom, it can be a blessing, and at other times, a curse. From an older sibling's perspective, they are the ones to experience the unknowns of life firsthand in hopes to report what they have learned so far in their journey. Though as a younger sibling, they have a constant mentor in their mists. To be the one to teach from right or wrong; at least *their* viewpoint on what is right. No one can prepare to be a parent; it is just a sequence of trial and error; the same can be said for becoming an older sibling. Rulebooks and guidelines are out for grabs, but how many actually snatch those? Some say the siblings are the other half's better portion or best friend. If that is true, I am in need of one straight away. Mr. Parker was ecstatic when he witnessed his little brother for the first time. A name was never devised at this moment, though it was in the process. One thing is certain; as soon as he looked into his brother's incognito eyes, he was and will be forever R2D2, while C3PO will continuously get him out of continuous trouble.

August was very hesitant about going into the room where his life would be changed forever. What if the baby did not like him? What if he cannot live up to the definition of a brother? All possible concerns flooded his mind with a constant reminder of what would happen if he fails. Wrapped only in a bathroom towel and embraced by his mother, the baby stared back at this soon to be an undeniably familiar face. Inching closer and closer to the bedside, August laid his hands on his brother.   Placing a hand starting from the forehead then making his way to the back of the hair, the baby did not scream or have any concerns.

Once the baby was able to be released, August gave him the grand tour of his room. Though there was not much to show, his room mostly consisted of medical equipment like oxygen tanks and spare parts for his tracheostomy. But what did his brother know? He thought this is how the average person lived. Communication was going to be a difficult concept for his brother to understand. There is a time and place for that, just not here. Before any sort of communication was devised, a name had to be established. Oliver. August enjoyed that name exceedingly. It had a nice ring to it. August and Oliver, or Oliver and August. *"The new inseparable pair."* As the pair grew older, the communication issue began to weigh on August greatly. Oliver became so attached to his older brother that he almost chose not to speak like his parents at most times in order to feel the connection. Using his hands more than he did his mouth, their parents began to be concerned for Oliver as he spoke less frequently.

Frankly, I would be opposed to becoming mute; words are not my specialty anyway. The only interactions I engage in are with Mother, Amadeus, and C3PO. Even when it comes to academics, the only sound students and staff hear from me is the sound of carbon dioxide, leaving my system or my writing implement making contact with spiral-bound notebook paper. School is an exemplary hostile area, full of cruel munchkins and admins. Teachers do not go out of their way at all to assist students, only to help themselves. If someone is struggling, they ask them if they were listening to the lesson! That is not considered teaching at all! I would be the best authority figure; I would explicitly go out of my way to assist my students. I would not want to see any of them fail because of my ignorance. However, I have not been called to become a teacher; that profession is for wiser, more extroverted people that fit the criteria. Nothing in the education field is screaming at me, other than the kids in the hall. They are jealous of what their inconceivable minds do not apprehend. Bullies only exist to those who will let them. Hypothetically speaking, if hostel and horrid comments were disregarded, bullies would be eradicated. In similarity to a horsefly, a bully needs a host to feed on. No host present means nothing is being consumed.

The effects are wearing off; I can feel the capsule leaving my system. The cancellation of sound becomes less apparent as the third scene reunites with my humanoid body. Never knowing how long it has been is a scary and mysterious feeling all within itself. The last thing I remember is visiting Amadeus and then returning home. Nothing about a change of clothes then strapping in this chair glued to a piece of paper.

My memory is somewhat veggie, but I do not recall having an extra capsule at my disposal. Where did this one come from? Or did I even take what I think I did?

Episode VI:
Vulnerable

Severe shaking and loss of control. Eyes roll in the back of the head. Mesmerized and undivided attention in alternate dimensions. Nothing in the computer database can give me an authentic answer. These are all of the actions Mother displays when *it* happens. I am questioning what it could be. I am extensively searching the internet for a possible diagnosis, though to no avail. Violently shaking, almost like slithering, is considered to be one of the symptoms, but it does not happen as much as the other ones. I did not bother inputting it into the search engine because I figured I would discover a plenitude of images on snakes. The inadequate knowledge of slithering is remarkable. Snakes are the prominent creatures for slithering, but I doubt not the only ones.

In every novel with prevalent themes of good and evil, evil is usually depicted in the eyes of a serpent. For this scenario being: *Robin Hood.* Identification representations are illustrated by the deeds and morals of the characters. Entireties of stories with this plot have good battle evil in hopes of banishing deceiving schemes throughout the land. The story of *Robin Hood* follows an English outlaw band: "*Mercy Men,*" who go on journeys with Robin Hood himself! The idioms and ballads of Robin Hood have two alternative narrative timelines. How can something have two timelines? Is it set in two distinct realms in which both timelines exist? No such thing of that manner would occur in *"Rescue the Lonely."* That would be tremendously complex, and I do not have copious margins of time to manifest such a prolonged plot. Anyway, the original plot consisted of Robin Hood on his adventures within the Mercy Men as the crooked clan commit crimes for personal gain. Later installations transformed the protagonist to a heroic vigilante outlaw whose mission currently deviates to steal from the rich and give to the poor. Robin Hood could not have been the main protagonist of the story because his character origin consisted of him being a criminal. Comprehension is a difficult task for me to achieve, but this is a whole new level. So, Robin Hood is evil at one point, but not as ruthless as the main swindler?

As for the ignorant or simple-minded ones who have gotten thus far, snakes are the epitome of evil. Ever since the beginning of time, they have been used to represent the crooked and most evil parts of society itself. But out of all of the animals and creatures in the world, why a snake? Why the slithering? Slithering has been associated with the depiction of evil and unlawful acts since the time of verbal stories would be said to children around the campfire long ago. Just like how demons can take possession of anyone and anything, serpents can do the same and will not stop until the host is discovered. Mother must be the perfect candidate because she has not been acting normal for the past two weeks now, approaching 3. What could she have possibly constructed to create such an outcome? This had only occurred one time when I was visibly present.

The 6th of September last year was not a very pleasant day to start with. Indeed, I woke up at least four times within that night because of sirens. Evacuation sirens to order people to desert residency to avoid imminent danger. The same sirens that come and go to warn people that someone is injured, the very same ones that exit those big elongated red trucks across from Amadeus' office. My community was compiled with various sorts of ruckus that night, neighbors departing from their homes to get a view of the commotion. A bright, glittering, radiant, light ignited the night sky in distress for someone to notice him. Though the creator never acknowledged him and kept burning for attention. For the simple-minded or merely confuzzled ones, the "him" I am referring to is the flare. It is a trick I learned in English class; I believe it is called a personification. Long name, yes. Though if it was up to me, I would have chosen anything less than a fifteen-letter word. Just looking at it is making me stressed. Finally, peering out of my bedroom window for the third time, I became just like the neighborhood that surrounded me, engulfed by the astonishing view of the flames as it made its way towards the Ohio River.

It was terrifyingly beautiful. I am in no support of violence and harm; however, nature has an intriguing way of displaying itself. The flames dwindled after 5:00 a.m. with no other sirens after that point. But silent sirens do not conclude the distractions. No. Reds and Blues flickered unsynchronized; the red was unbearable while the blue was pleasant—my favorite and nemesis in a constant battle in a color war. Have you ever analyzed a dying lantern? It rapidly blinks until it eventually evaporates. The fire was contained after some time between the hours of 6:15 am, and 7:00 am, keep in mind, this is only my speculation. Rejuvenated from my eventful morning, Mother was like how she always was:

Wake herself

Wait no more than 45 minutes before knocking

Announce breakfast (It is the same every day. 2 poached eggs with 1½ strips of Canadian bacon on the right all resting on a pile of hash browns)

All of this went according to schedule but what she did after was very unfortunate and questionable. I must have been in my room for no more than an hour and a half before a loud *Thud*! Descending down the stairs only to find my broken plate shattered on the kitchen tile, then Mother gawking across the counter at my empty plate before collapsing. If she is attempting to make me laugh, it is only making me confused and concerned. Consumed by guilt and fear that I might have been the cause, I ran upstairs, clinging to C3PO and hid under the covers praying the violent shaking would come to a halt. Discerning such questionable behavior from Mother is a surreal trait yet to be mastered. I am unconfident of when the viper started taking control of Mother; it could have been several days, weeks, or months prior to my awareness

Mother still said I could not have my fellow companion back until I admit to my "wrongdoing." (Positive it had something to do with my dirty dishes) I replied by admitting to her wrongdoing; no yarn will be shed on my end of the rope. Nothing I could do now could atone for what she has in store for me once I arrive back at my accommodation. The witch sent me off with a cold shoulder, and no admission of the protocol droid's whereabouts. Suddenly I have no recollection about where my focus feel-good drug is! Something does not add up here. No person would immediately forget where the treasure is stashed. In her eyes, I have not earned that privilege just yet. Or maybe now, she knows why I seem so intent on writing for these past days for prolonged periods of time.

The only occurrence I cannot accept the color blue is when it arrives in raindrop forms, much like today. Murmurs come to a shocking halt when scraping past copious amounts of feeble-minded fools is all I could do. The combination clicks, and with an ungainly lift, all my books come crashing down on the floor. The reactions are just as expected, laughter from all corners of the hall, then murmurs continue to the point where they cannot be categorized as that anymore. However, the *"Lonely"* glances at her locker mirror to be greeted by no one and them not thinking anything of it. Not a single student was acknowledging my mistake. Today is a strange day; I did see blue, but not in its usual form. It also has me questioning the reality of today, should I have seen bloodshed instead of rainfall? Whichever direction the wind blows, it does not matter anymore. The second period has arrived where time is an illusion, and ingenuity takes its first purposeful daily breath. Professor Skynyrd begins today's class with an insightful yet perplexing statement:

Fragments of reality compiled inside our minds form the world we view

Change is inevitable; how can a neophobe escape the inevitable? Answer: It is inevitable. No discussion about the quote or nothing, the words swirl through the prefrontal cortex of my mind, suppressing all other thoughts for a possible response for a petrified intellect like myself. No surprise, the professor calls me out amongst the crowd and asks me why I am not engaged in my work. Indeed, I am looking at him, but then again, I also am not. Everything is not what it seems anymore. Something horrific has occurred deep within. The students are doing the same as they did in the halls, but this time they are *"fragments of reality,"* as Skynyrd politely put it. Several minutes have passed and staying in composure for this extensive time is the most will power that has settled inside my soul. By now, I would have been long gone and most likely had my weekly rounds to the principal. It cannot happen today! Not in this class and not when Mother is already aggravated with me. Locks on the house will be changed, and my bags will be waiting at the door. Worst of all, if my vivid imaginations do seep through to reality, I will not reunite with Threepio.

"Sophia, whatever is happening inside of you right now. Remember, it will all go away soon enough. Just give it time. Can't you hear a word I'm saying? Look at me, look at me. Ignore everybody else. Keep your eyes trained on me. As far as you're concerned, we are the only two people in the room. You are disconnecting from our unity along with the class itself. You are not in any trouble; I would strongly advise you to please step outside."

Skynyrd is only doing his job, whether it is correct or not. But judgment is not accorded by me. I have not caused any commotion! He is the one who identified me as lost in the crowd. Who said I wanted to be found anyway! I pack my belongings and wait outside for the dictator to whip me into shape. Heads turn ever so frequently to see me still lingering around for someone or something to take me away. Useless! I quickly recall the one thing essential to my outfit is not at my disposal. A misplace of such sentimental value, that is quite impossible! I fully eliminate the option of my bag, my locker is the last resort. One, two, three, four, finally the fifth time it swung open. Discovering the professor behind me at a distance, a very unapproachable individual with arms crossed, knowing he will not strike up the conversation shows me what type of turmoil I have got myself involved in.

Observing this through the mirror, I ask if I can help him. Truly, the most incorrect question I could possibly ask at this point in the battle. He knows me being lost in space has become more frequent, but I cannot reveal the real answers in an anticlimactic setting. He tells me I have been acting strange in class and asks what the matter is. Yeah, tell me something I am not aware of. Sweat starts to seep through the calluses on the palms of my hands, and adrenaline skyrockets almost as if I were in a fight or flight situation.

Adrenaline can occur only in intense scenarios and happens when there has been an increased blood circulation and or breathing. It is especially prevalent in stressful situations, an encounter like this is a prime example. Why am I nervous? I have done nothing wrong to deserve this reaction within my body. Nothing that I have done will compromise my secrets. Nobody can know what I know. If anybody finds out, that will be it. I will be defeated.

Again, rummaging through my locker, the professor insists on me answering his previous question. Ignoring him is my best option. However, I know it will not last forever. Enraged with frustration, the locker closes in hopes of me turning in his general direction. I do what he says and turn but complying is something out of my pay grade. I do have to admit, the next card he pulls is a very intelligent move. In all of my days, I never thought Professor Skynyrd would threaten me. Well played, sir. I applaud you. Mother will have to get involved if I do not admit to my out of the ordinary behavior. Immediately I tell him everything…...he wants to hear. Creating fiction takes time and is never easy. Devising a believable story requires various factors, which may be presented by the following:

1) Keeping the story consistent

2) Attitude and appearance

3) Pathos (But most importantly, convince the listeners that they can minimally assist in the circumstance.)

Firstly, briefly explaining why my absences are; because of a much greater task at hand in which I cannot disclose. The use of the word absences is not in the generic sense; I am using it quite "dimensional." Physically I am all there, but mentally it is catastrophic, as you are all aware. The questions he continues to pester me about are relentless. Picking at me as if with a scalpel, sorry to disappoint Skynyrd, but my body is not intended for research purposes at the moment.

Next, I address the fact of the matter that my August is in critical condition with considerable surveillance. He needs me, I can hear him, the tender whispers caressing my ear.

Teasing is never a humorous manner. Why is it always associated with foul play? An answer I cannot provide. Whispers are undoubtedly a significant sign, but they also may mean something more. Sympathetic dimwit, my trap has sprung with a 27:1 odd deficit of escaping unharmed. You are right where I want you. The professor apologizes for his outlandish behavior and sends his regards. Admiring his warm-hearted gestures, I continue scavenging. According to him, appearing overwhelmingly distorted has its added benefits after all, and his assistance is much appreciated. It should have been hanging from my hook within my jacket pocket. Rummaging page by page, pocket by pocket, nothing poses the slightest clue.

Lucky charms are to symbolize good fortune. Looks like mine has just run out. "30 mg" is clearly visible resting upon my algebra textbook below the coat hanger. Skynyrd examines it, though why do the unnecessary? Why wait to answer when obviousness presents itself? Amadeus shared with me an acronym before. What is it! What is it?! R.E.D.! I.T.E.M.! T.R.U.C.K.! 4 characters are all it contained. Stop guessing beyond that?! Stupid! Stupid! It must have started with the second letter in the alphabet. B.L.A.K.! B.L.E.W! B.L.E.W.! Spelled Blew or Blue?? Okay:

[Step 1] BANISH

[Step 2] LEAVE

Last two, EW or UE? B.L.U.E.! Uphold foundation following exhaling. Explicitly trashing any step (step 2 was impossible) alters the rules, says the same man who I call teacher. Has nobody taught this man any manners? Could Professor Skynyrd not see that I was in the middle of my treatment? Interrupting someone's treatment like that, he should be ashamed of himself. Signs of disappointment turn and view me. At this moment, I wish I could be exiled to an isolated island in hopes of hiding with no seekers. Who knew one "word" could have such an impact. An explanation is not coming today, especially not for you. Shocking myself in the process, I would never bring one of those pills to this hostile environment. The school bell rings, then Professor Skynyrd creates distance between us. This next part, I am still embarrassed about, but people will do anything out of desperation, I now know.

"That is mine, sir. Please give it back!" I never saw anybody whip around so fast in my life. "Sophia, you are currently in possession of illegal substances. I will hold onto this until I contact my superior. I'm sorry young lady."

My best work is presented when I am under the influence, with an enhanced undivided attention. Inhaling all the air my lungs can withstand, it echoes throughout the entire building. -Almost to the frequency of cracking glass, not shattering. Attention, someone violently stole something of mine, who wants to get it back? Attacking occurs when one is intentionally sought out, self-defense is not deemed as attacking, keyword being defense. Twisted enough, that is not how the district ruled it as.

I cannot recall any details; my instincts take over in a flash. From what all I can piece together; the mission is a failure in retrieving the "30 mgs" and am now currently sitting with Mother in "our second home." The existence of the phrase insinuates my consistent visits. Great; the last thing I need is a lecture from Mother and the wicked witch after this whole shenanigan is dealt with: *Headmaster* ██████. No need to compromise her identity; she is no one of importance. I inform my legal guardian of typical nonsensical lies while Deja Vu encumbers the powerhouse of my human body.

Scrambled audio is difficult to recover, but no one said it was impossible. Syncing it together now and imagining it went something similar to this: "I'm sorry for bringing you in on such short notice, Miss. Collins. I realize this is not your cup of tea, nor is it mine. But we do have to discuss Sophia's attendance along with her attitude. It has recently been brought to my attention that your daughter's *disorder* has become a grave disruption in and out of the classroom. Miss. Collins, you of all people should know, this is not the first time complaints have come in; I want to apologize before I say that our school services can no longer help your daughter." Playing the silence game is fairly easy for me; however, near impossible when someone provokes me. Both ears weep even before the sound of the association to that wretched word slithers into my ear canal. No one human understands me like Amadeus does. He knows what I am capable of with my superpower activated. Emphasizing the term superpower rather than the wretched word for handicap requires patience and perseverance, both of which are useless among these incompetent monsters.

Out of courtesy, stepping out of the room only prolonged the ordeal. Plotting their scheme to rue the remaining of my days, thus being the ultimate consequence of all. Space is a terrifying aspect for me, fathoming a fantasy that plenty of people dream about traveling to the stratosphere and beyond. Must have been another thirty-five minutes before seeing Mother again storming out livid, signaling to pack my bag, and that was it. Unaware and quite frankly not too captivated by what happened in that room, school is no longer a priority apparently. Mother tells me that they were no-good, ignorant, buffoons, who do not care as much about me as she does. Therefore, she is replacing Professor Skynyrd, along with all other admins that attempted to teach me.

Seeing the same person 24/7 for seven days a week who has a resume that now reads two occupations; is exhausting. How and why would one hold two jobs if no added benefit is necessary to a second? People do have to make a substantial amount to support themselves or a family, but nothing like this torture. Distinguishing between the two personalities requires extensive amounts of practice. Though I am no expert, it has gotten easier throughout the weeks to differentiate between teacher and mother. Routine is nothing but a continuous loop of events only to have it overlap and fall into the next day. Monday through Friday is the same exact structure as real school, though some of the contrasts may include: a luxurious breakfast, no required dress code, the presentations of information, and no interactions with any other conscious mammals. When comparing it to real school, Mother surprisingly captures me with every single word that repels from her lips.

Class, if that term is even relevant anymore, contains none of the same elements that it once had before. Isolation is not a practice one naturally has access too. The practice is developed within the body by the use of experiences that leave the individual on the set reality of independence. Witnessing another chronic episode the other day, again falling to the floor to only stir the viper out of her. The Collins family are a good group of hosts; why else would there be serpents living inside of Mother. Knowing I only have seconds to spare, the wormhole grants me access. Not that I did not want to assist Mother in her troubles, but I sacrificed saving my desires rather than the woman who provided me with life. I did not bother investigating the common area or the surrounding vicinity for any sort of clue.

In all of the days living in this house, Mother's room is the one area where I am not allowed. Tread lightly for death may be creeping around, Sophia. I say to myself as I venture into the unknown. The light fixture provides a dim source of illumination whatsoever; it only creates the ability to make out the outlining of shapes. Unfamiliar territory has its way of generating fear out of the strongest. Gently shifting the bookcase for a source of entrance to this profound mystery leads to something dangling from the closet; time to put on my yellow trench coat. It would be blasphemy for a private investigator to continue without donning the entirety of the encapsulated look. Hypothetically speaking, of course. The mirror shows a latch which must contain infinite answers!

The taste of adventure releases flying critters within my stomach. Cobwebs are attached to anything and everything that has a solid surface. Boxes of all sizes scatter the floor like dead soldiers. Laying there, motionless. The first box contains nothing but childhood pictures and memories at a time when I was completely helpless. However, my red armed friend is fairly visible at the bottom of this useless box. Up here in the attic, you can hear everything the house has to offer, the toilet flushing, the hot water tank running, and everybody below. Exposed I will be if I linger in this confined space anymore, sweeping my tracks, I escape back to my original location with my protocol droid back in my possession. But as I do so, another box catches my eyes: *"Classified."* I will be back for you later. What do you not want me to know Mother?!

Episode I:
Symbolically Reunited

Concentration is impractical when the ear can pick up any sound frequency within 20-20,000 hertz. The slightest sound can rupture the silence—a terrible turn of events when it does occur. Precious planning is suddenly stripped away. Exhibition of my use of silence, too much of it can be a bad thing and vice versa. Music is nothing more than collective sounds strung together to create a melody. In addition to the vile, the tone and melody the classical genre generates is a plenitude of ideas, which then again calms my mind in times of stress. Experimenting with various kinds of solutions, however, a gradual improvement is clearly visible within this method of stress reliever. I am curious if the audience partakes in a similar reliever.

White noise surrounds us being anything the mind perceives as audible. There are two and *only* two distinct types of learners. First, there are those who live in solitude who want absolutely no disturbance by anyone or thing, simple enough. "Do Not Disturb" might as well be wrapped around their neck at all times.

Enter the ladies and gentlemen who deal with noise as if it has always been a part of them. Within this second type, these souls have harnessed the power of true potential. Minimal noise is bearable; although, once it reaches loud enough to where I can hear it from another room or outside within the world itself, then we have an issue on our hands.

Problem-solving has never been a strong suit of mine. Why do they call it a *"strong suit"* anyway? It is not like anyone is actually getting dressed up. If there so happens to be some sort of special occasion, no one ever informs me. Hypothetically speaking, if I were Webster, this confusing phrase should be trashed for one that does not make my mind sick. Possibly something along the lines of *"possessor of force."*

In the Star Wars universe, Jedis are the chosen ones who possess the power of a lightsaber with the supernatural entity of the force. I have never been a *"possessor of the force"* when it comes to mathematics. Insisting me to upgrade my skill, Mother cannot comprehend how difficult numbers are for me; she says just about everyone who is like me excels in mathematics. Sorry Mother, but I am not everyone!

Mothers two occupations are nothing compared to her professional career. She is phenomenal at it, she even works weekends! Mother works whenever she feels necessary. So, in other words, whenever she has a spare second. The company is very understanding and accommodating when it comes to her life outside of work. Leaving to go into the office is out of the question; working from home is much more preferred for her rather than exploring all mother nature has to offer. I ask her why she does not go into the office like everybody else, she asks why I already question the topics I already know. Correct, I already know the answer. But when pestering comes to the breaking point, then she will have to leave! I know. However, the reader is clueless on this aspect. Says she does not venture into the office because of me. What do I have to do with any of this! Do not blame your misfortunes on me, Mother! I have done nothing but obey and listen. Do not go blaming me when your plan does not go accordingly. Life does not come full circle like a carousel hoping to ride it again.

Realizing S.P.E.C.I.A.L. comes with various attributes, but I am not helpless and so dependent on every living soul like August! When college becomes more of a reality, I want to love my job as much as Mother does. Although, like everyone else, she has her fair share of positive and negative days. The one downside to her job is that she is constantly on technology, always creating informative visuals in order to capture her clients. Negotiations being a primary, does not sound like that would be up my ally. In question of how Mother does it all, some of the people she does business with are incompetent dimwits. She works for a small corporation within a larger corporation. I am still in question of how that works. I try my best not to think about it much. The graphic design profession captivates the strings of my attention whenever Mother discusses her occupation, but I do not want to do this as a career. Technology and I have a nasty feud, which is not a necessity to the story at all. A writing utensil and paper have always maintained a healthy relationship with me, even in the good and bad days.

The Parker boys, now developing functional brains, have partially understood the difference between good and bad. Bad outweighs the good for his brother August at least. In the mind of August, depending on everyone and everything constantly is a grueling task to manage, especially when the person being dependent upon is an introvert. Oliver, on the other hand, is an extrovert, guess opposites do attract. Up until the present day, August's other half is the longest relationship he has been in, and it has no signs of slowing down. This is all speculation at this point, and I cannot speak from experience from this point forward. Minimal research and eyewitness accounts done on my behalf suggest brotherhood is nothing more than a solid friendship with more significance. Brothers do the ordinary; bond, laugh, fight, repeat; but this is all presented on a pedestal no one else can fathom. Siblings, especially same sex, have a profound experience with a new definition of love. Parents allude to a unique love when comparing spouses to children. The same should be for siblings. I believe the same type of love and affection siblings share is comparatively, if not more remarkable, to a parent experience with a child.

Seesaws function when two people join forces, one side raises while the other sinks. The dynamic duo forces the seesaw to teeter; August's life is no different. This particular unique individual has been suspended, waiting for the other to do their job. Considering that every passing minute or any portion of time for that matter, is a moment that will forever be solidified in history. Yet August would not think about changing anything for that ideal picture of normal. Nothing is quite as it seems though. August was prone to false accusations and questionable people. People would make a conscious effort to go out of their way to question his condition. It was up to everyone else in his life to explain to onlookers that he was "sick." No matter how dull the answer is, people are compliant and pleased when someone acknowledges them. That is just the tip of the iceberg, patiently waiting to melt. When he was not under the public eye, he was freely roaming the isolated shelter identified as home sweet home. Complications were not as common for potential hazards as they were surrounded by strangers in a strange land. Though everything posed as hazardous to my August, frightened and terrified by the slightest sounds. Poor boy.

"Sick" may as well be an extremity in August's case. The word sick is almost always used in the manner of obtaining a mild cold, not when one is on trial with the reaper as the prosecutor. On an unknown evening, August was preparing for the nightly eight to twelve-hour rest as everybody else on this planet as everybody else presumably does, Mrs. Parker hollered out. Approaching the nearby room to find her son slipping on his pajamas. Stopping him to do one last thing before bed: changing the germ-infested tracheostomy to a fresh new breathing instrument. Done every thirty days, this was one of his least favorite activities to endure, and I do not blame him one bit. Being immersed in a liquid requires a vital skill. The average person can hold their breath from anywhere between 30-40 seconds.

However, that is not taken to account when the individual is unprepared and or not "average." Humans take almost everything for granted. It is not until it is stripped away that value enters the equation. Death has never been so vividly displayed. Picture being submerged, extending towards life as the room begins to close and darken. Radiant gold beams shimmer through silvers for a final curtain call. Although as soon as all hope was lost, the 15-second interval completed its run.

A series of knocks play upon the bedroom door, praying for the soul to investigate. As expected, Mother invites herself in, however, with a bizarre statement. With no time to spare, I pack the necessities into the car. What did I do to deserve such treatment? Is this actually Mother conversing with me or the serpent? Unsure of what is occurring, Mother's eccentric smile haunts the darkest part of me and proceeds to ask once again if I am prepared for what is about to take place. Need me to remind you that my actions have been nothing out of the ordinary. I figure it is best not to ask questions and to accept the situation as is. The route traveled is one that I have adventured numerous times before but never to this specific location. Questioning how Mother discovered this area anyway, no signs of life are present themselves. I observe my surroundings to unearth the coordinates of this specific hole in the wall! Though I have no measurements, this next part will be solely based upon an estimation of the structure. The area exceeds no more than 500 square feet with a surprisingly low roof; yet, with reinforced concrete walls. With every pro, there is always a con. For instance, this one deals with location.

Although it resides across from Amadeus's office, do you know what else lies on this cursed side of "the great divide?"

Exposed by various leafless buckeye trees, or by their proper name; Aesculus glabra, Black Birch's, and Tulip trees. Aesculus glabra trees appear normal once inspected. Seeds sprout, creating the fruit, which in the end, contains toxins and poisons. Research confirms the fruit as being fatal, and with that being stated, I do not condone ingesting these whether the individual believes it as safe or not. During the time of Native Americans, they would use the fruit as an ingredient in a dish they would often prepare. Now we know what actually happened to the ones that were once native to this land! Addictive in color and majestic in motion; the purple tulip trees overshadow the intensity of the nearsighted building.

Contents inside the structure are obviously more exciting than what is on the outside. After entering, we are then greeted by an employee who is exceptionally intriguing. Darting my eyes to and fro, we finally lock. Though it was hardly 10 seconds, I learned a lot within those precious seconds. Never have I witnessed anybody like this particular individual. At first glance, the average human immediately is repulsed by this creature, but us *"lonely"* find it intriguing and a challenge. The face is the most distinct feature that differentiates us from the next human, but never to this extremity. His eyes are the first that approach my personal pedestal, slanting upward to give the curvature of the rest of his features. Mesmerizing, I catch myself falling back into them with each spare moment, those ocular shaped wide eyes never cease to amaze me. Another distinct property about this gentleman happens to surface on the ears. Unusually smaller than the average joe, perhaps it may be pertaining to an evolved form of natural selection where the ear is propelled to a more advanced state. However, upon further examination, a hearing aid is fairly visible installed on the right portion of his head. So initially, we can rule out Darwin's theory of Natural Selection as one of the possibilities.

Clinging to Mother's hand and my eyes absorb everything there is in the room. "Hello, I called earlier regarding a golden retriever you had in the shelter. Is she still available?" Golden Retriever? I do not want a dog! Dogs despise me, and as do I them. Let me purchase what I want! Astonishment devours me as words flow from his mouth. "H- Hi! My-my name is Riley. What can I help you with? No dog here, sor-rrry. We have others, but no golden retriever." Mother smiles, and he leads us to where they keep the "prisoners." Not much of a selection to choose from; I have probably wandered past the same 3 dogs already. As I aimlessly wander, I run into the same employee from earlier. "I'm Riley. What's yours?" I know what you must be thinking. Why did I not erupt when he used a conjugation? And worse, two in one sentence! There is a fine line between someone who knows what they are doing is wrong compared to someone who is unable to recognize it. So yes, I have gone soft on this gentleman; but he cannot help it. He is the *only* exception. "Sophia." I say. "Do you want to be my ffff friend?" he asks. What an outlandish question to ask a complete stranger. I wish I were that confident. When I do not answer the first time, the question is repeated once more. Shaking my head in acknowledgment, I agree with his terms.

The young man is jubilant towards my affirmation and allows me to wander the shop neighboring him. The holding cells are as imagined, three or four mammals in an about two by seven diameter enclosed fenced concrete area full of divergent species of canines and cats. And this is what people call a shelter! Looks like a sure way to develop claustrophobia if you ask me. You do not have any other creatures? These are not my preferred animals, but I will make arrangements if necessary. Mr. Whiskers continued to call my name, -well, not really- an all blush orange cat except for the tip of his nose being rose-red, pressed *his* arm through the corrosive chain-link steel fence. I apologize; I should not be giving gender to this animal just yet; the genitalia has not been examined. It has swampy green eyes that scream help, but I am thankful for pathos, not devouring me. I very much enjoy looking at this fellow, but he is not the one for me.

I ask Riley once again if he has something other than four-legged animals. "No, I-I can't show you those. My boss will be angry, and she is very sc-scary when an-angry." "Riley, I thought we were friends. I do not want to lose you already; I want us to be friends forever. Now can you please tell me what else you have in stock? You can trust that I will not tell anyone. Please, Riley."

Persuasiveness is another one of my superpowers; I should mention this to Amadeus in our upcoming appointment. Acquiring it roughly the same time my primary ability emerged; nonetheless, it is a gem to use when presented the opportunity. He becomes hesitant as expected but longer than anticipated. That is never a good sign. "Okay. Only because we are friends. Follow me Sophia." After briefly scouting for traces of Mother, he then leads me through a small corridor hidden from everything else. Almost to a janitor's closet of sorts. That cat must have caught Mother's heartstrings. The hidden room consists of varieties of hamsters, fish, reptiles, and more! Immediately hovering to the aquatic section, the fish are just like the ones in Amadeus office, if not identical. Clownfish, Blue Tang fish, Betta, Angelfish, however, none of these are the correct ones I am specifically looking for. I ask the employee if they have a Raccoon Butterfly. Discouraged by his uncertain answer, I begin to exit when he suddenly tells me to look at his favorite fish. Squinting through the unfiltered cesspit of a tank to then find a familiar fellow. That is it! That is it! The racoon butterfly, with the vibrant gold color. It is more beautiful than I have ever imagined. I want this one! Proceeding to the checkout counter, we finally reunite with Mother. Riley shares his overwhelming interest in the amphibian, as do I, but that fish is more delighted with me than it ever was him. Asking if he can come visit the fish from time to time, I generously agree to his request. Take good care of him he says, with nodding in compliance, we exit the store.

Mother comforts me all the way to the car; why is she doing this? Why do I deserve a pet? Amadeus always told me it is better to stay silent than to ask questions in times like these. So, my intention shall be that precisely. Speaking from experience, it gets annoying talking to the same person continuously. So C3PO will now have someone else to converse with. Mother constantly looks back. Keep your eyes on the road, and less on your child. Someone may get severely injured; remember that haunting factor Mother. See-through plastic bags do not appear to be the safest material to package a live animal inside; what if the bag breaks! Although it is exciting to admire him, of course, that would not be possible if his remains are on the floor.

As soon as we get into the driveway, an attack is imminent. Thank goodness the vehicle is in park. Driving requires extensive responsibility, none of which is attainable at this young age. Change is constant with this fellow; I do not like this character because of it. August and I are as compatible as can be. We both resist change and remain on a set schedule. These diabolical demons violently thrust Mother against the wheel; I cry for them to stop, but nothing I say sells their attention. If I was their victim, stopping them would be no issue. Mother just does not have a superpower to fight them off like I do. Being fatigued must be a side effect after what occurred. An all-out war using the same tactics is a foolish move, Mother. Go into battle prepared. With her papier-mâché shield obliterated along with her weapon of choice, she enters her lion's den.

Right from the get-go, Threepio is pleasantly surprised, though I would not say energetic. My two companions now stare at each other with great intensity. Most likely studying one another based on physical appearances. I rummage through the kitchen for a home for Mr. Fish, there is nothing that matches the picture I have in my head; but I found something that may qualify. I return to find the fish happy as can be, bonding with his new friend.

It does not appear like that may be the case on the other side of the tank. The fish does like his new home, I believe. Do fish get claustrophobic? I think this one does because the vase I placed him in, has made him have a sense of discomfort. Brainstorming a wide range of names for several moments, nothing comes to us until C3PO devises the perfect name…. Corduroy; Corduroy the fish.

Inspired by Amadeus's fish, king Corduroy now has his own castle. August should be treated with such royalty; he is my king, and I am his queen, you know. This sad, sick, little, world does not operate in that manner, at least not through these "cracked" lenses. If something is cracked, then it is…...broken. If something is broken, it is usually...cracked. These words are used interchangeably to emphasize this fractured world. Superheroes exist to combat the "filtered good" humans cease to create. They are there to assist the common man, although the common man does not always need saving from an organism with extravagant abilities; sometimes, they just need another common man.

Adventuring out to eat is a treat; it is a pleasure to eat somewhere else other than your kitchen table. Thus, August and his family had good intentions about traveling to a local worldwide fast-food diner one day. The family did nothing out of the ordinary, ordered food off the selective menu, ate, and played on the inexpensively constructed jungle gym. As expected in the circumstances like these, the Parker family's time was limited, and the boys had to manage to do everything they imagined within a dwindling time slot. Oliver and August were at opposing ends of the structure, imagining their ways through miscellaneous simulations. Uncontrollably sliding down a central air shaft just like Luke Skywalker. However, rather than clinging to an antenna as the movie suggests, August is greeted by a foreign hunter in collection of his bounty at the bottom. The bounty hunter's ruthless behavior manipulates my miracle to perceive himself as a freak! Although I do not agree with this hunter's decisions, I do have to admit that he is persistent in his work. The torment continues for several more moments until a familiar face comes to the rescue. Spectating at what has just transpired to then vault out of the shadows and jolt the hunter to the ground. At that moment, August knew Oliver would protect his older brother and would vow to let nothing happen to him.

The same concept goes for Threepio and Corduroy. As long as I have air in my lungs, nothing shall get in the way of *their protector*. Throughout the short time of inhabiting my place of residence, Corduroy experienced the tour of my room individually. Relying only upon his motionless expression, I would say he will get used to living here. The agonizing pain my protocol droid is currently experiencing is solely due to jealousy. I have witnessed similar cases of this emotion, but on a human to human degree. One proclaims that they have obtained something, whether it be materialistic or something in between. The other begins to express the aspiration over that item or desire. Then opportunity *A* or *B* drowns their mind: *A* being stealing the content in a hostile manner; *B* having acquired it in a passive fashion. Throughout all of my years of existence, never have I heard of someone actually going through with plan *A*.

Mother reenters the picture as she calls me to the living quarters. Her stern expression signals disturbance. "What is this mess, young lady? This was not here before. Look, you left your dishes sprawled all over the place. Who do you think has to clean up after you! Take some responsibility, Sophia. Please, for once." Appears like it was me all along. I swear I placed my bowl in the dishwasher after I was done with it, guess not. See Mother, now the area is clean! Are you happy now! Mother then tells me that she has to go out for a little while…...alone. Is this a dream? Is this actually happening! She has never trusted me like this before. This would be the first time in forever that I would have control over the stronghold. "Sophia, hey; I will be gone for no more than an hour and a half. I have to run to the pharmacy than to the store." "Wait, can you get…. "A moment sooner, and I would have told her to pick up more fruit snacks.

Execute Order 66
1) Bike
2) Fruit snacks
3) Amadeus

When a parent lays down what is acceptable and unacceptable, the child experiments what they can surpass. Why does defiance intrigue the youth? With my list in hand, the child experiments. Knowing I do not need to do this one bit, there is no benefit for him, obviously. However, I have already made a decision. Depositing Corduroy inside the basket and with Threepio, my defiance begins with a pedal.

Every passing pedestrian and or vehicle cries in a disorienting manner. Confident it is not me they are gazing upon, unless I am that lavishly gorgeous. Though that is impossible now, sorry boys, I am taken. Remember, Sophia. Do not draw unwanted attention; that type of behavior only makes them want you more. Traveling the roads untraveled fools no one but himself, that is why everything has to be according to a plan. Remember all the times earlier when I mentioned that I do not enjoy seeking the unknown? Well, this time is definitely different. Diving into the abyss is almost a surreal experience, constantly reminding myself that I am going through with this ridiculous plan of mine. Animals are not allowed in public stores; look at service dogs, though. No one ever complains about the relevance of those creatures. Yet when I park, attention is drawn on me like a dog. That buckle that droops below your chin irks me intensely, incorrectly removing it each time and always manages to pinch me! The company, whoever designed these contraptions, should modify helmets in a way where the chin strap is Velcro. That way, the clamping of the skin issue will be forever resolved. Corduroy is lucky, he does not have to rely on safety straps, and if he did have to wear one, the smallest size would not even fit him. I am not admitting to people flocking us, but curious minds wander towards our direction to do a double-take. "Yes. This is a fish that I am bringing into the store; it is no different than you having to trudge in here with your service animal." Snatching one grocery cart out of pure instinct but now instantly regretting my decision, we travel over "the other dimension" as the automatic doors grant us access. Although this is absolutely unnecessary by all means, Corduroy is strapped in the cart and ready to continue our journey. The grocery store is a very confusing place for us; the aisle says it contains one thing, then contradicting the sign entirely. For example, we travel down aisle 07, which lists the following products: *Beverages, Produce, Desserts, and Pre-made Meals;* just as a horrendous maze as this place is, provolone cheese is nonexistent. False advertising is what this location is known for, cannot imagine arriving here every week to gather food on a weekly basis. Mother. You officially have my sympathy. Truly have I never experienced such a disorganized, overpopulated landfill. This place reminds me of an airport because of all the people having no regard for anyone but themselves, now I know how a school of fish feels. However, I am not here for cheese, I wandered the yellow brick road in search of the red shoes, and after forty-five minutes of searching, I finally found them; might I add in the most obscure of places. Whose bright idea was it to place fruit snacks in the breakfast area? If anything, they should be categorized under snacks. I am going to write a strongly worded letter towards the imbeciles we call employees.

Out of all of the options listed, why is there only a large and extra-large section? The medium will surely last me a month; I am not made of money, you know. Realizing I cannot do what I am thinking, that is illegal, surely will I be banned if done so. Seizing the "smallest" container, they showcased and then waiting in line. Boy, do I hate lines, knowing one of my unique abilities is not accessible, waiting in line with the other common folks is what I have to endure apparently. Halfway there to check out is when Corduroy decides to share one of the essentials of life he currently does not have. Placing the box of goodies on the floor along with Corduroy and asking the family of four behind me to save my spot, I run to the animal section in search of fish food.

Again, fish food is not listed as one of the products they carry. Grabbing the nearest employee, I ask him if he knows where I can find food. "Sorry, ma'am, we currently do not have any fish food in stock." Well, that is quite fishy. I intently stare into his blood-red eyes and whiff a stench of whatever drug he used earlier. "Are you sure you do not carry any? I ran earlier this morning." He reassures me and double checks the back. He then returns with a small container of fish food, the last one to be exact. Applauding his success and thanking him, my feeble soul returns to the line to only discover that my belongings were removed from the intended spot. Petrified as can be, I experience another episode.

I curl into a ball of clay than crying as loud as possible. This is both in the sense of using the voice box to propel your voice so everyone can hear and generating physical tears that construct my emotional mood as blatantly obvious as possible. Attracting the attention of every soul in the store now, someone has to approach me if they want these shenanigans to end. Helplessly lying on the floor analyzing and then concluding: *Special people require special needs. Funding those needs is out of my paygrade. Leave it to the next wanderer.* As you would imagine, I am fed up at this point and begin to take matters into my own hands. Inching towards the clerk, I ask her if she has seen a rounded vase with a fish inside along with a box of fruit snacks and a golden protocol droid with a complexion different from the rest of him residing on his arm. Hesitant as one would after the show displayed, she exchanges my mute friends for the cost of the items, of course, with its abiding currency. Exiting the building in search of my next and final destination. Note to self: Thoroughly investigate the situation before blowing it out of proportions.

With a clip and a pedal, I am off to his office though I pray he is actually there! Jumping a curb and continuing to follow the path as I always do in the car. Finally, I approach the sign: *[Rm225] Dr. Amadeus Richards.* Confronting the front desk, I ask for his availability, they then say he is with a client at the moment. Yes, I do understand that he sees other people besides me, but our relationship is stronger than what any other client can offer. We are best friends!! I need to see him; this is by no means optional! I have never waited in a waiting room before. This place is pitiful, with various magazines sprawled out that no one reads, a television that only has one channel, and annoying people who refuse to sit still. Is this what unprivileged people have to deal with on a daily basis? A young boy and girl walk down the hall murmuring amongst themselves, then decide on sitting next to me in hopes of striking a conversation.

"How do you know, Amadeus?" I politely ask. Both of them stare at me as if I had a dangling booger. "You mean Dr. Richards? Oh, we are one of his patients. He is the best one around, been going to him for four years now. I am guessing you know him too?" The girl nudges her brother to stop; who can blame him? Everybody loves fruit snacks. Quickly checking on the fish and averting my attention back at the siblings. "First of all, his name is Amadeus! Secondly, I have also been going to his services for quite a while, too, unsure of how long, however. Would you two care for any fruit snacks? I recently bought them at the store. Figured it would be best to munch on something while I wait." Giving them a single baggie, I ask what "superpower" they both have. She looks at me, surprisingly puzzled. Do they not know the essence of a power? What a responsibility it is to be gifted with one. As soon as she and he begin to ask for clarification, the front desk women wave me into Amadeus' office. "Excuse me, friends, but we may have to pick up on this conversation later."

Entering the room and only observing the fish for less time than usual, I mean, why do I observe them at all? I have one of my own now. I can watch this guy all I want. Lying on the couch and waiting for what word drips out of his mouth this time. "Sophia, I was not expecting you today. I have you scheduled for next week. But no worries, it is always thrilling meeting with you. I see you brought somebody other than Mr. Star Wars this time, getting replaced perhaps?" I bet you are all confused, Threepio is assigned out on guard mode. What? My bike be unattended, foolish of you to ever propose such an obscurity. While looking down at Corduroy, a squeeze of plastic enters the soundwaves. "No, he is still my special companion. I just wanted to bring my new friend along; he wanted to meet you. This here is Corduroy, the fish. He is a racoon butterfly just like the one you have in your tank there. Can I offer you a fruit snack?" Amadeus acknowledges Corduroy with a proper "handshake." It was a mental handshake; I can tell my bowled comrade appreciated it. Silence fills the room as my best friend studies my eating habits, but silence is soon broken by an outside entity. "Sophia!"

Episode II:
A Breath of New Life

Mr. Parker, on the other hand, had no one frantically searching for him. Possibly because he is not a rebel scum like me. Confidence was not August's strong suit, as we all know now, friend-making is no more difficult than a minor enlisting for the army during world war two. Granted, these are two drastically different concepts, but the process behind it is still present. On the left hemisphere, we have a proud American wanting to defend his country, and on the right, the idea of friend-making. Many issues come into play when discussing going into war. First off, the child would deliberately have to go behind his parents to mail his enlistment. With mailing the enlistment, he would have to lie on the form stating that he is at least above the age of 18 years old. Excluding real-world logic, for a moment, if he were to get past the officials with this flimsy lie, death does not come slowly. Roles are reversed; you are the punching bag, and death is the superstar. Relentless blow after relentless blow, there is no rest for the wicked. Judgment day will come, my little patriotic friend.

Anxiety can be reduced by becoming friends with your neighbors. Perceive the action of friend-making nothing more than speaking to Oliver, August. He will be there every step of the way. Also, I doubt it will go as horribly wrong as when I attempted to make a friend. These were his and Oliver's first real friends that they can freely visit whenever they would like. For timeline purposes, this next milestone occurred the same year the Parker family resided in their new home, upon a ferocious mountain dominating the town below. The house was substantially larger than their previous house; this one had 4 stories and is in the forest! The only logical explanation for this upgrade is because of August's father's diligence, and hard work had landed him a promotion at work. My dearest has never seen anything relative in comparison to this size. The more room he has to explore, the bigger chance of him getting a larger room. Thus, supersizing the opportunity to live a "normal" life. Directions getting to the new place of residency is abundantly more confusing than I created, though I do recall there being a lake close by. On the first floor of the house, we have the two-car garage and the basement. Nothing special on that floor, now advancing up the stairs to where everything else resides. As you enter the left and going counterclockwise: dinner room, kitchen/laundry room, living quarters, and last room on the checklist, the office with an outside balcony. Reciprocating the fraction, the second story is now in visual view. Speaking of outside balconies, get a load of this one! This one is inside the house! August was as surprised as I am right now, perhaps not *as* excited though…. intimidated, if anything. Traveling from right to left on the balcony, the guest bedroom, and then the right side contained August's and Oliver's separate rooms!

But with all this excessive area comes a much greater chance of becoming lost. Lost in one's surroundings, including the loss of thought, becomes quite prevalent when crossroads collide. The first night with August and his new home was anything but pleasant; while he was exploring the ancient basement, he became lost in his surroundings. Every which way he turned, everything looked the same. Replicating the scene from *"A New Hope,"* once again when Chewbacca and the gang enter the trash compactor in hopes of escaping from the stormtroopers. The walls closing in, and there seems to be no way of escape until R2D2 shuts off the compactors from the ground level control room above. Mimicking R2 to a lesser extent, August channels his fear into determination. Luckily, there was no monster lurking below him at the bottom. We do not want to get trapped in the same predicament Luke did. This house will have to get some getting used too, and I am not the only one admitting that obvious statement. I wish I could help him navigate; I am excellent with those sorts of things. I can remember things with a snap of a finger.

In the neighborhood of a week of being cooped in the house, the brothers decided to introduce themselves to their community. Notice what I did? If you do not catch that, there will be more examples as we progress; they will become more apparent as we move on. Recording the date as November 15th, 2003, is the day August and Oliver successfully made friends. He was sharing with me that he can distinctly recall that day perfectly. August saw a girl about his age riding her bicycle in her front yard. He really wanted to meet her, but he did not know how to start. Playing every scenario in his head, but none of them seem to be a plausible, realistic means of approach. So, calling on his reliable crutch, Mrs. Parker enters the scene. He tugs on his mother's sleeve in a plea of not going through with her crazy plan; he thought she was just bluffing!

The girl stops in her tracks, and August swiftly cowers behind Mrs. Parker. For privacy purposes, disregarding the identities of these people will be the logical move here. The two promptly introduce themselves, and the two proceed to get their other halves. Bringing both their brothers in their yard, the four of them instantly knew they were going to develop relations. The four spent an equal amount of time at each other's residence. However, August and Oliver enjoyed playing at their house significantly greater than his own because of one distinct house rule separating the two. *"NO M RATED GAMES"* Any spare time either of the brothers had, they would venture to the neighbors to play the video games that were forbidden otherwise.

Validating my input in the issue for the moment, this rule is absurd! What does it matter if a child is exposed to the real world at a young age? The world is not an *E* rated game where your wildest fantasies become reality. Where nothing bad ever occurs, and everyone lives in peace. News flash: it is mature rated! People do have their good and bad days, but most of all, they experience a broken world around their shattered lives. What Mrs. Parker cannot seem to comprehend is that there is no way around ignoring the issue. It is better for them to be educated now before subjects become substantially worse.

Forgive me for my outlandish statement. Shall we continue with August? Where did we leave off, ah yes escaping reality. Almost every day after school, all three boys would isolate themselves in the neighboring boy's room to stimulate themselves in a visually gruesome (at the time) WWII video game; *Medal of Honor: Rising Sun.* You know when people say, "what are what you eat," well, that cannot be any more relevant in this circumstance given. When the boys were not dominating the Nazi regime with a controller, they presented what they saw then brought it to reality's doorstep. Now the Parkers backyard was the primary place to be stationed when participating in the game of Army. The backyard was base camp, rendezvousing every time whenever in retreat. Which might I add was often, August was not the best with a "firearm" mainly because the condition of the weapons were not very durable. The headquarters devised a playset posterior to a massive dirt hill. Panning from left to right, the wooden structure had a yellow slide with a hut integrated into it, and two perfectly working swings operating as aircraft.

Pearl Harbor was an infamous attack on December 7th, 1941, forcing the United States to become involved in the war. Occurring at 7:55 a.m. PST which converted to my time would be 10:55 a.m.; the Japanese showered Hawaii with an array of airstrikes, thus commencing *Operation AI* or more formally known as the *Attack on Pearl Harbor.*

Sparking the movement of the Rosie the Riveter assembly line while the men fought for her. Her being America in this sense, not Rosie the Riveter, she is not real. Oh, did I spoil that for you? Sorry. Repelling down the work triangle factory work is one of the most tedious and repetitive lines of work there is. Correction: that criteria comes with every job. The question is whether it is tolerable. If I somehow had to work as men experiencing the casualties of war, let's just say I would not be employee of the month anytime soon. I would do the work, but no one said I had to enjoy it. Please do not label me a Rosie. It is estimated that a whopping 2,335 Americans lost their lives in this tragic, horrific, pacific event; that can be translated to 2,335 people who will never see their families and friends ever again, 2,335 people that left too soon. However, for the people who did prevail to tell the tale, records show that soldiers used warships mounted with anti-aircraft guns to defend the harbor and its people. Being the adventurous little men as they all were capable of being, they reenacted Pearl Harbor, but with no casualties, of course. Adrenaline rushed as they gunned down Japanese fighters with ease, then proceeded to infiltrate Japanese occupied territories for intel.

As well as expanding imagination, Army also introduced August to the traumas of war. Injuries are nothing to be taken lightly, especially on the battlefield. Though amputation was never a measure taken, contagious diseases along with agonizing abrasions ran rampant. The most common ones being scraped knees and lacerations along the back. Nasty wounds, these were. Who knew the Nazis could be so naughty! Nothing could be as agonizingly painful as the time the boys infiltrated a German bunker. Mission command requested the young men to retrieve any sort of intel by any means necessary.

My dear August did not dare intervene with those evil men, especially swastika wearing ones. Held in a secluded bunker covered by dense California oaks, the treehouse was heavily protected, almost to the extent of the Unknown Soldiers. The four Unknown Soldiers are soldiers heavily guarded upon every hour that represent unfortunate souls in each major war that the United States was involved in that were never recovered. Initially, I thought only missing four is an impressive number, granted that millions die for the country every year with funerals left and right. But stupidity got home-field advantage this time around because these four represent all unknowns. Maybe if I am lucky, I will represent the lonely! Of course, I would not have to be identified as Sophia Collins, but I bet I can arrange something in my time of passing. Fortified as could be, the treehouse contained viable loot within its walls that the boys were absolutely itching to get their hands on! August was the only one able to gain access to the bunker, of course. He is the star of the book anyway. That is the way it should be; would it not be anticlimactic and disappointing if he was unable. Seen only otherwise in movies, there goes my hero ascending up the rope dangling by the only point of entry. Evidence on my stopwatch reads "30 sec," although I know gadgets have a frequent tendency of malfunctioning; that is why I kept count myself for accounts similar to this. The estimated time of arrival by my count reads "10 seconds." Calluses enfolded the anterior position of his hand, especially where the finger meets the palm. Upon entry, despite the rugburns, lies a multitude of license plates and rations. Why so many? Was this their plan to take over the United States? Every plate ranging from and beyond California to Ohio, each one being uniquely different from the other, remarkable. Propping mine and his side by side made us seem that we are not so distant from one another. I fantasize about me majestically being swept up then going off with him. Sorry, August. Not me. Why in the world would I be a part of August's world? I apologize for my peculiar behavior; where is C3PO when I need him!

I am refocused and alert once again, shall we continue. Taking three more than prescribed. Prescribed, if only you knew who these were *actually* meant for. Desperate times call for desperate measures. The plates held great intel for the United States Army, but that is not the correct kind of information they were after. It is a grand achievement finding possible plans, agreed, but that cannot give them exponential height upon the pedestal. Packed inside a hollowed-out tree exposed an instrument. The Germans wish the Americans never got their filthy hands on. The most devastating factor revolves around the condition; this particular radio has seen not its best day in at least three years. Drenched in rust, disfigured antenna, and corroded batteries is not a good look. A major revamp shall be initiated.

Imagination has boundaries, you know; it can only exist for so long! I should know, C3PO and I can talk for so long. When the boys were not invading foreign countries on foot, the clan rode bicycles throughout the community. Their favorite game to play was one that involved waving at cars. I know the concept sounds obscure, but I can testify that it is immensely exhilarating. The sense of being a part of a community can change the game drastically. "*Sweet and Sour.*" Like what kind of ridiculous name is that? Who made that name anyway! August, I swear to God. The rules were simple:

Wave at cars and hope they honk
No honk=player(s) riding down a street
Loser(s) ride up street
Repeat

Seams self-explanatory, and you would be correct. The underlying issue was that August seamlessly always fell down the rabbit hole. Tedious as pedaling up and down the side street was, somebody had to do it. Everything becomes repetitive once performed numerous times, but this predominant game never became bland even when all odds were against the group. The majority of the people August waved at usually did not respond, so down the road, he went. This mediocre "streak" continued for countless days until on one fateful day changed that all.

It was like any other Thursday evening; did I mention that they only played "*Sweet and Sour*" during the evenings? Did I? I think I did. If not, well I just did, you are welcome. Sorry for leading you astray. Anywho, during one of the sessions, a stranger yelled out of their window to August. Everyone was extremely jealous, obviously, who would not? There are two distinct yells; the first one has an emotion attached; it does not matter what type of emotion, could be happy, sad, anything you would like. Now the second one is an attention-getter. I say that straightforward as I can possibly be. I like the idea of it being a jolly yell, but that is my interpretation, not the readers. Ruling out the obvious, it was a passing car that also honked, and it was either his teacher or girl he had a crush on. Memory is vague; I apologize for the inconvenience. "Hi, August!" was all that it took to create pandemonium amongst the kids. Frantically jumping up and down, they all forgot how to be civil members of society for a moment. This event occurred once and only once but let me tell you, August will never forget this.

The Parker parents (mainly Mrs. Parker) were unbelievably strict when curfew was a variable in the equation. August knew this because he became victim to this about every time he would linger past dark. Precisely at six o'clock every day, she would holler for August and Oliver to return home for supper. I have a question, though, why holler and scream; they are only across the street. As disappointing as this may be, I do not have a clean slate answer. But what I do know for certain is that August needed her orders the most to avoid this next atrocity. Boys are always one-upping themselves; I am guessing it shows dominance, not too entirely sure. Maybe if I had a brother, I would understand. The Parker boys, along with the next-door neighbors, were riding bikes throughout the yard one day. Now, if you do not know August's house like I do, of course, the lot is somewhat magnificent. The driveway is laid out as a backward S, the house is on the left facing the road northbound. Then next to their lot, lies the neighbors with trees scattered across rough dirt terrain. The clan casually was roaming in the yard when the neighboring boy proceeded to drift outside of the boundaries of the Parkers yard and over back to his, then back to ours once again. The term "ours" is used to subliminally involve August and Oliver; in no way does it pertain to me at all as much as I want it to be.

Boys will be boys, even mother nature cannot change that. Attributing all that it entails? I will never know. Attempting to mimic the neighbor kid as best as possible, August initiates a drift. I wish this next part did not take place at all, but what could I do? His black flame' bicycle did, in fact, collide with the dirt. However, it never seemed to make its way back to the pavement. Envisioning the incident so vividly, almost as if I were actually there. The wheels would not stop, round, and round they went, where is a speed gun when you need it! Granted, I am no physics major, but I do believe that when a stationary object is pulled by gravity, it is then set in motion. August forcefully pushed his bicycle, proceeding for it to roll; only then did he lose control, and it gained speed rapidly. Rolling down the dirt hill for what felt like a millennium, August frantically tried to avoid the oncoming bulldozer of an oak tree ahead. His delicate young mind could not register the actions of evacuation. Training wheels are equipped to prevent accidents, not to cause them! If August had never so naive, this all would be avoidable. I would end up in the same situation, too. If this is any correlation.

Wet tears and bloody screams were all that could be heard throughout the community after that point. Like emerging into a thick fog, everything was a hazy reality. Guided only by a hand, Mr. and Mrs. Parker absolutely flabbergasted by the sheer magnitude of what had happened. August's mouth was nothing but blood with a gash separating gum from teeth. Mrs. Parker applied whatever she could to soak up the damage, but a dam can only sustain for so long. Once were cleaned bathroom towels, now look like they have been through a massacre. This issue would not resolve itself; professional help would be involved. It does not take a genius to figure that out. Leaping into her car, Mrs. Parker and August rushed to the local hospital.

I do not like waiting rooms after experiencing that epidemic at Amadeus'. Anticipating the wait, dying to know if you are the next name, is truly pathetic if you ask me. Hypothetically speaking, if an appointment is registered at 2:30 and you are waiting for 15 minutes beyond the requested time slot, that does not look very punctual for the company. As much as I do not like waiting rooms, apparently, my knight in shining armor is not fond of them either. Though he has a completely different reason, it is still plausible, nonetheless, more than mine. I swear this always occurs to me; whenever I am in dire need of something, I can never find it. This happens to others, I am sure, but it feels like it only happens with me. August can, with confidence, relate to this. Mother and son waited for an excruciating eternity until they were finally called to the emergency room where privacy was held by a thin baby blue curtain. The two waited for at least forty-five minutes before the "doctor" was able to see them. This person should not have the title *doctor* if he has no clue as to how to suppress the pain. Any other person would be more qualified than this nut; he should be exempt from all responsibility. Time wasted and bedtime approaching, a plan B needs to be advised as soon as possible.

There is not much open at 12:30 a.m.; everyone is sleeping. However, circumstances are different when involving my August. Denied phone call after phone call, Mrs. Parker finally rings up the boy's dentist out of pure desperation. "The dentist will see you know, Mr. August." Rummaging around someone else's filly, disgusting mouth has never been mine or August's cup of tea. Just the thought of someone else going to that extreme of lengths is mind-boggling. What is up with the hundreds if not thousands of tools they all have in their drawer of secrets? The one instrument I dread the most is what I can only identify as "the scraper; I apologize for the unofficial name, but I can care less about what it's wretched name is. I immediately get chills just thinking of it, that goes to show the reader how much I despise this tool. From my existing knowledge, it is used to scrape pockets of pre-existing food between the teeth, all while counting incorrectly. Its geometry is quite impressive, as it is terrifying. Built like a pencil without its initial eraser or lead though and initially placing dual wield hooks at each end. Darth Maul would have great pleasure killing Qui-Gon with such an upgrade. Enough with the jokes, apologies. I am having extreme difficulty putting this down in words because, with every passing moment, all that enters my ears is the screeching of the tool against my teeth.

If any of you have been to the dentist, you can surely sympathize with me. Enough about "the scrapper," I am getting nauseous just thinking about it. Now let us discuss dentists' ability to count; shall we. The number system only has numbers that are in the mathematical realm of things; there are no such things as variables, especially when involving human teeth! Variables are there as the unknown factor and not part of the solution. Dentists are equivalently clueless as to the children in my old school.

Silence is golden…...in certain circumstances. Now I understand operating in silence, but how about when your patient is in agony! "It will take longer if you scream, stay still!" the wretched dentist says. As the reclining chair's leather begins to show its insides, August pleads to have his insides intact, unlike his predecessor. Moments feel like years, and an hour feels a century; the pain is absolutely and unequivocally unbearable. With several stitches along the crease of his gum, a mouthful of gauze to the wound sometime later; her "Masterpiece." she calls it, is complete. Does not look like much; let us pray it can get the job done. Paralyzed as can be, August spent the rest of his days in bed moping for his ordinary; average, life to get a jumpstart. For weeks Mr. and Mrs. Parker watched over their "helpless" August, feeding him, sleeping with him, chauffeur him around, the normal chores parents do. If only Mr. and Mrs. Parker knew me, I would be delighted to be on August duty. I would not mind having those responsibilities at all, let alone the second one.

My Prince Charming changed the playing field with this next move; only he could think of such a marvelous plan.

I am just ashamed I did not think of this first. August, mind if I borrow this one? I will be sure to give you credit once it is a success. The plan involved becoming so bedridden and helpless that one of the adults (preferably the more reasonable one) would give into the individual's battle symphony, as a result of buying gifts for the *lonely*. I am not sure whether Mr. Parker gave into his sympathy, or it was some other factor entirely, but the provider provided his offspring with an exclusive *Xbox Vol.5 Exhibition disk*. Now for who may have gotten this far, I have taken into account that there might be a wide demographic reading this; so for the younger, elderly, and adults, or even millennials who may have no clue what this product is, bear with me as I attempt to inform you. Refreshing my memory is a wise idea, as I am not as in-tune as August is when it comes to video games. I digress; the Xbox entertainment system was produced by Microsoft in the early 2000s as competition to Sony's PlayStation and Nintendo GameCube and was a major success. It had exclusives like the Halo franchise, which also popularized the first-person shooter genre and released several playable game demos to advertise upcoming releases in the form of exhibition disks. However, for the purpose of this content, that is more than enough information needed to understand.

Plopping the disk in as if there was no tomorrow, August has longed for a day like this, a day where commands and suggestions about his health were a side quest. Divulging into a fictional world where he can control the outcome was all that he needed at that moment. The majority of the content on there was unsuitable for August, so his selection was narrow and limited. There were maybe three possible titles he could immerse himself in, two of them being sports. Why play a sports game when mother nature wants to enjoy your presence? I will never understand people. That is why I am better off by myself. The only one left that he could actually play was an original arcade run and gun game remastered to console: *Metal Slug 3*. It would not be a physical cure for the pain, but rather a psychological one. Though there is absolutely no scientific explanation as to how it happened, over time, he did begin to improve as the frontal lobe of his brain was processing the video game. Meanwhile, the rest of his brain and his body were focusing on healing the damage sustained.

Meetings are in place to enforce order among a certain group of individuals. Discussion topics within meetings can range from a magnitude of topics; these meetings are quite serious and involve copious planning. Planned sometimes months in advance to discuss products for the upcoming quarter or an issue in the workplace, requires leadership to bring people together in an organized fashionable manner. With that said, professional meetings come with risks and constant work; but an intermediate family meeting is monumental.

Mrs. and Mr. Parker pulled the boys down for an exciting piece of news. The boys jolt down the stairs in expectation of a materialistic item. August and Oliver were set up inside the kitchen, leaning over their dark green island with a black marble surface, all while the parents were sitting at the marble "cliffhanger," viewing the family quarters from the kitchen. The Parker boys drown in anxiety as the parents waited for the right moment. August could not take it anymore; he needed to know. "Are we getting a new TV?" he says. Oh, August; you silly, silly, boy if you only knew. This will definitely change your life more drastically than a television ever could. They must have rehearsed this for months; I say this because, at the same time, they both shouted, "You are having a little sister!"

Instantaneous dread crept down his elegant skin; August knew this revelation would bring more competition than there already is. Two comparatively to one is quite a substantial difference when you actually think about it. The parents would be more affectionate and attention oriented towards the younger children. Pondering the thought more adequately, the more it makes sense. Younger the child, the more recognition it needs. It needs more mental stability than an older child does. Though all of my time knowing him, it is of great concern to express my attitude towards August's gut-wrenching fear of loneliness.

I would not suggest August does have monophobia, though he does feel uncomfortable being without someone for a short period. In essence, to further specify, comforting himself with his mentality to sustain stability seems to be an effective antidote. Nonetheless, it was anything but effective on the day of delivery. With this being no exception, Mr. and Mrs. Parker rushed over to the nearest hospital while the boys were left with family friends. Frankly, I do not want to get into the essence of the delivery process; it is quite disgusting if you ask me. But from some prior pre-existing background knowledge of mine, doctors create "interdimensional portals" for babies to enter into our world through the stomach; how? I care not to swim in those waters, thank you very much. Again, I deviate from the event at hand, August and Oliver wander around a clothing store for what seems to be hours until they get confirmation that they are transferring to the next chapter of their lives.

Mr. Parker brought the boys back to see their mother, who was heavily dosed on painkillers and resting at the moment. Who knows where Oliver ventured off to in this next part, but all that matters is that I know where August is. The father of his newborn daughter asked if his son would like to see her. As passive as he is, he ever so graciously nodded his head. Both enter a long hollow corridor emerging in the nursery. Mr. Parker points at her; she was encapsulated in a tiny glass see-through rectangular box. August gently walked up towards his sister and peered into the glass. "August, wrong baby dude. She is this one over here." Granted, all of the babies had this contraption over them, and they all look the same, so who could really blame him. Do not be ashamed, my dear, I would have made the same mistake as you only I would not forgive myself as quickly as you did. Grabbing her small delicate hand with her noticing a sense of touch. He looked at her healthy baby sister and reflected on why he was the chosen one. The chosen one was born with complications but not impossibilities. This same, one with a name for the new addition: Maddie.

Episode III:
Postponing the Inevitable

"Can I offer you a fruit snack?" That was the last interaction I initiated towards Amadeus before being rudely interrupted. How did she manage to find me? I am positive I did not leave any sort of clues behind; she must have just been superb at hide and seek back in the day. I am the only one in the room thus far who has yet to face the doorway, even Corduroy has! So much for his "undivided" attention, Amadeus is not even paying attention. I want you to help me, that is why I came here on such short notice. Now, if you kindly avert your attention away from the figure in the middle of the doorway and make your way back round to me. He is not being a very faithful best friend at the moment; I shall mention something to him later about this little misbehavior.

"Um, Sophia; please explain to me why your mother is furiously standing in the doorway of my office." Amadeus, you are not listening to me! I need to tell you about August. "You worry too much; she is none of my concern." These were a poor choice of words on my part. I take full responsibility for my stupidity. She is fed up beyond belief because she invites herself in, and if you know Mother, you know that she usually asks permission to enter a room. Intrusion was unforeseeable, but I guess I am the exception. "Young lady! Let's go. You know I never say anything twice. Now, move your tush off that couch." Tugging me with such grip is quite painful; I do not wish this on my worst enemy. Well, in order for that to happen, I would need to meet people. Right as my right arm exits his room, I proceed to throw him a fruit snack. "See you next week!" I yell and as imagined; Mother was shocked that my expectation of seeing him next week would be a possible reality.

You know how in movies, most prominently kids movies, where the child does not want to leave and creates embarrassment for the parent, let alone everyone around them as they latch on the door frame and try to crawl back in? Well, that was me. Never thought of committing myself to idiocracy, but keep in mind; I need my best friend. No one else understands me, not even Mother.

Progressing down the hallway is anything but pleasant; her handbag continues to hit me. The same siblings are still in the same spot as I left them earlier, do your parents even know you are here! Mine does; I am still trying to wrap my head around how she even found my whereabouts. We are almost out of the door when it happens again. Onlookers draw their eyes as Mother's head collides with the floor. As expected, everybody goes into a panic, and someone calls 911 in an attempt to rescue her. "Hello, 911, yes we have someone who is experiencing a seizure, please hurry." This is karma, Mother; you should have let me stay in there with Amadeus. I was going to tell him about you. About the demons. But look at you now. Flopping on the floor like a fish for heaven's sake. If you are so desperate for some attention, I am proud to offer you some; but this is a tad dramatic and excessive, would you not agree? Strangers shift chairs and tables away to create a more open space. These episodes are increasingly getting worse, and might I add, more frequent. If there is a super-entity God out there, what are you not telling me? What are you hinting towards?

Simultaneously while all of this is happening, Corduroy and I are over by the siblings, eliminating ourselves from the equation. "So that's your mom! I am surprised you are even able to contain yourself in a time like this." "I never know when they are going to stop, sometimes it can go for three minutes, other times at least a near eight. This is nothing new, but this is the most violent they have even been, and in front of people too! Why do they embarrass her?" Perplexed as the little girl must be, the boy then proceeds to ask who, while still munching on the fruit snacks I gave him earlier. Looks like you are enjoying the show, bud. "Who are they? Are you okay?"

"I am sorry I have yet to explain this complicated situation. The serpent's......demons, poltergeists. She is possessed." The girl finally responds with an over-exaggerated, and might I add, prolonged "oh." Your brother asked, and I answered. Figured you two would not understand, hardly anybody does, and for a second, I thought you were different. While all of this is occurring, Amadeus jolts out of his office to assist. "Mr. Richards!" they yell. Promptly glaring at them in opposition to their remark before I continue towards my good friend with what I would imagine a plenitude of questions that need immediate answers. When the first-word leaves, his mouth is simultaneously when the demons are done with her...for now.

She looks like her morning self, groggy as always, and hair disheveled; the only difference you have now apart from the morning, is an audience. If I did not know any better, I would say I have been completely bamboozled into another one of Mother's schemes and is awakening just in time for the paramedics. Rushing from all sides, they sit her up while she is completely hysterical. I cannot blame her a bit; I would be too if I was caught in the same circumstance. Escorting me into his office is none other. So, we are going to have our meeting today, after all? Quite a change of heart now that no one is pressuring you. It is like we never left, sitting in our identical positions as we were once before but with a twist. The topic of discussion did not revolve around me this time, rather her. Which I completely understand one hundred percent, I cannot be hogging the spotlight the entire time. Understudies need their time to shine too. So, before we get into it, I would like to comprehend the fact that since Mother is of more importance at the moment, jotting notes about me will be irrelevant.

However, on her, conditions are different. "I am so sorry, Sophia; you must have been terrified! I would be too. Does your mother have a history of seizures, or is this the first time that this has happened?... Please take all the time you need. This must be a difficult time for you right now." He says all of this after adjusting his spectacles. Needless to say, this is nothing out of the ordinary, but what does he know? Animals do not talk, I know that for a fact; though Corduroy is communicating with me in such a way that is hard to explain, yet profound at the same time. He says I should tell Amadeus about Mother's condition for the safety of everyone, especially his and hers. His reason is a considerable one; nonetheless, what if the result of sharing will make Mother even worse? What if when I share this valuable information, the demons will get at any and come attack me for my betrayal! For all I know, she is still breathing because I have not told another commutative mammal to seek help. "How did you like your fruit snack, sir?" Amadeus looks at me puzzled, then remembers the packet I tossed to him on my way "out." Lord knows that the first session was nothing more than an inconvenience, for us to later meet up to operate a prolonged and more productive meeting, thus landing us to where we are now. Including you, the reader. "Sorry, Mrs. Collins, haven- my apologies; have not, had the opportunity to eat them yet. I thought I would eat them while you share your experiences with your mother." I exhale a great amount of oxygen then swallow the remaining absence of food from lunch. "Humans are a complicated creature, you see. We are the only species on this earth where we can never be certain what the other is processing in their mind. The most viable and simplistic analogy I can give is one of a tree branch. Compared to a tree branch, we can be calm and comfortable in one state of mind; however, when that branch breaks, rage and discomfort usually enfold the brain. In other words, Mother's branch has broken right off of the tree and is being viciously stomped upon by various passersby as we speak. Also, to answer your previous question about the history: this is not the first time, more like the fiftieth. This is an extreme exaggeration; I have not been counting whenever this has occurred. This is an internal war between her and her only. There is nothing that an external force can do that no one has not already done before to save her."

Amadeus is a very passionate and caring friend. Throughout the entire time of me explaining the situation to him, he is showing full compassion as if he were to care about Mother as much as I do, a possible reality. Patients are, but never should be, curious about their files. They are for the doctor's eyes only to assess the patient on their lifestyle and or cooperation pertaining to the diagnosis. As mentioned before, I am clearly not the subject at hand. So therefore, I glance over at whatever he is writing but to no avail. None of it is legible, perhaps to a chicken it is. Tapping the pen repeatedly against his lower chin, Amadeus questions the identity of the demons as expected. He is not keen on the history as much as I am, so I will give him some leniency. I retell the exact response as I once did to the siblings in the hall; only this time, the receiver did not assume I was a loony. After several tedious time increments, he finally understood the relevance of her demons and how they play into the story. Then I proceed to explain to him the first time I caught Mother experiencing an episode; you know the one, with the conflagration illuminating the night sky as a result of waking me along with the entire neighborhood. Yeah, that one.

Meanwhile, I open another one of my fruit snacks and sprawl them out on the glass coffee table in front of us. I start by arranging them by color. If you did not know; within every package, there are precisely twenty gummies in total. Every package is different in the variety of quantity but always containing the same fruit flavors: strawberry, grape, orange, banana, and blueberry. Inevitably three out of the five flavors are always going to be disregarded in the essence of superstition. I will not waste my breath clarifying which ones I do keep; the reader should be able to use context clues by now. As I do this throughout our discussion, he asks what is point of doing all of this "nonsense." You may think it is nonsense, but to me, it is an action of gaining lady luck on my side of logic and reason.

Reluctantly, lady luck has been gracious enough to let me divulge in more blueberry flavors rather than strawberry. "Speaking on behalf of luck, have I ever told you the incident with Professor Skynyrd and me? It is a disappointing one, I do have to say so myself."

"Yes, I believe you have. But you never did tell me what you two were fighting over." He responds. I know for a fact I never told him the story. But what is the use in arguing? In the end, I know I am right. Such a shame; he is missing out on a fantastic story that he could possibly share with this family, and I would be okay with that outcome. "A lucky superstitious dice? What? I don't understand. Why is that of so much importance? Never once have you mentioned that." Instead of exploding, yet I contain my composure in the calmest manner I can attempt; emphasizing the importance of the dice whenever I am- sorry, *was* at school. Halfway through our organized session, Corduroy hints towards his desire for food, as does Amadeus, but he does not need to tell me. How funny you are, and here I thought the protocol droid was the king of comedy. Amadeus' kryptonite must be plastic wrappers. I say this because as soon as he opens them, they run rampant across the carpet. As a result, we burst out in laughter.

Apparently oblivious towards the man's "studious and serious" sector I am, because never before have I acknowledged his framed family portrait resting upon his desk facing out at us for all to see. Well, I assume it is his family. It would be awkward if it were not. Time to embark on another relentless mysterious case. Corduroy! Where is my trench coat! "A recent one or one you got out from the attic?" I quickly ask without the slightest hesitation. "Sorry?" "The photograph of your little family of three. Mother does not allow photos to be as decor in the house…. Correction: she does have *one* in her room. Of the three people coincidentally, I do not recognize the other two people in the photo, only her." Understandable, I unload on him right away. It would make sense for him to pause and decide which topic to decipher first. "I am going to go at this from a chronological standpoint Sophia. First off, that picture is a newer one, yes. We were at the zoo, and my son wanted all of us to be next to the red panda bears. From my understanding, the Cincinnati Zoo is one of the only places that keeps red pandas. Secondly, do you have any idea who the others might be? There any distinguishable features you can point out? What about your mother, from what you have shared in the past, she lets no one in her room, was this an exception?" Please stop bombarding me with questions, sir. There is no possible way I can answer all your ludicrous questions at once. I have never been to the zoo in my entire life. What is it like? What kind of animals reside there? I bet the possibilities are endless. If I were to choose, I would definitely want to see a gorilla.

"What is your favorite animal Amadeus, Is it the panda bear?" I calmly pause as a way to transition towards my next topic of discussion. "Your son. I never knew he existed. I know of your wife, but never him. As for the people in *my* picture, one of them is certainly Mother in her younger days, I presume; the others are a baby and a strange man." Mother looked so happy in that photo; I still wish that were the case today. The doctor continues by writing everything down as it is happening, probably a good idea. You do not want to forget any of this. May I have my own pad? I need to jot down notes of my own too. "Interesting. Very peculiar." He says nonchalantly. Immediately, I knew he had the answer. But a smart move for him not wanting to tell. The detective, inside of me, needs to do with no outside interventions. I am a detective, after all, not a dependent child. Nothing like August, of course. He knows I am toying with him. I imagine he does not mind a bit. "Indeed, red pandas are my son: Riley's favorite animal. Mine-" Whoa! Hold your horse's cowboy. Let us click rewind on the Walkman for a second. Riley is your kid's name! He must not be the same one I am thinking of. Just an odd pair of coincidences. Yes, that is it. Do not overreact yet, Sophia.

He has not told you the punchline yet. Wait. "All this time, and you have never met Riley, have you? He happens to be coming by right now after his shift at work. I will introduce you." If the next words that exit his mouth are that he works at the animal shelter, then I will officially have lost my marbles.

Below and behold, the next source of information is just that. It is the same exact person. I hesitate to share I have already met him. Perhaps best to disclose that information for now. This is all too much, too much for my brain to process. Is it rude that I pack my things with the intent of rushing out of there with no prior explanation as to why? Surely, he knows he did nothing wrong; it had to turn out this way. Rushing down the hall, then immediately noticing Riley in the distance. He is walking towards me! I cannot let him notice me; it would be too awkward and embarrassing. Shielding my face, I pass him; however, without success. But how?

Riley tilts his head, guessing for a better angle of me. I mean, who can judge him. "Corduroy? Sophia? What- what are you guys doing here? Did you see the fire trucks outside? I've always wanted to dri- drive one." I am conflicted in this predicament; I do not know whether I should play the hostile or hero…. Hero, of course, I do have a superpower anyway. And so does Riley, apparently. Still in question on what his is, though. He is one tough cookie. I love cookies, next to fruit snacks, nothing comes close to chewy, gushy, flavorful, goodness. Cannot go wrong with a batch of snickerdoodles or red velvets. I would bet that Riley has a preferred flavor also. I should ask him about it. Another time, when the mood is more appropriate, and I am in a calmer one.

Generously replying to his questions with admission that I am the cause of the trucks being here. Priceless; his eyes widen, jaw drops in awe, and everything. He is on the edge of his seat, adorable! Careful, we do not want you to get injured. Anyhow, the paramedics are here, so if he does get hurt, it would be the most appropriate course of action. Why did he ask if I saw the ladder trucks? Assuming my vision is at a certain healthy standard, there are by no means any outside from what I can see. Paramedics and ambulances block the office building only. Understanding his confusion because I was once him, so cutting him slack is something a friend would do. Origins of anxiety rise to the surface. "Riley, I really have to go. Mother is in intimate danger; I need to see what the verdict is. Please, I hope you understand. This is by no means an excuse to blow you off. I will talk to you later. Okay, Riley?" Extreme disappointment rushes down his body; I can literally see the goosebumps exposed. "That is fine. I understand you have a life too. I-I was sooooo happy when I saw you he- here. I never wanted this moment to end. But I guess all things do. Your mother will be in my prayers, Sophia. All re- rea- ready for a speedy re- reco- reco-." "Recovery?" I interject. "Yes, that word." We say our goodbyes, and I swing the door open when I hear him yell one last thing. A speedy one for Corduroy also!

Belligerent as always, "A speedy one for Corduroy also?" Riley has definitely mixed his medicine. What does he know! There is nothing out of the ordinary, look! Well, I do have to admit, he may be right to a certain degree; his scales have the impression of being flaky. Although that might be due to consuming his food too fast. An older gentleman wearing a paramedic jumpsuit catches me and asks me to confirm my identification. Then shares that Mother is in stable condition, and she is waiting for me at home. Home leads to two paths; *A* or *B*. *A* is typically the more routine route where ignorance is bliss, where everything returns back to normal, and never to discuss my little deviation off the beaten path. Of course, with side *A* comes side *B*.

Treachery invites torment with this one. Nothing will stop the lecture of disobedience from Mother, and she will stop at nothing to make it crystal to never do this kind of foolish idiotic act again. Now that we have the possible outcomes explained and out of the way, Mr. paramedic here informs me in cases where the patient has recurring experiences in such instances as this, no call is required but she is unable to drive due to the severity. I nod my head in compliance then explain the formidable actions taken I cannot own up too. It happened so fast and I could not control it all; I am only one person, you see. People get scared of what they do not understand, but if father time were gracious to me, I would turn back time to prevent wasting your valuable time on something innocent. He was a nice fellow, a courageous, confident, approachable fellow, who must have lots of fans just waiting for a rescue.

Little whispers should have been alluding to something greater, but they were not. It was my own maniacal personality blowing it out of proportion when it obviously should have not been a big deal at all. Once again, Corduroy and I pair up with Threepio outside, only to learn of some unfortunate news. Our "TIE fighter" we flew in on has now suddenly disappeared. Who in their proper functioning mind would steal a bicycle when they most likely own a motorized vehicle? Unless it is another child who needed that bike more than me at the moment. Assuming my method of transportation must be in a nearby shrub, I scurry over to ravage for the loot I so long for. Ruling out the possibility of misplacing it all while my head spirals down the files of sequences. My heart rate skyrockets with crippling anxiety just around the corner. Butterflies materialize inside my stomach; with these innocent insects inside me comes the formidable urge to vomit. My dull fingers smear across my scapula while simultaneously pacing back and forth in a prophetic manner. I hyperventilate then immediately cease. While a healthy pigment identifies as pick, on the contrary, mine shifts to a dangerous blue, and my two loyal comrades are the only crowd I manage to gather. Equilibrium is no exception. Like anything else, it can give way and or fail completely, as I directly foreshadow an upcoming event. Record this one for Guinness because this one is record-breaking! I continue to fail and cause a scene and commotion for a while longer, but I simply do not care. At this time being, any passerby is more than welcome to interject and assist me in my heartbreaking issue. After an immense tantrum and a revolutionary makeover later, I am once composed and ready to take on the world again. I accordingly followed the steps of B.L.U.E. to find a comfortable piece of mind. As I take input along with suggestions, The fish nor the humanoid robotic droid bring an ounce of valuable insight to my attention. Drowned by defeat, I drag my feet along the barren, desolate, empty city I call home. The walk back is much longer and frightening than I recall. Reckon I have not exercised like this since I was required to for school purposes.

Staying afloat is hard enough, but how about when your life preserve gives way and shore seems an impossible reality? Every gram and protein of energy converted is solely focused on keeping you conscious. Saturated by moisture residue of the tears of an almighty, mystical, unforeseeable entity, trudging through and to a source of familiarity. August is in the same boat; the only difference relies on the key fact that he is aboard the Titanic, and I am aboard the Sultana. For the curious and unknown, prior to some extensive educational research to inform my audience, I was also lost at sea on this one. The Sulanta was a Cincinnati oriented steamboat while having an existing timeline in history of two years. Constructed in 1863, its intended function was to serve as a cotton vendor. Commercially chu chuing as it traversed the Mississippi river, passengers regularly became accustomed to her whistle. As I did not plan this at all, merely an ironic coincidence, she is named by some to be the *"Titanic of the Mississippi."*

Alter-egos can be proposed as a second identification form, less known notably. Just using our context clues, we can already hypothesis what kind of fate she will craft. According to various websites and historical manuscripts, the destruction of the Sultana is the worst maritime disaster in America she has ever witnessed. While also serving as a cotton transport, the Sultana also functioned as a passenger-carrying vessel. Rookie mistakes are the ones that will get you killed; I am looking at you, Sultana, and your distant cousin Titanic. A full diagnostic is widely suggested; luck has never yet been gracious with tragedy. Around the pitch-dark hour, the ships three of four boilers suddenly exploded, and roughly 1,200 out of their 2,000 passengers perished by either hypothermia or her platonic nightlight flames. Historical records date it back as occurring on April 27th, 1885, but you cannot believe everything on the internet. After commencing such dedication research for such time, I am astonished to learn that this catastrophic tragedy has always been overshadowed due to Lincoln's assassin just days prior.

I know what you are all thinking, surely my boat may be worse to board, but let me assure you, August is currently in suffering as I have already met my demise. Stairs can be the most ordinary and bland piece of architecture to date or the most intricate; it all takes shelter under the hospitality of deception. Up to this point, Mr. Parker thought he experienced the worst of it, however that never seems to be the case in real life now does it. Usually, it will get worse before it gets better. The adolescent years are some of the bewildering and exhausting steps a human has to conquer. Everybody packs differently when traveling but relatively loads similar items when evolving from childhood. Teens inventories almost always exist with that one over-encumbered element, yet my beloved August is unable to dispose of this mission-specific item. Before there was labor induced exercise, the ramifications of any sort of factor of exercise were obscene and obliterator from a standard perspective. Physical education killed August in every possible way, especially the physical running aspect. (Obviously due to his severe throat condition) Running was a quintessential portion of the PE course at his middle school and was mandatory if you strived for anything above a C-. Any sort of alternative is practically despised due to their high tiers, so we can officially erase that one off the list of ideas.

With that "added benefit" of a rapid increase of demise, my knight pierced his armor more times than I can recall...all ultimately due to bullying. I am just lucky they did not target the critically fragile chainmail! I remember him sharing that every day my August would return home drenched in tears, thus breaking his mother's heart in the process. Initiating vengeance among the wicked one revived a strange comfort in him. Of course, it was merely a recurring thought within his young adolescent mind; he would never act upon it, would he? No, no, Sophia, foolish answer. Physically amongst the two, there were never any altercations, but traumatically it was a horrendous train wreck and imprisoned within the rubble, the sole survivor. The term survivor refers to someone who remains alive after an event in which others have died. Coincidentally, I do not find beauty in the literal.

For me, more so August's sake, the definition that greatly resides, corresponds to a person who copes well with difficulties in their life. None of it was better when the enemies' distance was within a dangerously close proximity. Talk about putting it to the test. He ultimately was not ready for what was going to be bestowed upon his head. Ruthful, despicable lies left him vulnerable than ever... for now. I cannot remember precisely what he shared with me, but I do recall August stating the things said were mostly revolving around his uniqueness -that being his throat- despicable statements along the lines of "If I had what you have, I would kill myself right now you ugly motherf***er." I can surely relate to August's struggle. I was once picked on for my power, and I know the exact reason why; they were jealous. Jealous, my power has been bestowed upon me and not them. I will forever obtain an ability they can never possess. Though it never was a reoccurring event unlike August's, he is much stronger than me, absorbing all that torment to ultimately make it into something positive. Remarkable! Transpiring into a physical altercation was never an issue except for one instance. Well, physical, if you can even classify it as that, considering the protagonist provoked the antagonist, which ushered injury. I will give him the benefit of the doubt; the warning sign signaling not to tease the ferocious lion must have not been visible for him.

My little gazelle was being chased by not only one but two lions! The great African safari applauds foul play in her royal arena. Any method is overruled in hopes a victor emerges. Grotesque and gruesome as ever, the mane monsters muster for number one rank upon the leaderboards. There are rare occurrences where the great African landscape intervenes to whips their wild beasts into obedience commencing a conclusion to a lesser successor. Make no mistake, the gazelle is severely wounded, but not down for the count. Mr. Parker still has some fight within him. The bully slowly fades while physical education parades the streets. I assume the majority of the audience, if not every single one, is dazed beyond confusion. Let me rewind to where we last left off. Remember, we already established the connection between Mr. Parker and physical education and the bully, yes? Well, the three-go hand in hand along with the African analogy. Them being the two lions and August being the hunted gazelle.

Pain is a funny little creature, chronic defeats acute when discussing an appropriate adjective in order to unravel the intensity of one's certainty. Reasons become knocked out are realistically due to the underlying factor that it is too egotistic to get into the ring with a whole lot of fatal flaws. However, with advantages surpassing it by the entire nine yards, chronic pain can just as easily submit to justice; just ask August about his story! Pinpointing precisely what the root of the downfall was is nearly impossible; we can only speculate.

Reducing his physical status from shockingly significant standards to only a couple of months. August was slowly dwindling away. Obviously, by the one thing we can all use more of; exercise. Third class hour metaphorically insinuated him waiting for a hospital gown transfer affirmation. For an entire school year, 180 days, to be precise were slowly enabling the demise of my smuggler. This Leia cannot survive without her Han.

Two laps off campus grounds around a public park equate to one mile or, in other words, 1760 yards total. So, in direct comparison, the students had to run 880 yards to be considered 50% into their mission in progress. He could barely do five minutes of running! What makes you; the authority, think he can run a full uninterrupted mile! Each passing day grew increasingly difficult for my one true love.

Absolutely reconsidering what Riley mentioned earlier, Corduroy does seem unusually quiet with seldom eaten any food in the past few days. Riley might be onto something, but too soon to concrete anything obviously. I will keep a close eye on you. Sling-shooting time into motion once again, I am still convinced it is still an utter miracle August survived his entering the junior high school year. In retrospect, summer is the epitome of fun; the time to scope out the beach, explore well past dawn, and most important of all, enjoy the water! Reimagining the word summer is so foreign to us Americans because we believe all of our ideals are blueprinted and ready for production. All to do now is to start production; however, a dimension has been miscalculated time to remap. The particular dimension in question is an instance of that which occurred in the first or second week of June. It was only a couple days out of school when action was initially taken. Personally, if I qualified able to test drive, procrastination would not linger for as long as it did. Mrs. Parker, do us all a favor and pass over the guardian papers over here if you would kindly.

"Honey, August! August! Are you okay!? I'm calling Cincinnati right now!" Now you may be thinking the location is done purely out of convenience, perhaps, although the reader knows nothing about me beyond these pasted words. I cannot imagine this is really happening; just imagine, me and August finally together at once! I cannot begin to express how excited I am at this moment. Cincinnati has been a safe haven for the Parkers even before I entered the picture. That is to say, if he were to venture somewhere else other than this specific location, he would have no chance of survival. These folks are the best in the business in what they specialize in and were recently ranked number two overall in this year's children's hospital of the year. Overperforming all other 86 qualifying contestants, August needs to go to the best of the best. Losing my baby is not an option!

Firmly gripping his now overflowed tank, the three of us acknowledge our existence with a loud slam. Extracting one capsule from C3PO's makeshift plastic head, I am once again fully submerged within the Parkers' world. Returning that excessive water back to the ocean, persistently, I watch Mr. Corduroy become less agile in his gestures and altogether; frankly, I find it disturbingly peculiar. Just when things could not get any stranger, a pair of feet cushion the welcome mat!

Episode VII:
Finding Beauty in Unchartered Waters

One last adventure with the family: *The Capitola Car Show*. Located 10 miles from Santa Cruz, they host tons of public events such as this one, but this is by far the guys' favorites. Every year people bring their hot rods and custom classics admired by many, and may I mind you, the majority of them are impressive. Personally, I am not one for motorized vehicles, but who is that to say for August. It was on that weekend that he found his dream car, a vintage 1965 Shelby Cobra 427.

Internet exploring is difficult for someone like me to accomplish. Repeatedly I fail to find an image a little higher in resolution; I do hope I am searching for the right car. *Single, double, triple* clicks later and finally, stumbling over this man-made marvel. If August were here right now, he would give me a pat on the back. Although a pat would be much appreciated, in the end, it serves only as a distraction.

Absolutely lost for words, let alone the revolving world, stunned by its mirroring metallic blue guarding an impeccable sublime white stripe dividing the machine at the sagittal plane. You know what the people say, *"If you love something, set it free."* for all to see, and is that not the truth! I am roughly estimating the time on this next section, so please do not butcher me if I am incorrect, but 60 dedicated minutes were spent just looking at one car! Do you know how long 60 minutes is? 3,600 seconds to be accurate. That is one hour of your life you will never be able to exchange with Father Time. You know how many side projects I can get done in an hour alone!

Despite that, not all was lost; souvenirs were included in the weekend getaway. Next to the amphitheater at the center of town were kiosks stocking everything and anything hot rods. Though August did not find this too appealing, now Mr. Parker… that is a story for another time. Wandering around the various tents, the sponsors presented their finest products to car connoisseurs. From gaskets to merchandise, the list was endless. Now he wanted not just a temporary item; No. August wanted what the sponsors could do; promote and advertise. He wanted actual proof that he was there, word of mouth deflects in effect over time. Records claim the date was Sunday, June 13th, but who really knows the exact date except for August himself? Intel, thus far into the eldest son's story, points to him purchasing a mud brown, long sleeve shirt exhibiting an image of a black skull centered around triple flames with scissors at the base all encapsulated with the event name. The sleeves are unlike anything I have seen yet before, one long strenuous faint blood red flame outlined in black on each arm. The back duplicates the front image but projected in a larger font presented by what I can only guess as the main sponsor under a pristine black exposed beauty 1930 Ford Model A chopped hot rod and the words: *8th annual* on the left deltoid muscle.

Gurgling engines and exploding exhausts occupy airwaves, forthcoming their departure. Leaving only an echo in their wake, filled once again when she (being the ocean) conducts her waves. Brushing against trillions if not billions of sand harmonizing with the lyrics of crickets, her waves send as our moonlit "natural night light" signals guidance.

Doing my research like the good girl I am, I have discovered change is as much of an opposition to him as it is to me. Another common factor we both share; check that off the list of compatibility. Now arrived in the Buckeye State with a taxi as their source to get from point *A* to point *B*. Predictable as ever, their minimum wage chauffeur, of course, drew a complete blank on the desired location. I advise this man to get a new profession! I am shocked he made it to the airport by himself, to be perfectly honest with you! Observing the bickering from the back seat, voices are then placed in the trunk by attractions dominating three alternative scenes in the metaphorical sense, of course.

Little more to go until our paths can officially intertwine, but what is distance when you are truly head over heels. Crossing over to my world, reality as we know it has been permanently shifted sideways. Entering a special privilege house whose only residents check the box for any complications greater than or equal to grievous, cold chills run down his spine as he convinces himself of being an unwanted guest.

Funny of you to mention that August because speaking of unwanted guests; there are currently four feet pattering around the ground floor when there should be no more than two. Like a child, I grow increasingly fidget then ever so delicately, press against the bedroom door. Intently staring at the white wooden door as if that were to improve my audio receptors. By no means am I a bat, but I predict the interaction went like this:

He greets Mother, and before he could say anymore, I hear a slam at the door. How rude, give the youngster a chance! Nothing more than the current pitter-patter I now hear down below. "Why now? Why now show up after all of these years." A deep pause can be heard and deep enough that it takes a moment to regain her train of thought. "You know what; I should have never let you in, in the first place. We are fine, I appreciate you checking on us, but you need to leave Jeremy." Mother enters the kitchen with the premeditated thought of a welcoming gesture. This Jeremy character must be an emotional slob; I need a rowboat just to get out the door!

She then offers coffee; a reply can be heard from the man, and the conversation picks up where it left off. "Where is she?" he asks "-she's the other reason why I'm here. Look, I know you have full custody of her now, but I haven't seen her in eight years. By the way, did it ever occur to you what the real reason for me being here is? I got a chilling call from the doctor. Apparently, I was the number one person on your emergency contact list." Mother corrects him while also catering him the caffeine morning beverage. "It's been 10 actually, but close. She's grown a lot, you know; she is not the little girl you remember. Let's say I do let you see her, right; you're a stranger to her." Guess Mother really is Mrs. Parker in the flesh, hmm, it never occurred to me once. They become less agitated towards each other as the two finish their drinks in the kitchen. The stranger (her words and also mine) requests access to see me until the tyrant finally grants him an opportunity to do so.

Intently listening as he is gliding his hand all the way up the railing as he approaches my door. While simultaneously for minutes on end, I devise a battle strategy. Good thing, the stairs are somewhat strenuous. He unlocks the door with the special Morse and invites himself in. I am sorry sir; did you not happen to see the *"Sophia's Room: Do Not Disturb"* warning sign visibly present on the doorknob. Clearly, you cannot read either. My "welcome greeting" is anything but as he pokes his bald head, though, and is immediately greeted by my E-11. A standard trooper blaster, the difference between me and stormtroopers...I will not miss. Admiring my bed as much as any eccentric enthusiast would makes me rethink my initial perspective. "Woah! An AT-AT bed. It's got a full cockpit and everything. This is awesome!" I continue to stay silent until I look at C3PO for encouragement. After I ask him who he is, I direct his full body away from any possible exits, for I command him to face me. The classic hands held high the head surrender pose is the image he is going with. Smart move. "I would not dare mess with this rebel if I were you." I confidently say.

This next action displayed by this soon to be familiar "stranger" sold me. I say the word stranger extremely loosely to capitalize on the essence of its importance. He inches towards the vigilant armed soldier while his arms are kept vulnerable still. "Obi-Wan never told you what happened to your father." A smile shows, and I cannot help but play along. "He told me enough! It was you who killed him!" More confident as I have ever been in my life, it is safe to say I rest assured in the identification of this dicey smuggler well before the twist is revealed. "No, I am your father." Intently staring at him, the exact same Luke did to Vader. "No. No. That's impossible!" The only exception I will ever use a contraction. Ever. Extending his hand outward in hopes as he finishes the iconic scenes with a bang. "Search your feelings. You know it to be true. Join me, and together we can rule the galaxy as father and daughter." Withdrawing son and depositing daughter in its place. It seems unnatural if I did not modify the line to my liking. It is my book, anyway. Of course! That explains the photo in Mothers room. That man must be him. The dots are finally aligning. The bondage of hands signals my acceptance towards this rash claim of his. "Please, Father, explain yourself, or is it alright if I call you dad?"

Blaster now holstered, he guides me down the ladder and starts by making up for lost time. Kneeling down to my level, he proceeds to ask about school. However, as dad does so, there is a hollow-sounding clank erupting from his knee. Guess I should not have stared for as long as I did; he caught on pretty quick. Ever so slightly, he clenches his fist. He taps it a couple of times for demonstration purposes. Why does his sound so different than my knee? He must be an intergalactic alien! -It is the only logical solution. I mean, why else would his knee make a sound like that? Perhaps he is some sort of cyborg. Either or, it does not change the fact that he is here with me at this moment. He leans in while I am in the process of straightening my cluttered hair. With a majestic soft whisper, he shares a secret. "Prosthetics are overrated; but your mother still thinks I am still fully intact, little does she know. I only put this on, so I won't get another lecture. You've had your fair share, I reckon. I much more prefer wheelchairs. I got mine stashed in the truck out front. But shhhhh, this will be our little secret, okay, baby girl." Compliance is extremely important in this household, or else there will be consequences as you have already seen. So, I respond the only way I know how to: by nodding my head in a rapid motion pledging my allegiance. Forgive me for being too curious, but this visit could not be random; he had to have a reason for being here. Loving me is not a strong enough valid answer. Inhaling air, I began to regret my decision. "It is your mother." He finally says. He asks if there has been any suspicious activity around the house. When are there not any suspicions? Sorry, this is not the time for jokes. This is a serious matter. Mother's life may be in jeopardy, and I will not go and jeopardize another mission, my sincere apologies to Dad and my readers.

Anyway, school has not been a highlight of my existence, and now he is aware of that reality too. Bowing his head and directing his attention towards the ground, I then hear my first curse word. I have heard of them in various forms of media but never in the real world. My body retreats as my voice lets out an expression of dissatisfaction. "You still going to Amadeus? Huh? Or did she take that away from you too?" It is hard to connect the dots on something that does not have an already pre-outlined path to take. How in the world does he know Amadeus? I am no mathematician when I say this, but this does not add up. Having to repeat the question a second time, he recognizes the dilemma. "Who do you think set you up with Amadeus honey? Mommy or daddy?" Is it not blatantly obvious, of course, if someone words a question that specific, you can almost always count on the person asking being the initiator! Dad tells me that he was the one who arranged Amadeus with me and not Mother. She was too incompetent, he says, too irresponsible, too stubborn he says. Apparently, Dad and Amadeus have been lifelong friends, the best kind of friends. Then glancing at the time and kissing my head, Dad exits my life temporarily. I watch as Mother observes the last few moments of our encounter together, smiling and feeling what probably was self-regret. What else is she hiding? From this day forward, I vow to never trust that deceiving, maniacal woman again.

Dismissing the fog pressed against my window, I watch as he gets into his modified truck then drives off into the distance. I have so many unanswered questions like how do you drive and stuff like how did you lose a leg, and why has Mother never mentioned you? Officially shutting her out of my life and also the door please. I have some very important work that I must attend to, so if you would kindly operate someplace else; that would be much obliged. At this time, I usually feed Corduroy while also conversing with

Threepio but today was different despite the blue drops in the sky. As I normally do, I feed him fish food but refuses to eat it. I apologize for not getting the correct brand, but I had no choice. This was the only one they had at the grocery store, and I was not about to travel all the way across town just for you, no way. I had to get my food too, you know, it was more convenient this way. Killing two birds with one stone sort of thing. The action of brainstorming usually regurgitates brilliant ideas, but like I mentioned earlier...today is unusual.

Being the diplomatic service droid he was always programmed to be, Threepio suggests a clean environment will make our inseparable friend bubbly once again. Awarding his fast thinking with a thumbs up, I then bring them all to the residing room across the hall. Flicking on the lights and closing the door, I immediately get to work. Plopping him in the sink while simultaneously waiting for a lukewarm tub, I start by cleansing the tank with a new and healthier aurora as from when I got it. Smothered all over the walls and even the decorative rocks below, feces. These once turquoise rocks are now browner than mud on a mucky day. After minutes of making the same non-compliant repetitive motion over again, a change of action is recommended. As I exit the room, I witness the protocol droids hand directed towards the sink, but the action has yet to register in my mind. Foolish me, but everybody does make mistakes from time to time. Jolting downstairs like some kind of superhero and opening up a cabinet in the kitchen. I know precisely what I am looking for. *Operation Extraction* is currently implemented as we speak. Everything is going according to plan, no hiccups whatsoever until Mother emerges from her room. I am guessing from all the ruckus I have created.

"Sophia, what are you doing? Stop making so much noise. My head is killing me!" Shriveled up like a sponge, I apologize for my actions depicted in promise to be much quieter. She is hesitant to travel back up the stairs; her movement comes to a halt as she begins to ask something, entirely disregarding the concept of confidentiality. "How was your visit with your father? It seems you guys were inseparable. He truly loves you, you know." "Unlike you." I say this while still scavenging for supplies. Creating no eye contact under any circumstances though to drive the nail deeper. First a grunt, then the lingerer spies on me as to see what type of mischievous work I am up too. If attempting to be cunning is Mother's way to appear invisible, I have to admit that this is the utmost pathetic and embarrassing way to execute such a plan. Who appears to be acting like a child now!? Curious as to what we did? I will inform you, Mother, we did quote-unquote "stuff." Stuff she cannot fathom, stuff she has no control over, and frankly, I would much prefer if she does not intrude on mine and Dad's life again. You had your chance, Mother, to make things right for 16 years in fact, and you blew it! Well, we all have to move on at some point.

Persistently buried inside the pantry cupboard; shifting pots and pans out of the way, I search for some sort of appliance to delay this conundrum; ceasing duty after becoming alarmed by a startling *"BAM!"* Poking up from down under the cupboard, Mother vanishes from my peripheral vision. Whipping around the corner, I do nothing but stare in awe at this horrific event I have foreseen numerous times before. Not wanting this chapter of my life to end just yet, Mother's phone is the first destination I run to. Good thing too, because Dad gave me his phone number in case of emergencies before he sped off. This would fit the definition... correct? The more time goes by, the more worried and stiffer my body becomes. If there is a purgatory, my heart just plummeted towards it because next, I am greeted by a voicemail. "Hey, you reached ██, I am not available at the moment. Leave your name and number, and I will get back to you as soon as I can. Thanks." Four or five times later and the same belligerent response. Not sure whether it was four or five times I dialed; at the moment, I am too overwhelmed, as you could understand. I did my part, now do yours, dad; answer the phone! In total disbelief, I come to an epiphany. Amadeus! Why did I not dial him to start with? He will know exactly what to do!

Phone calls particularly are not my specialty, as the reader can probably tell; if I cannot properly execute this, I am out of options. He identifies my voice immediately. Then that; is when I begin execution "Do me a favor and shut up and listen. Forgive me for coming off as rude, but something happened to Mother! Correction, it would not be labeled as something if I know the roots of the problem. Never mind that, she made them angry. No, not angry, livid. They are relentless in their pursuit, and I already called Dad multiple times but to no avail." Finally, I gasp for air. "Remember, in your office, when the paramedics came? Well, that was because the demons attacked her too. But now it is significantly worse. Help me, Amadeus, you are my only hope." I know it is a lot of information to take in, and it may be confusing to someone like him who does not know the origin of these traumatic events, but he will come around soon enough.

Lost for words, he starts off by stating how many questions he has. As one would in such a predicament. For him, it is probably like opening a book towards the climax and him not knowing where to go from there. "Warning, Sophia, take this with a grain of salt. Judging off personal accounts, I presume your mother is suffering from-" Enough! Nobody likes a spoiler. Revealing the matter at hand so soon, please, and especially in a time like this. Not your best move Amadeus, not your best move.

Accompanying me in my mist of sorrow, my good and honorable friend apparently decided to show up to take Mother away. Amadeus tells me I should not be home alone and to be there for Mother when she wakes up. Your positivity is reassuring, however, something from a Disney fairytale. Shall I suggest the term *if* rather than *when*- she wakes up? Shutting down the offer by expressing my dedication to the other task at hand, I have in the bathroom above. Still, he feels uncomfortable about leaving me alone, I perfectly understand, but I am not a child Amadeus. I can take care of myself clearly, as you can see. Before leaving with Mother in his arms, he tells Riley to stay with me. Was he in the car the entire time? Why did he not come out to at least say hello? He is an odd soul, let me tell you. The mentor leaves the premises, and now it is just two naive rascals roaming as they please. Let the fun begin!

"Hi, Sophia." Riley says while swaying back and forth. I say hello as I am gathering my instrument from the kitchen. Transcending back up the stairs to finish what I started before I was interrupted; he is still in the same position. He has not moved since he has gotten here and is staring at me like he is studying me. In an attempt to be a good friend, I stop in my tracks and include him on my mission. "Riley, I have to finish something upstairs. Would you like to come?" I already know what he is going to say. Of course, he wants to be involved; he would be foolish not to. "So-Sophia, I- I would very much like to Th- Thank you." My eyes widen at him when I whip around. "Wait!" He is startled and, as a result, jumps back down the stairs. Sorry, Riley; I did not mean to startle you. If it is any consolation, I scared myself in the process. "You want coffee?" What kind of friend would be I if I did not offer him a welcome beverage? "Yes, please." He says gently. What kind manners you have, young sir. You are 10% more of the human I will ever be. I applaud you for Amadeus raising you in such a pristine prophetic manner.

Is it too late to tell him I have never made coffee, as a matter of fact, anything on my own before? Well, he will soon find out this disappointing reality through my work. Some wife material I obtain, no man wants a woman who cannot tend to their needs. So much for any sort of directions either, there is no systematic order when it comes to coffee, guess common sense is applied to these "simple tasks." A simple task. Give me a break. I barely know how to start this concoction! Riley butts in the mists of my suffering. "Do you even know how to make this? It is okay if you do not know how. I can just have water. Hey, Sophia, look! The sun!" I need to finish what I started. If you originally wanted coffee, you will get coffee. However, it may take an hour or two to figure out how this contraption works. So, if you do not mind, I need to concentrate. Locating the coffee beans inside a glass jar out of the corner of my eye and dropping what I think is a good amount for two people. This is the moment when disaster begins to brew.

"Riley, how much water do you think I need to put in? And do think I need to heat it up?" Looking away from the window, he suggests filling it halfway and to heat up the water. His reasoning being the water will not heat up in the coffee pot; it just blends the two together. Smart thinking Riley. Honestly, what would I do without you. After heating the water, I dump it into the pot and click *"Power on."* Placing myself across the kitchen table from Riley that is against the window, I wait for one of us to strike up a conversation. Riley fidgets with his hands, caressing them back and forth until he finally gets the courage to break the ice. "I am sorry to hear about Mother, honestly. Do you know how it happened?" Stretching my hands upward, pretending as if I possessed the power to pull the sun right through the clouds. "You see Riley, that right there is a loaded question. If you really want to know how it happened, we have to start all the back to when I was still in school in Professor Skynyrd's class. But I digress, yes, I know how it happened. In layman's terms, she has been in an awful collaboration of events that lead to her becoming possessed by demons from hell. One day, she pissed them off so bad that they have been relentless ever since in their pursuit." His eyes widen once I finish; along with his heart, I can only guess. "You were in Skynyrd's class too! Now I remember seeing you. You were the one having a blowout and dis- disru- disrupting the class one day before he pulled you outside. I was one of the students watching you on display. I want wanted to tal- talk to you that day, but I was too sh-shy." He has been there from the beginning! That is astonishing. God only knows how many tabs he has on me! He is like a chameleon, hiding in plain sight. This is revolutionary information. What else does this friend of mine know? Adding onto what he was previously stating. "Mentioning the demons from hell, would- would- would..." Spit it out, man, we only have so much time together. "......would you like to go to church with me and · dad in a couple of weeks?" Starstruck for a moment, not by the question, but rather the offer. I open my mouth when I am interrupted by the side activity on the counter, feet away from where we stand.

Uncontrollable shaking as if it were to mimic Mother, I race towards it but too late. The pot now has a mind of its own, frolicking all about and dancing upon a lifeless stage. Motion after motion, the performance almost becomes unbearable. Almost is used as a filler word here; it actually is unbearable. Maybe I should not be so open and admit such things because my words apparently have a crushing impact... Literally. It shatters upon impact with shards of glass and splattered coffee redecorating the room. We both say nothing yet look at each other, thinking the same exact thing. Fetching the dustpan, I start to collect the pieces. Riley begins to help almost immediately. I bet he feels bad that he was the one who ultimately caused all of this. But really, it is not his fault one bit. It was inevitable, it was bound to happen at one point or another. I am just glad he is here right now to share this memory with me. Containing our silence no longer, we both burst out in laughter. Whipping away his tears for him, he looks down into a shrinking puddle of coffee. I poke my head next to his both staring back at our reflections, sometimes I catch myself staring at his reflection and vice versa. The house is abundantly filled with silence, only Riley and me both intently observing our physical features like never before. It was so unreal; I would even admit almost magical. It happens so fast I am lost, paralyzed if you will, and then this man does the unthinkable. He leans in and……

Whoa! Whoa! Whoa! Did you think Riley…. And I? No. We are only friends. Good friends but not *really* good friends, if you catch my drift. I am grateful to have Riley in a part of my life, do not get me wrong. But he can be nothing more than a friend to me; my heart is only for August Parker and all that he represents.

Riley pulls me into his chest and initiates a hug. His comforting posture invites me in, almost like a shadow does to an unclaimed piece of territory. Nonetheless, I am proud of myself for not going into a panic or blowing anything out of proportion. This marks the longest duration where I have not had an episode. I will be sure to thank Amadeus for his efforts next time in our next scheduled visit. Politely asking him to do the sweeping, Riley immediately takes up the offer with no hesitation whatsoever. While he is making the kitchen less hazardous, I, on the other hand, am soaking up the spilled coffee off the walls. My heart sinks six feet under. "Oh my gosh!" Racing the clock now, up the stairs and nearly tumbling in the process. Riley is not far behind.

Gaining my attention the same exact way from the last time I exited the room, Threepio directs me towards my powerless aquatic cold-blooded companion. Friendly reminder, native bound sea creatures require water to exist. Water is essential to fish comparatively as oxygen is essential to mammals. But why am I telling you things you already know. You are here to read a story, not a lecture. Though I deviate from the beaten path, inhaling all the water possible into his gills, I am in utter shock at my blissful ignorance as I stand there paralyzed. It is Riley once again who saves my life. The one to restore water to Corduroys suffocating gills. What I would not do for a friend like him. He is the absolute best friend a girl could ask for. Obviously not taking Amadeus into account, of course, he is in another category separate from his son.

With quick thinking, the atmosphere is now stable, thanks to the actions done by Riley. Returning his gift better now than ever, a gentle yet affectionate wrap around the shoulders indicates my true feelings for him. I just hope he does not get the wrong idea. Riley is my first actual real friend, and I want him to never be in doubt about that. I know I do not display the best attributes of a friend at times but believe me when I say I am trying really hard not to mess this one up. I know this is silly because, realistically, we have only seen each other for weeks at a time, but I feel a surge between us. I am the flint, and he is the steel, just hoping a spark will ignite. After our endeavor in the bathroom, he asks permission for a change of scenery. Plopping him down into his now squeaky-clean environment, I then introduce Riley to the most important room on the foundation.

Encouragement, caring and giving. These are ingredients to only one of a plethora of recipes for friendship. With mine, the guideline I always follow includes an optional ingredient; directiveness. Directiveness is one of the core building blocks to a successful friendship or relationship for that matter. If you cannot be upfront and personal with the people you interact with, they are rewriting the soul definition of honesty. Directiveness may come in all shapes but most prevalent in the form of authority figures. Perhaps that is why August feels lost at times because they are trying to hide the gripping reality, but actually, by building a wall around him, you are only damaging him even more.

Mr. Parker and his protege are greeted after being buzzed in. The middle-aged brown curly-haired woman leads them to a side room of the house. My question is, why is it called a house? Yes, it resembles one, but if this house can hold seventy-five plus rooms, I believe it would be categorized as a hotel; tell me I am wrong. Argue I will not. Logic has baffled me once again. There they establish the ordinary check-in procedure and something for August as a welcome gift. The bag had a red pigment to it with white text overlapping it inscribing the name of the location. Within the bag: boxed snacks, hygiene equipment, and something he still cherishes near and dear to his heart to this day; that of a custom-made blanket by one of the many volunteers who work here. Obviously, he could not choose what design was appropriate for him, but he did with what he was presented with. A giraffe textile patterned blanket lined with a thick fleece coat. The woman soon finished up and escorted them to their temporary living arrangement.

Phasing through the morning, then late afternoon, the Parkers arrive for their scheduled appointment, not a moment after the moon settled. Not an appointment per se……procedure would be a more applicable noun to use here. Unlike anything he has done before, doctors made him be part of a "monitored observatory sleep" in simpler terms. Mind elaborating more doc? I do not want you to do anything to my August without my approval. As long as you promise you will have all eyes on him 24/7, you have a green light on my side. August, what do you say? Who am I kidding? It is not like you have an actual say in this sort of matter. From conversing with the team, the Parkers reassured themselves with the now definite plan. Departing from the elevator and led by someone from around the front desk, she leads the duo down a long corridor to a room at the very end.

At least to me from a personal standpoint, the current floor where the Parkers are located strikingly resemble Amadeus office. With the added concerns of hysterical children accompanying more germs with them on their bodies than a public playground. So much for only admitting children to Cincinnati Children's Hospital! August is 13 years of age; he is well beyond a child's age! Guess this particular intricate individual has special access due to his long-recorded history with the company; countless years dedicated to one organization means a lifetime membership;

where do I sign up? Placing sticky pads in vital areas upon his body, the pads are then linked to a monitoring system unforeseen by the patient. Authority tells him to sleep as if nothing were to be out of the ordinary. How can he, though, with these atypical sensory readers strapped onto him as if he were some type of suicide bomber? As Mr. Parker's prodigy get situated for slumber, the staff observe in a nearby room while Mr. Parker stays with his son as any good father would. Only a few hours later, August is brutally awoken by various members of the staff alongside Mr. Parker, expressed by a face best summed up with concern exhibited by his actions and facial expressions. Emotions of confusion and horror play out as my poor boy loses all self-control, water secretes from his eyes. The most hysterical I have ever seen him yet, the staff continues to do what they were doing previously. From the words of Mr. Parker to August, he apparently stopped breathing throughout the night and had to instate oxygen through the nose. Judging by this unforeseen catastrophic incident, he does not need a confirmation from a man in white to determine the severity of the situation.

Hazy by what seemed to be a nightmarish dream, mornings reckless judgment pursuit continues. Wheeled out of that wretched cesspit of a room, having an ancient phone by today's standards to his name, and filed into what is only known as A5. Surpassed any sense of expectation, the eldest son was now provided with his own room with surrounding neighbors—a significant upgrade from the night before. Side conversations ignite persons from all over entering and exiting the contained floor as they please; drone out anatomical nuance cries of children with fates yet decided. If it is anything to the audience, August had a window room overlooking the dilapidated decaying Cincinnati streets; then again, everybody had the same viewpoint he had, just from various angles.

What a coincidental change of scenery, Riley and I are now at the hospital also! Not the same one as August, although that would be quite something. Hypothetically if that were an option, would I decide to visit my dying mother or my dying love? There is no immediate answer I can give, not without ruling out one completely. Although, karma has its fair share of weights. A fair amount has happened since you last left; such a shame I have to repeat myself once more.

So yes, Riley saw my room, and to my surprise, he thought it was magnificent. No one else has seen my room before, besides Mother and now; Father, so to have someone else's opinion on my personalized room is an appreciative comment. Introducing himself with no explanation needed, my artificial intelligence humanoid droid says it is a pleasure to meet one of Miss. Collins associates. Taking into consideration the awkward interaction, Riley respectfully nods his head then averts his attention back towards the one non-inanimate object in the room. I pull up for him an extra chair as he is intrigued by the stacks of paper on the wooden desk filled with clutter. "Astonishing! Look at these. Did you do all this? They go on and on." Grabbing a neatly organized color-coded stack and tossing the read pages scattered across the floor. Do you recall when I gave you permission to play Sherlock Holmes in my room? Me neither, please getaway. If you want to see them, I will show you…. and handle them with care for that matter. "Excuse me, sir, these are in pristine condition and would greatly appreciate it if you do not ruin my work. This is very important to me, but that does not mean you cannot be curious. If you do want to look, I would be more than welcome to show you. You just have to ask before going and manhandling registered property." Wiping something from his eye Riley apologizes for his unprofessional attitude, then tries again in his best effort.

It still has room to improve, but I will not make you perform a due over. Embarrassed, he was most likely and in front of a pretty girl! The recollection and gathering of papers continue as Riley is more than reluctant to assist in the accident. Firstly, expressing what an honor it is for an opportunity to arise for us to spend quality time together, in conclusion, to reveal the importance of those papers, Riley currently has his fingerprints on. "All these stacks of paper you see here in various colors with sticky notes everywhere; this is my book. It is still in the works, of course, but it is coming along nicely if I do say so myself. However, I may be a bit biased, so it is in your best interest to share your thoughts on it too." Riley cautiously grapples the cover page, if you can even call it one; and reads the title aloud. "Res- Rescue the Lonely. Why is it called that? Sound Sounds condemning." Taking a sip of water, I roughly explain the plot. "A lonely is, or dare I say are; the ones more advanced than everyone else, more specifically in the mind, body, or soul. The premise revolves around a young man by the name of August Parker and his sense of purpose in this shattered world we call home in the various stages of life and the challenges he has to overcome. An example being when he legitimately could not breathe on his own and was dependent on a special device to assist. Another time whe-" He interjects right as I get into the heart of the artichoke, metaphorically speaking. "Soooo, who is this character based on? Is August me!?" I can tell it took him a couple to finally get the words out. Prophetically confident as an opportunity like this does not occur often, I elucidate my troubled friend that August Parker is a mere product of pure creative imagination who takes characteristics from various individuals but never is he defined by a single soul.

Just as I begin to conclude the topic, we start to hear alien sounds on my property. Signaling the man to protect the woman, Riley quietly removes himself from the chair and inches towards the window as I patiently wait in my room for clearance. My heartfelt like it was ready to leap out of my body, and my hands, along with all the other limbs, vibrated a chilling sensation down to the nerve. I hyperventilate, waiting for some sort of response. -Any for that matter! But I continue to see Riley look out the window motionless, then I hear something. "*Slam!*" Clearly identified as a car door than silence…. for nothing more than a moment. With not a second for either of us to react, three hard forceful pounds connect with the door. Finally, pulling him away from my room, I lead the way to the front. Both of us are hiding behind the door. I look through the peephole one last time before hearing another pound. I see nothing, yet I still open up.

"Sophia! Thank god, where's Riley? He is still here right; do not tell me he did not happen to leave." Just started non-compliant as if a stranger to me; however, Riley pokes from around the door. "There you are. Guys, we need to go to the hospital. Sophia, it is mom. She is not doing well at all; she is very ill. Riley, your dad is watching her over there, and I came to pick you guys up as soon as possible." That seems like a justifiable reason for an interruption; thank you, Dad, for including us on your ever so endearing endeavor.

Now that the reader is all caught up, there should be no need for confusion. As I was saying, I am at the hospital for Mother's sake, and I have seen nothing worth mentioning. The only thing remotely interesting, if you can even call it that; would be the dedication of a nearby hipster; I say that out of sarcasm; there is an old man two chairs away within the waiting room, digging for gold, to put respectively. Repulsing as the sight is, I glance back every so often as I look past Riley and the tv, as Dad is in preparation for us to visit Mother. Geez, she has never needed any sort of preparation before this life-threatening attack. I bet the demons are grateful she has been such a compliant host. Riley darts his eyes back and forth in my general direction, and he thinks I do not notice; little does he know. Licks his lips, and then he cannot decide how to position his feet. A couple times, we touch hands, but that is it, and none of us know if we should advance. Best we do not test our luck. Finally, after getting a sip out of that water bottle from the vending machine he got 15 minutes earlier, my friend finally succeeds in gaining my attention in hopes of god knows what. Being very vague and shy with what he is asking, I tell him to speak up. The stuttering does not help the mumbling one bit, as you could imagine. Tired of attempting to decipher his encrypted message, my body leans across his chair. "So, do you want to?" "Want to what?" I ask. "Can you be any more cryptic?" Threepio can be hard to read sometimes, but never this difficult. "Go to church with me this Sunday. I want you to ssssit next to me." Extending my hand, the same way the businessman does in an office meeting, Riley latches onto my hand, and our eyes interlock. "Save me a seat."

Just before my dear friend can get a breath in, Dad waves us back. By this moment, anticipation usually kicks into overdrive but nothing this time. I am in awe this time and do not know what to expect. I try to brace myself for the worst possible outcome, but I do not know what that would look like. I would like to imagine it would result in becoming motherless, although how far can that rope extend, a physical absence or mental absence? Brain damage would be extreme, and I have lived with extreme circumstances before; it is nothing I cannot handle. The only difference now being Riley and Dad acting as an added lifeline if necessary. Riley runs to Amadeus as soon as we reach the room while I pause before going to Mother. Her skin is pale as ever, and when I touch, goosebumps form, running rampant along my arms. "Mother? Mother, wake up! You okay?!" I yell. Clearly, she is not alright; however, it is an appropriate thing to ask whenever someone is not themselves. I would ask Riley or Amadeus the same question if they were in the same predicament. Dad whips my hands away to pull me aside before I perform my version of defibrillation. Good thing he did so because I do not know where I was going to go with that. If my actions had followed through, Mother could have ended up with broken heart syndrome; I am not saying that figuratively either.

Crouching down to my level while in the background the Richards are courteous enough to leave the room, Dad reiterates what news the healthcare provided with him. "Mom is very sick, and frankly, I don't know if she is going to make it through the night. I was talking to Amadeus earlier, and he said you knew about her condition for some time. Why didn't you tell anyone! We could have prevented all of this from happening. I am not mad; I'm just disappointed you did not tell anyone sooner." After he does the same and meets his longtime friend outside.

Placing myself on the edge of the bed and caressing her hand, I start to ramble. No one really knows what to say when they ramble; it kind of just happens. You do not think at all when doing so; at least that is the case for me. I start off with how sorry I am for not sharing my secret with Amadeus, predictable, I know. But it was bound to come out at some point. As expected, she does not respond, but somewhere deep down in the abyss or wherever her soul is trapped, I am certain she forgives me. Forgiveness does not come gently for people with autism; we have a difficult time with the social aspect of humanity. With that being said, I just pray, Dad can forgive me also. I can tell he is unpleased about my previous actions. Nothing I do or say will resolve the issue now. Think of it as an open wound. Injuries like these almost always require time augmentations with dissolvable stitches.

Instinct kicks in as my conscious zombified body is subtracted from the barely conscious being, exiting the room with an idea after Dad pulls me away. An idea that will certainly make Mother forgive me for all the years of "torment" I have caused her. Believe me, I am the least of your worries, Mother; now that Dad is almost done playing detective. Trying to decode all that you have done to me over the years. All the pieces are starting to align quite nicely, would you not say? Familiar voices are unsuccessful in their efforts, but the voices cannot persuade me from my mission. If I derail from the tracks, who will steer the train to safety? Racing down the hall to the same spot where Riley and I absorbed some well-nourished quality time and swiftly grabbing a pair of sunflower plants off of one of the receptionist's desks, I began to make my way back. I doubt the receptionist will mind if I borrow these for an extensive amount of time. It is for a good cost, of course. Sunflowers have always been my all-time favorite flower, and also interestingly enough, it is the epitome of conjuring good fortune. But that is not its defining trait; a single flower is made up of upwards to thousands of smaller flowers expelling from the pedals. Informative answers are my forte; however, I cannot scientifically explain the process if I cannot even comprehend the gravity of that fact. Although it is not Mother's particular choice of flower, it is okay because it is not like she would be able to object to the matter anyways. I return with the ideal plan, placing flowers upon the window. Cracking the shades inconspicuously, the sun ricochets off the plants gracefully surfing across Mother.

Positioning myself closer to Mother this time as I approach her in a knelt position, an indecisive entity fills the room. Nothing hostile, no, but rather something passive.

Encircling Mother and me, we feel surprisingly content by its presents given the circumstance. Perhaps it must have been due to the sunflowers' integrated healing factor. Debating my next move cautiously and quickly grasping her hand for a request, I have yet to mention it to any of the adults for some time now. "Mother, for weeks now, ever since the first initial advertisement has been for public viewing, I have been obsessed with seeing *Star Wars Episode VII: The Force Awakens*. Would you and Dad care to accompany me?" A long-overextended pause fills the empty space. "Oh! Can we bring Riley also? I am starting to think he can be a keeper...potentially." Just as I begin to wrap up, a nurse comes in to escort us, visitors, out. Correction; not really us, more so, me. Just before asking for a third and final time, Mother, ever so fragile, gestures me with a tap of the middle finger upon my wrist. "The Rebellion will crush The First Order" are the last words she manages to hear within the correct calculation of an appropriate earshot distance.

Individuals do not cope well when addressing tragedy or trauma. Trust me, I know this far well to be true. There is a severity when it comes to these hardships. Within every complication, there is the kind that creates temporary traumatization. All of these symptoms usually include and correspond in both levels of mood shifts to a depressive or angry behavior, anxiety, and an act of consistent fatigue. Ordinary! No. These signs are by no means, not ordinary. Popular signs like these are a great indication of when someone is struggling but do not ignore obscure signs, especially when they do not appear present. Though August does appear to be suffering from similar conditions to something I can link to soldiers in times of war. It is unlike anything else I have seen before, a slight case of post-traumatic stress disorder that disorients the brain and triggers ambient sounds emitted from hospitals. It is hard to explain if it is not relatable, but imagine, the slightest trigger has the possibility of simulating that one tragic event throughout the complete duration, filing down to a fraction of a second. All memories surface to air, as you relive through where you were in the moment of desperation.

I knew when Augusts demons were coming, but August himself? Well, you will soon find out. If I were in August's current situation, which I most definitely am not and have no desire to be in, my first order of business would have been to analyze the procedure from the previous night to hypothesize an issue. Although that is not a realistic plan, however ideal, nonetheless. Next, I would survey the room, scoping anything deemed suspicious in particular. This is not about my course of action as much as it is Parker's. I tried to warn him about all the signs; however, stubbornness got the best of him—a tragedy truly, what ended up occurring. I feel so helpless, knowing there is nothing I can do to help my other half. My partner has been through enough already, has he not! Right now, if I could trade places, there would be absolutely no hesitation without a doubt!

Episode VIII:
Colossal Circumstances
for a Small Person

Dear Lucasfilm,

I am writing you this strongly worded letter in regard to the latest entry in the beloved Star Wars film franchise. I saw the premiere with my parents and a good friend of mine this past weekend. The film overall was phenomenal, and while taking heavy inspiration from <u>A New Hope</u> was not a discouragement on my end at least, I do wish it were not the single thing that it would constantly lean upon. I found the new characters extremely likable, however, not as adoring as the original cast. This now brings me to my next topic of discussion; notice how I have not used my strong words yet. Do not worry, we will get there soon enough. You will soon find out I am very particular in my wording and want to address my issue as clearly as possible, so this kind of thing does not occur in the future, either to me or anybody else who may happen to fall into a similar predicament; just so we are on the same page. Anyhow, as for the original characters, the way they were placed in the movie to drive it forward was fabulous, and glad it was not just another five to ten-minute cameo. For the lead protagonists who will protect the galaxy from The First Order, Rey is a spectacular character along with Finn. But me being a biological female, she does not per se dominate the movie, outplaying Finn or Kylo Ren in their respective roles. However, is a shift within the galaxy we all know and love. Speaking on behalf of the Star Wars galaxy, I would now like to call forth and announce my strong words for the upcoming issue for the remainder of the letter. C3PO's arm!

You people should be ashamed of yourselves, stealing an innocent girl's idea and using it solely as a cash grab—shame on you. Threepio's arm turning red is my idea! It happened to me first. Lucasfilm,

you could have at least asked permission to use it in the movie. I would have generously obliged, but since you did not, I am suing you! It all happened well before the movie was being advertised for public viewing. I was in a deep slumber when I was suddenly awoken by what I have now rationalized as red paint upon the walls. Its point of entry is still unknown, and the paint still leaves a stain on bleeding through my bedsheets as we speak...or write? The red paint is quite persistent if you ask me. To make a long drawn out story short; most of the stuff was washable once I ran it under the bathroom sink. Though since I waited longer than anticipated to do his arm, my CP3O figurine is now and forever the etiquette protocol droid whose color scheme is not fully intact. So, you see, my idea was stated well before your company ever took any initiative. This occurrence happened roughly four or five months ago in the scheme of things. So, if you would do me a favor, please Lucasfilm, own up to the mistake you made. May the force be with you!
    Sincerely,

Sophia Collins

P.S. Can you bring Mother and Corduroy back, please? If you are not aware of my dilemma, Mother and my fish Corduroy recently passed away due to uncertain circumstances. Though she could be controlling and manipulative at times, deep down, I know Mother loved me in the same way a mother should love their child. She is bossy at times, especially when I am running late as an example, but I know there is nothing I cannot do to make her stop loving me. A few days prior to her demise, she was admitted to the hospital to deal with the various demons inside of her. We all know now how that ended up.

Demons:1 Mother:0.

Unable to fully diagnose, let alone cure her, they released her that Tuesday, and that Friday, we saw the movie. As I mentioned earlier in the letter. My good friend and I got seats inside the theater while my dad got the popcorn, and Mother was arriving. Mother was running late because of her feeling ill, most likely due to the medication; they gave her. Immersed in the full 136 minutes, I went to stay with my dad for the night afterward while my friend accompanied me. Mother traveled back to her house, but she never made it back. Those wretched demons found their perpetual time to strike. Guess the doctors so happened to forget to mention that the patient is at substantial risk by driving a motorized vehicle. I thought it was protocol to go over all the rules and regulations prior to graduating from in-patient to out-patient. By now, you have most likely realized that my parents are not married; from my understanding, they divorced a long time ago from something I have yet to discover. But believe me, I will one day.

By no means do I actually believe I will go along with suing the company. I just did that as a tactical method to strike fear into them. I do not know the first rule about commissioning a protocol like that, but I would imagine it requires an absurd amount of filling out informative papers. A signature here and a signature there. Which ideally, I currently do not have the time for or the willpower to start an all-out feud with one of my favorite companies. Let us say I do go through with my irrational pretend plan of mine, then who would finish *Rescue the Lonely*? Yes. That is what I thought too.

"You ready, baby girl? I will be in the car." Putting the finishing touches on and wiping away the remaining tears, I meet him in the driveway. "Who will all be there, and do I have to say anything?" Dad is very compassionate with his answer. "Only a few people. No more than twenty. Mostly consisting of your mom's side of the family, but you can hang by me if you want. Although I think you will be surprised by how many people you do know. As for a speech, that part is entirely up to you. But you do not have to if you do not want to." Whenever we hit a stoplight, Dad checks on me in the rearview mirror.

I understand why you are checking on me, but you do not need to. Trust me, I am okay. I am just processing it differently than you. The time is 10:00 a.m., and the destination is across town, and yet we are the first important figures to look over her headstone. Where are all of the other guests? They should all be here by now. If she could see it now, she would be proud of the aesthetics. "God, I miss you. Why did you have to leave me so soon? This was not how it was supposed to be! You were supposed to live forever and be by my side through thick and thin like you always are! What am I going to do without you or Corduroy…....? I love you, Mommy." Out of nowhere, tears roll down my face, and within a flash, Dad surrounds me the only way he knows how to. With a big hug with a kiss on the forehead.

I collect my composure after an appropriate time of weeping, brushing the autumn leaves out of my hair as I see the guests come over the hill. Forgive me, the term guests would not be applicable in this instance. Guest is usually used in situations involving parties or a proper gathering in which you invite them. Instead of calling them guests, I will refer to the collected people as mourners. Rays of light cut across the grass, all while birds sing their songs. You know, this place is not as bad as they make it seem. Then again, the sun is out, and I am in perfect view of all of my surroundings. Nothing is obscured in any way; I do have others with me to make this experience less frightening. If the reader has not guessed it, this is my first visit to Vine Street Hill, let alone any cemetery for that matter.

I believe this is where Mother would want to be buried if she was able to express an opinion right now. Now she will never be alone, even when we are not physically here; she has all of these stone statues guarding her soul. Serving to protect the dead as they were always meant to. I just hope Mother believes in superstitions too. Clear of any obstructions, Dad reassures me that he is right by my side, no matter the circumstance. Thank you, Dad, I needed that. Especially in a time like this. The mourners arrive at the headstone, an eloquently displayed sense of community surrounds the remaining members of the Collins family. Some of them with flowers and others with umbrellas. Might I ask why umbrellas? Clearly, the weather is anything but wet. What? You thought it was dark and rainy; that is too cliché. The sun is shining brightly for all of us, waiting to compliment her. Umbrellas are not considered formal dress code, or am I missing something completely. This is an exception for circumstances where they are appropriate? Imbeciles!

Dad is held upon a pedestal as he pushes the service into motion; metaphorically speaking of course, because the cost of an actual pedestal would probably exceed the budget. Additional to the fact that he is currently bound to his chair. "First of all, I would -excuse me, both of us; would like to thank you all for making it." I stand in front of Dad, his hands resting on my shoulders as he continues. "As most of you are aware if not all, our marriage didn't last. Excuse me," Dad swiftly looks at me and corrects his mistake before I go berserk. "-did not last. But that still does not mean that I did not love her any less. My wife was ...complicated, to say the least, and judging by some of your faces, you know exactly what I am talking about. But that is beside the fact, she had that special flair about her that made her irresistible." Chuckling replaces an initial pause. I take some time to survey the crowd. I can hardly point out any of these people! This is my first time ever seeing these older beings! Dad lied. So much for me knowing anybody. There is nobody here remotely close to my age! Did you know that eyes can relay information we physically see into our brains as an instrument to perceive what we know as reality? According to a study I recently learned about, everybody we see, whether it is a one-time occurrence or multiple encounters, has the potential to appear in dreams. So, these mourners that I am glancing at for a split second may appear as nobodies in my dreams even though they actually are somebodies.

He chuckles and begins to reminisce about a time before I was even conceived. "I remember we had been dating for a little over two years by this point and decided to go bowling one night. Well, actually, it was candlepin bowling, a similar variation to the traditional thing. Slightly altered rules but logistics and endgame are the same. Anyway, it is the middle of the second game, and we are having a fantastic time when all of a sudden, she starts getting cocky. Can you believe that? Her! My ex-wife! Cocky! Never heard of such a thing."

My apologies for desperately wanting to interrupt your soon to be a romantic story, but was that sarcasm you just used? If Mother heard you say that she would not be very pleased with you at the moment, Dad. I am trying to look out for you. The audience is laughing; *They* are laughing. Dad, you are making people laugh at a funeral. Guess this is better than crying. I am not going to judge the way you run things if they appear to be working. After all, you did orchestrate this entire event. As you were saying ... "So, she strikes up a little competition. If I win, she says, I have to join the army, and if she wins; she gets the naming rights to our future baby. Good thing I always wanted to go fight for my country. Now finally reflecting on that day, that bet was extremely stupid, then again, so were we. To make a long story short, she won the bet, and now we have living proof of the best thing ever to happen to both of us. Sophia."

Claps and snuffles fill the air as we disembark in an attempt to get lost in the crowd. Moments pass awkwardly as ever, waiting, praying, for someone to take the stage. Looking back at Dad, I ask if he is aware of who will speak next. He informs me that there is no set roster; if someone feels so inclined to speak, they will. He already went over this in the car with me, but I have no control over it; I am nervous beyond measurement. Seeing someone emerge from within the crowd filled with mourners, Amadeus steps into view. Just before he begins his eulogy, he ruffles with his spectacles and bow tie while I, on the other hand, spot Riley from across the way. I link up with Riley, and he is anything less than overjoyed to see me, although deeply saddened by the circumstance, as we all are. First, admitting how great it is to see me and then saying he is sorry for my loss. You are too sweet Riley, I wish you walked into my life earlier; truly, I do. Then you could have gotten to know Mother better than that first and only encounter at the pet store. He pulls something out from behind his back. "I brought some flowers. Wh- Where sh- should I put them?"

"Hold on to them for now. We will personally go visit her once everyone is done giving their speeches. You look appropriate for this occasion. Your jacket is exquisite." Riley whispers something so faint that I almost have to do a double-take. "You look exquisite too, if I do say so myself." At that precise moment, both of us dart our eyes away and become increasingly embarrassed by displaying our quivering smiling faces.

Throughout the duration of my good friend's eulogy, my eyes begin to secrete water. Riley soon notices and asks what is wrong. Even though he knows what is absolutely occurring, he still obviously says it as a way to comfort me. My demeanor shifts as soon as I stare into his wide hazel eyes. "Riley, I- I do not know when it is appropriate to cry." Without expelling a sound from his lips, Riley's hands does the communicating as he embraces me, and I begin to let loose as my beloved friend constantly reassures that it is okay. My cries practically mute the speaker. Sorry, Amadeus, this was not intended in any way, believe me when I say it just happened. Riley pulls me away from amongst the commotion out of respect, and I finally become like everybody else, like Riley, a mourner. I cry for some time, telling Riley the typical things a mourner says. Like how much I miss her, and I wish it was me instead of her. Well, maybe not that last part. I begin to be more hysterical as time passes through our fingers, and I tell Riley something I thought I would ever admit to him. "I love you, Riley. I want you to know that, okay. I will never let you go." He hugs me tighter then solidifies the thought even further with a kiss on the forehead. "Yeah, me too." He replies.

After calming me down some, we return to our rightful spot amongst the crowd. Riley does something next; I am sure he will never regret for the rest of his days along with what had just occurred moments prior to this. Ever since meeting me, Riley has had a thing for me. I could tell from day one. If the reader could not tell by now, I am very observant. I just do not look like I am. Just as we toon back into Amadeus' riveting story, his son inches his hand towards mine, trickling its way into my palm. You would think he would look at me, or at least I would… but no. I just hold on.

"I remember the first real-time I met ███████. It wasn't until Jeremy and I got stationed to go home. You see, we were in Iraq in 2004, and that is where I met my soon to be best friend. Hey! I thought you lost that bet! You don't get to join the army. How did you get roped into that?" Dad then shouts out from among the crowd. "She had no say. It was my decision. We already had Sophia. The bet was long over." "Ah, I see." He says, and Amadeus then continues. "Well, as I was saying, He invited me over for dinner one night. Must have been no more than 12 weeks after Riley was born, that I finally met his wife and Sophia. Little did I know that baby girl of theirs would become my most ravishing patient to come." He does a twinkle in his eye to me while further explaining how he and Dad began to drift apart.

He begins to explain about how I was the elasticity that kept the rubber band stable throughout the duration of their lifelong friendship from terminating. The story goes that apparently, Dad gets discharged from service early due to combat-related issues. Guess there is no more mystery about the leg ...or at least what is left of it. Anyhow, after his arrival home, Mother's demeanor drastically shifts within the 8 months he has been away. Once a loving, nurturing, and spontaneous wife, to now being a paranoid, overprotective, mother. Reality hit Mother in the face hard. Perhaps, this is only mere speculation at this point. You do not think anything bad will ever happen bad to *you*. How could it? Bad things only happen to everybody except me. News flash: you are still among the minority, and the minority just became the majority. She soon convinced herself Dad was unfit to operate as my father due to his violent past experiences apparently. So, not even 30 days go by, she separates him, and now Dad is in the picture no more.... or so I thought. He was relentless in his efforts to see me once again, but he could not get past Mother. She was far beyond saving.

Eight years go by, and that is when Amadeus enters the picture. I know this may seem like excessive over-explaining, but it all comes full circle eventually. There is a meaning to this. Take me on this one. Have you ever played the game of telephone when you were little? The game comprises of two items but involves three parts. Imagine Amadeus and Dad as the two cans at the end, then me acting as the string that holds them together. In essence, if I were not a part of Amadeus's life, nor would I be of Dad's. I'm unsure if this is the best example I can give, but this is the first analogy that initially came to mind, and the more I think about it, the more it makes sense. If it still does not make sense to the reader, I would advise them to sleep on it, see how they feel in the morning.

If Mother were present, I would have no complications with this next affair. Forgive my inconvenience, nonetheless... there is some sort of animal which becomes fully independent once the mother abandons its young. If I can remember correctly, the species of animal I am referring to are harp seals. Just like these arctic seals, Mother has officially abandoned me now, forcing me to drift along the ocean's unpredictable currents without warning. So much for that so-called "mothers unconditional love." And just like that little harp seal pup drifting across the ocean, life seems to act as a vast body of water for the time being. I finally buckle down, muster up the courage, and walk into view of everyone once Amadeus finishes. It does not hit me until I finally see all eyes trained on me. What did I do! I am so stupid, I could barely speak to Mother without flustering or mixing up my words, let alone an undivided crowd! What better way to kick off the headliner, am I right? Though I am going to go out on a limb on this and confess what the reader is thinking, I am not the headliner everyone was expecting.

There is a distinct difference between the haves and wants of people. Having implies that you need it no matter the circumstance. You only need five things: sleep, food, water, shelter, and air. The rest: meaning everything else in the world; would be filed into the *want drawer*. *Wants* are completely and drastically different from haves. *Haves* are the qualities that are necessary for survival, *wants* are materialistic items, beliefs, along with many more that the heart desires. For example, purposely for clarification, although I find it hard to imagine that anybody does not understand this concept by now, that is beside the point. I *want* Mother and Corduroy to come back; I can clearly see Riley *wants* me to like him back in the same way he sees me. By any sort of obligation, do those things ever *have* to happen; we may *want* those things to happen for our own benefits, but never *have* too. I want to say something; I know it is by no means mandatory. But I want to do this for me... for Mother.

"Hello everybody," I start off. "some of you may recognize me, but I probably will not recognize you if you come up to me after." Everyone giggles; that must be a good sign. Thought of throwing in a joke in there, or two. The atmosphere was too blue...see what I did there? "Honesty is the best pill, tell me I am wrong. No, but seriously, with all jokes aside, I want to give you some more insight into what kind of person Mother was. Mother was the best mother I could have asked for, and I would not trade her in for the world. That will not change now that she is no longer with us; that just makes her memories even stronger. She could be very protective at times; more times than most, I might as well add if I am completely honest. Whenever I got in trouble, which was a fair amount for a young teenager, she would immediately take away my C3PO figurine I carry all around with me. It was immensely aggravated, as one would imagine, to say the least. But now, looking back on it, I would just love for her to take him away from me one last time."

I accidentally shed a tear, but the show must go on, nonetheless. "The first time I truly noticed her declining health, I did not want to believe any sort of negative aurora could happen to Mother. But I had to come to grips with reality sooner or later. I am going to be blunt and I do not care what any of you say, Mother was possessed by demons. Persistent with a side of resilience. There was no way of tracking them, no set time when they would appear. That is what finally got her in the end; Mother was spared during the battle, but ultimately defeated in the war. I convinced my good friends, Riley and Amadeus, of their existence as well. All this time, I knew from the complete duration of time this was occurring; she did not attain the required will power to abolish the possession of her demons in the slightest. It was all a tactic I thought up in my head to convince my feeble mind from interpreting a real logical and rational truth to all of this chaos. The scientific truth in which I was later informed by Amadeus is that Mother suffered from epilepsy." Another flow of tears reenters the atmosphere and at that precise moment, I will never forget what he did for me; Riley joined me up on the platform and just looked at me and held both of my hands as I fought to get through it.

"I know she fought as long and as hard as she could, but that car ride home was a fateful one. At least she spent her last moments with the people she loved. So, in conclusion, we cannot bring her back no matter how hard we try, no matter how much we want to, but she will always be a part of us. I love you, Mommy."

Tears roll down my eyes once again. This time, I am not the only one. Weeps cover the stratosphere for it to only reside to normalcy after an accumulative amount of time. Dad rolls his way up to me, at which point I fall into his arms. As I continue to weep in his steadfast arms, Mother is already in the process of being properly buried. I am curious as to which method Dad chose, was it his choice or one of Mother's dying requests to go out like this? Using the process of elimination taught to me by schoolteachers, I can eliminate the cremation course of action, which then leads me to the direct path of the widely popular, traditional, decomposing body in a casket sentence.

I am just going to put this out right now before I forget to mention it when it is too late and time has already taken its course; if I were to suddenly die of natural causes or whichever cause best suits my style of death, I would request that I go out the same way Darth Vader did in *Return of the Jedi*. With my lifeless and unresponsive body decaying at the sound of crackling embers, roasting over a log fire deep in the heart of a nearby forest while Riley, Amadeus, and Dad, attend along with people I will form a bond with in the future years to come.

Pulling him up close and personal, we are now towering over the tombstone. "She only lived to be 37? That's not long at all. My dad turns 42 this year." Riley exclaims. "No, it is not Riley. Not long at all." I say in a sudden reply. Next, Riley then takes a sigh and begins to slowly shake his head in a swinging motion. "I hope you know that I know that we are and always will be the bestest of friends, right, Sophia?" I reveal something out of my pocket in which I only know the contents of at this point. Riley sees something shimmer out from my pocket and asks the question the audience is all probably wondering right now. "What is that?" Dirtying everything else up except my dress, my nails are covered in dirt and small pebbles while I dig within the confines of the earth without blatantly asking permission first. Creating a small crater within the earth, I then place my raccoon butterfly attentive listener companion, Corduroy, down under. "Mother never trusted me with Corduroy. I had to almost force her to let me buy a fish at first. Over months and months of trying by my pessimistic nature and insistence, something clicked in her. She must have figured finally buying a fish would shut me up. Well, you want to know something, it worked like a charm. Riley suddenly disappears from my peripheral view, nowhere specific to my knowledge. Now it is just me and her, a mother, and her daughter.

"Since I already gave my eulogy on my behalf, I am finally going to make a confession. A confession you and Amadeus have wanted ever since you two were in speculation. The pills! I have been stealing your pills. You know the ones, with "30 mg" etched into the clear half of the orange capsule. I have been hooked on these Adderall pills ever since you began experiencing seizures, perhaps even before. Nevertheless, my pulsating desire for them grows rampant. That one day you took C3PO away was one of the most excruciating days for me because he is not only my comic relief partner but also my reserver.

A reserver, or as it is officially known in its proper synonym form, a placeholder. A reserver is a person by my definition in which he or she can refrain an item or substance from use or is able to refrain for future use. All thanks goes to Webster on this one; I can take no credit on this one; plagiarism is a punishable crime in the state of Ohio. Surely, I am surprised you or Amadeus did not do any further digging into the matter. Assumed the matter would be a prevalent one for you of all people, however once again, my assumption proved false. Now that you, my initial supplier, can find no vacancy on earth, and I express that in the most literal way; Mother, you can no longer provide my creative side to thrive. Now the question for me becomes, how will I get more?" A vow is not valid unless set in stone, something in which I second-guessed and was too naive to comprehend at the time given. Hallucinations are a force not to be reckoned with. Now for future references, I know to only take the prescribed dosage per day."

Holding materials provided by none other than mother nature herself, Riley returns to the spot where he once stood before as he reenters the picture. Without a word spoken prior to the action depicted, he places two slightly disproportionate sticks overlapping each other. A cross now sits on the head of Corduroy's burial site. What a lovely addition! If Mother and Corduroy were still present, they would both immensely appreciate the gesture done here today. "Thank you, Riley. This means the world to him." I say.

"I can only imagine." He settles near a patch of fallen leaves off to the side, without signs of any physical display of attention whatsoever. Lost in his own thoughts? Possibly processing all of this like the rest of us, wondering how I will be able to progress further in life being dealt an atrocious hand. Do not worry Riley, I still have you and Amadeus. Let alone Dad, to help me get through this, it will be okay.

Covering Corduroy up in a blanket of dirt and worms, I begin to comprehend what just occurred. Never would luck have it that Sophia Collins would lose two family members so close to each other. "Corduroy and Mother both died on the same day...evidently. Both were ill at a time when these two figures were an immense part of my life, although Mother suffered much longer, that is beside the point. This is by no means an accident occurring at the right time and the right place. No, this was definitely something more...paranormal." Pronouncing Riley's name no more than three times in total, his attention is averted back to the existing reality.

"So- sorry w- wha- what? Yes! You are right, Sophia." Supernatural activity is seldom yet effective. So, I hereby officially propose a proposition, suggesting that Mother and Corduroy's passing's are done by the works of an ungodly, spiteful, mephistophelian, demonic presence. "Could it be possible that when Corduroy got severely ill, Mother started experiencing more episodes? Like telepathically connected?" I announce. I only wish we had the same positive outcome Elliot and ET had. Riley then responds. "Hon- Honestly, Sophia, that would fill in some of our gaps we orig- originally had. You- you- You are very smart. I would have never thought of that being the underlying cause." Startled, as one would be when hearing a suspicious voice approach from behind them. "Excuse me,

Sophia?" it says. Riley jolts his head up well before I ever make any attempt.

This is an unexpected turn of events. Look who it is! This is the last person I would ever expect to show up at a place like this and especially on a school day! "Skynyrd? What brings you to this part of town on a Wednesday afternoon? If my memory proves me right, which it always does, you have a class to teach at this very moment. Correct?" Professor Skynyrd smirks at the fact of my over embellishing confidence, or would that be my ego? He has not changed one bit since I last saw him. "Hmm, you always did have an exceptional memory. I admire that about you, and yes, I am supposed to be at school at the moment. But as luck has it, I just got back into town. I returned from a vacation with my wife a couple of hours ago. I was walking my dog when I saw you up on the hill here, and I could not resist but to make my way to see how things are with you." Wanting to be desperately noticed, Riley waves at Professor Skynyrd without disrupting the mood, and to my satisfaction, Skynyrd remembered Riley. Well, he is in his class after all, it would be quite concerning if he did not know who he was. Skynyrd averts his attention back towards the conversation at hand. "Well, Skynyrd, a lot has happened since I left school. Mother pulled me out and is now homeschooling me, and I got a pet fish from my new friend here, Riley." Skynyrd's eyes illuminate, then wrestles for his vanilla Labrador dog to calm down. "Awe! So, how is your mother anyway? I have not seen her for quite a while." Viciously shaking his head with bent arms passing each other in a horizontal fashion. "It is okay, Riley. Thank you."

I am quick to interject. "You want to talk to her; she is right here. Be my guest, I bet she would love to hear another familiar voice. We were just talking to her before you approached." I point down to the tombstone, and the makeshift cross Riley made moments earlier. Flabbergasted as an unknowing soul would be, Professor Skynyrd sends his condolences and little did I know that would be the last time I see him in a long while.

Dad calls us over. I could already tell he called it a day and wants to go home. "Sorry for taking so long, Dad, we made something for Corduroy. Not that you care or that is any sort of viable excuse, but I thought you would like to know that Riley and I were being productive." I holler over to my guardian for some sort of affirmation. On the way back, Riley asks something of himself that I find a bit intrusive if I can be frank. "Since this is a hard day for you, do you want- want to hang out later. Possibly a slee- sleep o ov-er?" Way to be slick about it, I would have never thought we would already be getting to this stage already in our relationship. Let me ask the opinion of the audience on this one. Do girls have their guy friends sleepover? Or does that usually end up in grown-up stuff?

"You know, I am not the right person to ask. I cannot make this tremendous decision for myself. There are too many factors that go into this. Tell you what, let us ask Dad and Amadeus and get their opinion on the matter." I clarify the situation to him.

Amadeus's response: "Sure kiddo, you know what, Riley, you are a great friend! I bet Sophia is glad to have you aren't you, Sophia?"

Dad's response: "I see no harm in it. Sounds like pizza tonight for dinner. It will be better to end today on a good note rather than what your boring old dad had planned tonight."

Fast forward to later in the evening, Dad leaves me in charge while he goes to supply us kids with dinner. For my first rule over my dominion, I suggest to Riley we go upstairs with the intention of inviting See-Threepio along to join us in our adventures. On the way up, Riley reminisces to the last time he was in this house. Ah, yes, Riley, I remember. How could I forget, the events were merely a chapter ago...literally. Onward with the story, we get up to my room, and I grab my little friend off the desk. Meanwhile, my other friend trends into unchartered waters while my awareness attempts no effort to notify me. "Riley! What are you doing! That is Mother's room. No one is allowed in there!" Now I am no expert here by any means; however, the face Riley reveals to me once he turns around shows the embarrassment down within. "But-" I know exactly what is about to be expelled from your mouth, and you are correct. Defiance is nothing but a word to me now. Before, it signified punishment if caught. But who will catch this mouse now if the cat is nowhere in sight? "I never said we could not venture forward. Proceed with caution." I say.

"This is no different from my mom's room at my house." Riley shares as he continues to explore further within the contents of the room. "But does your mom's room have this!" Pulling down that same hatch I stumbled upon so long ago, I reveal to Riley the attic crawl space above the closet. Again, covered with as many cobwebs as last time, with the exception of a few being spun together as we speak. Hope Riley is not afraid of a little spider. Light is absent for the genre of suspense to roar louder, as the dark alludes to magnify mystery and eeriness to an otherwise bland atmosphere. The sense of dread is most definitely present in this place. Actively listening as he reads a handful of the names on the boxes aloud: *"Baby Years, Toddler Years Through Age Ten, Classified, Teenage Through Present."* Abruptly ceasing him to a halt and demanding he repeats himself. "Baby year-" Ugh! Give it here. It appears as though I have to do everything myself. A slight shove is all that it took to get him out of my way.

Heavier than I would have imagined, thus making it no more complicated as the two of us cautiously descend down the ladder safely with ever so precise foot placements. We collectively place the box in the middle of the room to give us both an exponential amount of space for us to explore the contents inside. "So- so what is the deal with this box? Why this one in spe- specific?" I gawk at him in such a way where I should not even be needing to explain the reason why. "Maybe because it has the word in big, bold letters and is in all caps, **CLASSIFIED**." Does that not intrigue you at all, Riley? It certainly intrigues me." Riley goes first, taking out what looks to be a brown worn travel journal with the binding scarcely intact. He flips through the tattered thin pages while I stumble upon a canteen along with some old photographs. This one shows Dad in his uniform just before he is about to deploy on a mission. He looks so happy, him and his platoon! Another one shows him getting ready to board a fighter jet of some sort. And look, he has both legs intact this time around! Riley trades me the journal for the box and its remains. Skimming the dates month by month, year by year; then it abruptly stops with no warning. Here, I will read an entry for mine and the audience's sake.

Thursday, April 29, 2004

Today has been a good day, an eventful day. My team and I infiltrated a small bunker over the horizon we have had our eyes on for a couple of days now. The base was home to a few hostels but no casualties on our end. On the contrary, I wish I could say the same for the other guys. We were low on ammunition back at base camp, and this was just the edge we needed to push forward. That plus a little motivation never hurt anyone.

Also, rumor goes; there is one new squadmate who will be joining my team and I on any future missions immediately starting once we rally up and rendezvous back at headquarters. I don't know much about the guy except his name is Amadeus. Look forward to meeting the guy.

-Till tomorrow comes

Amazing... so Dad and Amadeus's relationship must have just been a seedling way back at the recording of this message. Just then, we both exclaim, "Look at this!" simultaneously. I show my friend the journal once more, and he shows me a picture once more. "Look! Look! That's my dad and your dad Sophia!" He exclaims. I wish I could have said something with more emotion behind it than a simple "Woah." But the past cannot be altered as much as we want to at times.

Ever so stealthily, Dad enters the room, not intending to startle us. But that is definitely what took place. "Did you guys not…... Hey! I remember these! I thought your mom tossed these out after she tossed me to the curb. Guess not." Riley, all of a sudden, looks bewildered. "How did you and-" Before he is able to finalize his thought... an interjection occurs. "No Riley. Remember, he already went over this once before in the funeral." I say. I could instantly tell; the memory came back to Riley just then. He must feel embarrassed now, but do not be discouraged my friend; these types of things happen to everyone once in a while. Finding the canteen, we placed off to the side earlier, Dad finds this as an excellent opportunity for us to venture down into the kitchen. For us to get some food and perhaps for him to clean that rustic jug of his.

This is atrocious! Abysmal! Why would anybody think putting pepperoni on a pizza would ever be a good idea? Before Dad left, I specifically said for him to pick up any kind except pepperoni! Obviously, my opinion is considered nothing more than white noise in the air! Wrinkles bridge the gap between my eyes to my nose, and my upper teeth clamp down, enough to expel the faintest exhale. My eyes do an excellent job of paraphrasing the exact emotions I am in resentment towards, and I then somehow manage to express them in verbal form. "Specifically. No pepperoni, I said, and what did you do? Get pepperoni!" Fazed by none of this at all, he and Riley begin by collecting slices of pizza on their plates but not after stating, and I quote. "Sophia, this is not for you."

"Okay, then Dad, what the heck am I going to eat?" He never raises his voice, explaining the situation the best he can before I lose another gasket. "Apparently, you did not see the other box beneath this one. I got a cheese pizza too. Now, if you would have let me speak before, we all could have avoided that tantrum you just had." Now I most definitely feel like a fool. Talk about Riley being embarrassed, look at me now! I feel astronomically worse than he ever did. This will haunt me for the remainder of the night.

Multitasking is a very difficult task to master, but never one to prioritize. Apologizing to Dad as I watch him effortfully clean his canteen. He obviously forgives me from earlier, and as repayment, I assist him in his efforts. After all, two is better than one. Cleaning the cloth in which it was originally concealed in, while Dad attempts to get at least 10 years' worth of grime out from inside the stainless-steel container. On the surface, nothing seems to be out of the ordinary; however, upon further examination, there is more than meets the eye. An intricate symbol is out on the outside bottom surface of the beige-colored cloth where the canteen is holstered above.

It is carved nearly deep enough to be able to pierce right through as well as the literacy being fairly illegible. I show my findings to Dad in which he stops running his hands under the sink and pauses. "I made this to remind myself I always had someone to return too once they sent me home. Whether that be Mommy or you. It is a triangle with yours and Mommy's first initials inside." Shaking my head in acknowledgment and before I breathe another breath, Dad then begins to tell us one of his riveting war stories about how the sketching came to be. Dad grabs a chair from the table, and Riley and I make room, making dinner now our second priority.

"So it was me and your dad Riley; we were posted up on a nearby hostile rooftop providing cover for the rest of the squad while they were infiltrating a small village; maybe a hundred yards out for intel on our target. Amadeus finds this rustic battered canteen a couple feet away from our initial position. He pries-" I cannot help but ask for clarification. I could distinctly tell by looking over at Riley that he needed some too, but he appeared too shy to ask. "Wait! You did all of this with only one leg!?" Dad looks at both of us in shock. He then specifies the timeline in which this story takes place abundantly clear. "As soon as I lost my leg, my run was up. No more getting sand out of hard to reach places, no more unexpected sandstorms, or journal entries…. But you guys did not come here for pity and sympathy, did you! So yes, this happened before I lost my leg. Anyway, Amadeus pries the canteen away from the sad, innocent corpse. "Here.-" he says. "-Had his canteen holstered on his pack, so it only makes sense for me to do the same. Brothers in arms!"

Then we look at each other. Riley and I are both very confused. "But how did you get the etching on the pack? The triangle." Riley asks, then Dad apologies for veering off the beaten path. "The etching…. the etching. Okay, so what happened again? Oh, his arm. Oh. Oh. Oh yeah! Yeah! Yeah!" From a murmur so indistinct, it would nearly read *10* decibels when read on a meter, and back to his original frequency, he finishes off this long-overdue story. "Let me just recollect my thoughts. Sorry guys, it has been a long time since this happened, and my memory is not what it used to be. Anyway…. Somehow, somewhere, a silenced bullet rips through the air, and believe it or not, my canteen saved Amadeus's lower abdomen… his arm …not so much. Don't worry, it only grazed the first layer of skin. I had to act quickly, Dad to the rescue. I was wrapping it in layers of cloth, then the bleeding subsided and almost stopped immediately. As a gesture of gratitude, he offered me his satchel, which I now have possession of thanks to the detective skills of you two. Then we continue to march onward towards the fight." Us kids look at each other in astonishment. "Our dads are heroes!" We finish our pizza and thank Dad for the story, then head up to bed. Dad kisses me goodnight while Riley goes onward up to his temporary sleeping quarters to make his makeshift bed, with my permission of course.

I then enter the room to find Riley pulling out the extra mattress pressed against the inside closet door as instructed. It takes the two of us to situate it in the middle of the room with enough available walking space between the both of us. Supplying him with an already folded blanket, Riley brushes his teeth in the bathroom. Two minutes later, the toilet flushes, and he reenters the room with a white t-shirt complimenting some green polyester pajama bottoms. Complimenting his new look, he then does the same to me. The light that once illuminated a portion through the one window of my room is now consumed by the surrounding darkness. Riley wrestles with the covers while I need no readjusting whatsoever. Staring at the blank ceiling just inches above, a voice fills the room not far after. "Do you know what you wa- want to do wh- whe- when you're older Sophia? My apologies…. when you are older."

A slight pause, then silence vanishes in the room. "No need for an apology Riley. If you could not tell already, I have made an exception with you and *only* you. But I do appreciate the correction, really, I do. With that being said and for clarification purposes, my choice of words will be and always have been precise in the way that they are delivered. As for your question, I am not sure when it comes to the widened spectrum of things. However, I do know that eventually; I would want to visit August in California one day." Appearing on the wall farthest away from me, his shadow reveals more than necessary. The shadow coils in fear then retreats back to where it was once comfortable, into darkness. Unlike his shadow, Riley makes his presence quite apparent in the room. "Have you been?" He asks while displaying an enormous amount of confidence; it is almost contagious. Please, if you would be so kind as to pass it over towards my direction. The outline of my face is fairly visible enough for my friend to witness my reaction. Returning to my original position, I ruffle amongst the covers as I find my sweet spot once again.

"Riley, I have to be gone early in the morning. I may be gone before you wake up, so just let yourself out if that does happen to be the case, okay?" Without hesitation, he kicks a flourishing flow of powerful communication into motion that is impossible to deviate from. "That is perfect; I have work early in the morning as well. We can regroup after I am done." His jubilance is cute. "That is a more than likely possibility Riley." I reply. He asks me to dive more into depth as for my reasoning behind my departure, but all I manage to do is stare. Lying will do nobody good; it is in my best interest to be honest with him if I want to continue to keep what we have sacred. Then finally, the words leap from my lips. "I am going down to Children's Hospital to visit August. He is in a very vulnerable and unstable state at the moment and cannot be left unattended." His response is almost immediate. "Who is August again? I remember you mentioning him to me once before. It does not matter; I bet I will find out tomorrow. I- I will meet- meet you there when I get- get off work. I was unaware August was in town. Send him my regards if you will."

I have never understood asking someone to send someone else's regards or well beings to them. I do understand if you are unable to make it to tell them yourself, but if you will show up regardless, why not them yourself. Do not ask me to do the work you are unwilling to do. Passing on one simple task from your checklist will not make life substantially easier.

The next morning, I wake up at a reasonable hour as I continue to stand firm on my commitment to myself and Riley. I start by getting ready to conquer the day. Equipping a winter coat alongside fur laced Ugg's, to battle the frigid winds. I venture onward towards Burnet Avenue. I presume Riley will leave soon after, so best not to wake him for a goodbye. After all, I will see him later on, so we will initiate a proper departure then. You know that feeling when you feel like you are progressing up the ladder of life, but in the grand scheme of things, you have merely moved inches? Through and through, that is my current identity against the harsh winds. Cigarette smoke dissipates as I blow my way through. That is one way to keep warm. However, not an ideal method. Among all the ashes and discarded butts I have presumably stomped on thus far, rationally, I decide it is best to see August on a full stomach rather than an empty, hollow one. A shuttle bus stops a fair way up ahead, but I opt-out on taking it. What is the adventure in that? There is none; I will save you the experience.

An expedition is about what is experienced along the journey. Would the audience not agree with me? Cars excessively travel beyond the recommended speed limit; each one zooms past me, and I maintain a more than recommended distance between me and the shoulder of the road. The noise from a nearby truck is gut-wrenching, almost unbearable with all of its sirens and horns. It enters the roundabout circle of assistance vehicles at the same time I do. Upon entering the automatic doors, another set of doors nearby also swing open from that nuisance of a vehicle. Two emergency medical technicians step down from the back of their truck with each taking hold of a side of what I can only imagine as an unpleasant, uncomfortable, mobile bed. The two rush into a special sector of the building in which I, the common folk, have prohibited access to. The victim is in an irreparable state; I got a glimpse before they completely disappeared from view. Or so I presume, but what do I know; I am just a concerned citizen. I pray that the child will once again be able to become a functioning member of society like they most likely were before the incident. May God enlighten their soul.

What a *great* way to introduce the very hospital where August currently resides. That was yet another attempt at sarcasm if it was unclear to any of you. Upon entry, I begin to follow a little girl who appears to be no more than the age of nine and her mother for some strange reason. I do not know what has become of me. Do I follow them for directional clarification purposes, or is my curiosity wanting to gain exposure? It is up to the reader to make their assumption, for I cannot identify a reason myself. My footsteps create an echo once I connect with the tile flooring, as does everybody else, though. So, I am in no way unique, just another common folk. I begin to follow the family of two into the cafeteria but am immediately sidetracked, all thanks to my peripheral vision.

My peripheral leads me to the presence of another mother and her baby. Out of pure joy, I start by covering my eyes with my hands and "magically" making them appear, creating giggles amongst the child. When the baby boy rapidly claps his hands is when what I can presume as only the mother of the child, takes notice. Upon further examination, I find that the small child I have been interacting with for the past 120 seconds contains no hair follicles and has a tube securely fastened with tape to his foot, administering a constant supply of medicine within his veins. Well, this baby boy is in this institution for a reason; perhaps he could be battling with the invasion of abnormal cell growth that has the potential to spread throughout his body we intellectual beings have identified as *cancer*. Realizing I have most likely overstayed my welcome, I curve my four fingers repeatedly to gesture a good goodbye.

Stretching my mouth in a silly form to gain one more laughter out of him, the mother simultaneously mouths a thank you. Finally, upon entering the beloved food court, I hear that precious giggle.

Approaching one of the various counters located in this monopoly of a health center, a few of the cooks in the back distract me as I watch them dispose of a batch of freshly peeled potatoes into multiple skillets. Mesmerized as I watch as the spatula effortless flips the patch of nicely stuck together peels once appropriately cooked, accidentally burning a small portion of the food employees in the process. A cashier approaches the register in hopes of taking my order like any other ordinary customer. She starts the exchange of words by formally greeting me. However, the employee did not seem satisfied to see me. Odd, I did do something to make you uncomfortable in any way? Scratch that! I did no such thing. You ma'am, should never begin your days drowning in sorrow because in the end; your pity will multiply to another host soon enough. So, if you would kind and knock the attitude off.

Presenting my most prevalent foot forward, I ask for a cup of water above ordering anything else. The cashier slants their head down while simultaneously forcing a smile. The person sighs and then proceeds to fetch my water, accompanied by my full complete order. "May I have two poached eggs and one-half strips of Canadian bacon and an enlarged hash brown overlaying the two, please? The presentation of the food should be accurate as I will not attempt to touch it otherwise." The response I give stupefies her. The employee operating the register clears her throat of any mucus I presume, and states the following: "Excuse me ma'am, but we do not have that. I do not know what you were looking at, but that is not listed on our menu. Now, if you would like to order some other dish listed on our menu above, I would be more than happy to comply with you."

The adjective that is serious nearly does not describe this situation; by no way does it illuminate the person's change in demeanor towards me, stern does perhaps. This adjective homes in on all emotions present while also excelling in the atmospheric setting. Glaring in utter disgust with a dash of confusion, "What do you mean you do not have it? Mother used to make for me every morning and this morning; is no different!" It snarls back at me; I wait for what next expels from that wretched gullet of hers. "Well, mommy isn't here is she. So, I suggest you order something that we currently do have; you are holding up a line!" Amadeus says to just stay calm in times like these. However, that is easier said than done.

A long time ago, within the confines of our meetings, Amadeus once told me to avoid aggressive confirmations at all other costs. Shame, I did not retain possession of that useful knowledge beforehand. But you know what they say: *You live, you learn.* To some degree, that statement is correct, more viable now then above all else. But not without derailing towards a plummet down the rabbit hole.

Acting the same way I did once before, in the grocery store with C3PO accompanied by Corduroy, although slightly altered. Unleashing a gut-wrenching scream located from the bowels below, the cashier cowers, and a curious profusion of eyes are suddenly all stunned beyond belief.

Sudden degeneration of the left sole of my shoe begins to originate blisters on my heel as I amount to ridicule this particular customer service upon this embarrassment of an establishment. Clenching the counter outward from my current position, I then demand them to add my order to the menu and for the cashier to never use such a congregation again if she knows what is good for her! Sitting on the far-left side of the counter, there my water ripples. With at least mouthful spilling, I snatch my cup and seize an unattended, unopened, fruit salad just before exiting the vicinity.

Retracing my steps back from which way I originally came. If my memory proves me right, I seem to remember bypassing an elevator adjacent to a comprehensive layout of the facility posted on the wall, all while led by an admissions desk. I can guarantee August had nowhere near the amount of trouble passing through as *some* people do... so I hear. Now for someone as charismatic as him, the situation proved no threat, as for me, that is an understatement.

Approaching the desk and then swiftly greeted by a security guard. Well, I hope he is a security guard; it would be such a shame to announce the incorrect title he was properly given prior to this encounter. Though if that were to be the case present, then why does it appear for this man to be wearing a questionable, although respectively, sky-blue button-up with federal organizational badges stitched within his uniform? Personally, if it were my doing, I would not have worn those hideous pants today! Obviously, this is not his doing, it is his wife, of course, and all men know; denying a woman consequently sends the husband to the couch sooner or later. Or it could very well be part of the establishment he is employed for.

Anyway, back on topic, the uniform could also pose as police attire. It is either one or the other, police or security outfit. In the jist of things, what does it matter anyway? Both professions operate in the same manner; one is just of lesser rank and less appreciated than the other. Which one you ask? That indication is all based upon the reader and how they view the subject at large. I am merely a messenger delivering knowledge; my opinion has no weight here and should be viewed as irrelevant. It should neither be perceived as a way to approve or disprove the decision. It is ultimately up to the individual to create their own conclusion.

An exemplary amount of syllables, thirteen to be precise, consisting of something along the lines of "Hello ma'am, how may I assist you this morning?" is the mature approach to someone who is involved with individuals and their needs. That is how I, along with the person after me, was greeted: in a well, formal, professional manner, willing to answer any astray questions. "Excuse me miss," I say with an unintentional pause, "do I need any special authorization in order to permit clearance for me to visit my friend August Parker who is currently residing here?" The race car races round and round the racetrack of my mind, recycling any and all accounts of a denial of access. What if the guard does not let me in? What if I need a guardian with me? Nor can I confirm or deny the precise location of my August if asked of me. Do they need that information from me, or will that be provided regardless? Before I can provide any more clarity to my previous question or perhaps ignite any more thoughts, the receptionist crosses her designated work boundary and equips a bracelet detailing all sorts of important information, including my name and other contents of that nature around the circumference of my wrist. I nod then ask what floor my friend is at. She, along with the guard, is quick to get me on my way and sense an impatience in me. Though that is furthest from the truth.

However, I do acknowledge I am not the only encounter they have today. "What is your friend in for?" The desk lady asks. In response, I slightly adjust my neck upward to reach a polite and respectful eye to eye contact. "Forgive me for not knowing the proper medical term for his condition, though I do not actually think there is a name yet for what he possesses. August has a superpower that impairs his breathing, but it is not a lung issue if that is of any use." The enforcers' strict yet friendly demeanor washes over me, and I am mesmerized at how calm this man has been throughout the entire duration where *my* superpower has probably been more exposed in the past twenty minutes than it ever has in a thirty-day increment.

"Your friend should be on floor *A5: Pediatric Airway Reconstruction.*" My dimples begin to show as I express my gratitude, and a stamp is smudged on my right hand in return as the last interaction I have with that security or patrol guard, or whatever his profession may be. For someone who has never ventured to a hospital before in their lives, let me assure you that the maps posted around here are astonishing, with grave detail poured into the craftsmanship to a significant level. The legend is fairly easy to read despite the levels in elevation, and I only lose sight of the "*You are here*" red arrow indicator no more than an undisclosed number of times as I am a respectable distance away, for I do not want to obstruct vision for anyone else who may be lost.

Staying conscious of my surroundings, I enter a significantly downgraded tower of terror. Although this attraction is, without a doubt, notably more frightening, almost all the passengers on this free public transportation attraction hide a portion of their faces with a variety of facemasks. Some appear to have childhood characters on the masks like Elmo from Sesame Street for example, or various zoo animals like a yellow, realistic, affectionate, giraffe for instance. Well, you understand my point, as realistic as a fake giraffe stitched into a piece of patted fabric can get. I proceed to imprint my thumb onto the round steel button when it illuminates a hostile, fluorescent, blood-wrenching hue around my thumb upon energy transfer. My arms are strict to any sort of movement, so I have to ensure the passionately waiting game once I reach the designated floor. Addressing all who enters and exits the elevator with a wave and a smile soon results as they are soon to follow in my footsteps once I depart. Perhaps footsteps would be an incorrect use of grammar. A more appropriate grammatical form would be: They are soon to follow in my *gestures* once I depart.

Thought the floor would appear more barren. No, desolate, being this early in the morning, but thoughts can be deceiving…. or is this section really that unpopular? Either or, I do not need to further clarify; the audience has been with me thus far and should have the capacity to understand what exactly I mean by now. By no means does becoming sidetracked provide excuses to ignore the larger problem at hand. Though I am in no way associated with this particular couple, a man, along with a woman, trail a distance behind me. Assuming these people are parents would be a generational assumption to make. I apologize for self-indulging and getting ahead of myself, where obviously I have no business being at the moment. For all I know, this "couple" is nothing more than two gender opposite strangers. Mindful as these two are, they shield themselves from their cesspit of germs confined within them, adventuring out of the way to isolate themselves whenever mucus builds up in the form of a cough or sneeze. I truly do have immense respect and gratitude for parasitic individuals who take the time to be cautious of their surroundings.

Stopping to observe from only feet away, I watch as the people who were once behind me now gain the lead. I catch my left side lean against the rough, golden drywall as my shoulder orchestrates a divot in the plaster. The man can be seen with the same type of lanyard badge the woman downstairs gave me, waving it in a rapid motion in front of a keycard access control system. A lime green flash glistens in a controlled vicinity, and a faint beep can be heard granting access finally upon the fifth aggravating attempt to what I can confirm by now is a couple. The husband shelters his wife through the operational metal double doors, and just like a snap of the fingers, they are gone. My physical body surveys the area, approaching the technologically advanced door while my mind collapses any possibility of any sort of hiccup. I am not absolutely positive in my decision, but I feel a sudden ominous presence in this room with me. If there is a chance I am able to reach the other side of this portal, I am more than certain I will be free from this dark entity.

Reenacting through the motions as the gentleman did before me, the door does create audio, yes, but what it does after I was not prepared for. The same color as the elevator button, the same color as those large trucks with ladders across from Amadeus, exactly the same color stuns my vision to an extent. Trying the same method multiple times around gets me nowhere, and all conclude in the same treacherous results until immediately bounding myself from the extensive universe outside. I resist an outburst, and for the most part, it is successful. Guess my mind does not always seem to get the best of me. Reassuring myself that I cannot leave until I see August, I plan to linger around until someone else attempts the door, then I will slip through the access point. A good plan, would the reader not agree with me? Thought of it by myself. Not long after I devised this foolproof plan, the universe presents the opportunity; a do-over above all else, and it came in the form of a middle-aged man with a scruffy appearance dressed in a light blue uniform accompanied by a cap of the same color; a doctor I would presume. An angelic being must have been by his side because he got through the door with such ease...and not to mention, as do I. Thank you, you scrub. Did the reader laugh or chuckle at the very least? I had that joke planned for a while now, do you get it? See, I called him a scrub because he is a doctor, and doctors wear scrubs! I bet if Riley or Amadeus were here, they would approve of this humor.

"August! You are here! I cannot believe that you are actually here. I have missed you so much." I never anticipated how difficult this chapter would be for me or let alone him. I see him down the hall from me upon the successful attempt of my plan, isolated in a captivating room. You know that feeling when you feel like you have known someone for a long while, but in the end, it turns out that you have not actually had a single encounter with them prior to this interaction? Well, let me say that this is what I am feeling right now, and I hope he feels the same as I do. Leaving the sliding glass door cracked open a bit as to not be too conspicuous in my revolving actions, he looks at me, then out at the skyscrapers reaching the sky and back at me once more. I do nothing but smile in awe and am in utter disbelief of how perfectly the stars had to align for our separate encounters to intersect. August begins to explain to me that this whole situation with him having to be reconstructed once again has gotten Oliver and Maddie in a frantic but more so Oliver than anything else. Apparently, once my beloved returned back to his little town in California, Oliver would push him against the wall or trudge into his room with Mrs. or Mr. Parker tending to his needs and exclaim something along the lines of:

"Stop it! Your baby boy doesn't need your help. He is fully capable of doing things by himself." and "If you didn't have that thing in your neck right now, I would punch you!" I know deep down Oliver never had harmful intentions for his older brother; he was just angry at the injustice of this particular circumstance brought onto his brother, as he rightfully should be.

Knowing his mental mainframe, it will not be long for August to develop post-traumatic stress disorder because of all of these events. Truth be told. Although my dearest's speech is coincidentally incapacitated for my untimely visit, that does not exclude us from a connection. He shares by sign language that it is quite aggravating having no choice but to be so dependent upon people for even the simplest tasks.

Wanting an immediate change in subject, I tell August about my day, including the days leading to this dreamy event also. He comforts me as any man should comfort a woman when delivering heart-wrenching news. Revealing the unfortunate passing of Mother and Corduroy sends him to tears, which in turn makes me shed a few as well. "It is absolutely unfair that you, August of all people, have to go through this traumatic tracheal reconfiguration experience again for a *third* time when he does not deserve one bit of it. Well, you know what the saying is, *third time the charm.* Let us pray that this distinct statement is true above all else because nowhere in my agenda for today do I have *August's passing* listed in the to-do list. "I have already lost Mother and Corduroy, please do not let me lose you, August. I do not know if I would be capable of moving on without you." I begin to uncontrollably weep, and Mr. Parker holds me tight as I never want this moment to dissipate. He continues to hold my embrace as I continue to share to him how important he is to me, that he is my vessel that keeps me afloat. The one person in this god-forsaken world that would second guess to judge me for my attitude or any mishap for that matter! Unbeknownst to me, a sudden noise interrupts our intimate time together. "Where is August?"

Episode IX:
To Alter an Altar

Stunned, as one would assume, or might I add, *caught off guard* for an appropriate alternative describing word for a depicted reaction. "Excuse me? Sorry?" I somehow manage to sneak out before my vision can be fully restored by the secreting precipitation streaming down the sides of my cheeks. The voice grows closer with every impatient moment wasted, the person behind the voice asks again where August Parker is. I have still yet to unveil myself beneath the crescents of my hands. Finally, it brushes my hands away from my face and wipes my tears for me. "Riley no. Stop. I can wipe my own tears away." But Riley is neglectful to obey. A frigid gust of wind happens to seep through an apparent sliver of a crack in the window, which in turn creates a hazy thickness around the only thing Riley can use to perceive reality. Wiping the obstruction from the lenses, my friend then adjusts his spectacles and refocuses his visibility. He intently stares at me almost as if he were in disappointment or upset with me.

"Soooooo, who wh- who were you talking to?" He finally asks upon occupying the chair that is residing near the end of the bed. "Talking to!? Is it not blatantly obvious Riley, the only other person in this room besides you or I." I watch as Riley suddenly shifts from a face of confusion to distress. In all of my years of being a private investigator, no amount of experience could help me solve this implausible case. If only Detective Tracy was here to lend me some assistance, I would surely no longer be stumped for such an unfortunate and indefinite period. Flipping through all of the possibilities that I have ultimately concluded in all of my years as a professional private detective; I have never met a trail that has gone cold. Lifting my head in utter shame and embarrassment, my dearest friend admits some news that is almost unbearable to hear. "Sophia, there is no one here. In fact, there has been no one in this room besides you. You have been sitting in an empty room talking to no one. You are starting to scare me, and you look like a crazy person for doing so. Ho- how long were you sitting for?"

My heart sinks down into my stomach. This phrase has always been a hard one for me to grasp the true meaning of. I can never decipher the meaning of it by myself and always rely on research to do the heavy lifting in a sense. I would like the reader to enter the mind of an autistic for a moment, to be able to ponder the same question I am currently reciting. Why does the heart sink into the stomach? Why, in fact, is that an actual saying? It is such an odd literary device. Grammatically, the saying is an expression of impending doom but let us decipher this in a literal sense. If a heart quite literally sank down to the pits of the stomach, hypothetically, it would create internal hemorrhaging within the body and destroy vital bodily functions, I would presume. As this is an imaginative scenario due to the impossibility for these two events to concur precisely.

Soundwaves ripple through the atmosphere, ricocheting off the walls than out of the confines of August's room to a more populated and condensed area of the A5 level. "Liar! That is not true!" I soon scream and a couple of the metal rings holding up the room's curtain clatter against the sliding glass door once I abruptly exit. I immensely regret this; Riley is my friend. Correction, *Only* friend. Who am I kidding? Surely, he will not imperil our friendship over this...will he?

A whirl gust of wind lifts the back end of my coat up by the time I hear the *lonely* voice call my name one last time. To impatient to use an elevator for that would be more of an emotional wreck then I am already currently in. As a way to avoid anybody who were to witness me in my present state of mind, I resort to an old-fashioned way of transportation; an ancient method is what the younger generation are now starting to call it. Flinging an oddly shaped doorknob open if I have ever seen one, I transfer from one flight of stairs to the next. This barren, abandoned, silver, childproof, gated, safety rail guides me all the way to the ground floor destination. I am just thankful that stairs have stood the test of time, not being eradicated by all the technological advances of the world.

Pressure from my shoes clap against the cold, desolate, concrete floor upon every step that I take, and it screams to be heard with every one of my progressive steps.

A rapid succession of one of the overhead lights irradiates an even portion of the steps to a belligerent yellow tint—no wonder why exercise is so orthodox these days. I can now understand why. People are starting to forget what good a little bit of exercise can do to the human body. From this day forward, I vow to never use these wretched, hazardous stairs again. Have I mentioned yet that I fell? If I have not, then here it is: yes, I did slip on the last few steps before reaching the lobby and obtained a physical memory of a minor laceration on my knee as to why no one takes the stairs anymore.

Not being aware of my surroundings and or considerate for that matter, the stairwell door swings open, but luckily a stopper was there to prevent idiots like me from causing property damage. Once the door makes contact with the stopper, a force explodes within its confines down its skeleton. Thus, commencing a restless disturbance of equilibrium, otherwise persistent with the stopper itself. Burying my head around the same corner where the administrative desk resides, all while cutting through these cords of asinine people, I finally find a place to rest and collect my thoughts. Planting myself on the same bench where I met that baby earlier with his mother, and a considerable distance away from the cafeteria, with my head between my knees resting upon crossed arms; the very same bench that faces outward towards the roundabout.

Tears continue to roll down my face and eventually, a considerable amount ending up on the floor. Where is the wet floor sign when you need it? Still distraught, if not more than what I was experiencing with August and Riley. Or I guess it was just Riley, so it happens, come to discover August was never here in the first place! "What is going on with me? Maybe I should admit myself into a psych ward! It would be no challenge whatsoever occupying August's room. I am sure he will not mind. I bet he would be proud of me for acknowledging I have a severe issue, and I am taking the necessary steps to recovery. God, what is happening to me? Is this how insanity develops?"

I am gaining an abundance of onlookers, I would quite imagine, but I am not their problem, so why would any of them help a poor hysterical stranger? As people continue to play the passive game, my eager ears feast on any sort of approaching footsteps. I occasionally glance up to see if I am the only occupant on this intricate wooden framed seat with a burgundy lace. To my dismay, I still am, but that all changes sooner than later, thanks to a pair of poorly tied tennis shoes -if I have ever seen it, approaching my direction. The shoes indisputably look like they have seen better days, but any sense of pride and maintenance of this footwear are nonexistent. The logo is almost unrecognizable and charred to a fraction of the size. They might be *NIKE*, but who really knows? However dirty the shoes may be, that is the polar opposite of the resemblance of the person who is wearing them. "Sop-" With arms wide open and before he can even finish his word of choice, I embrace the man behind the voice. I know that voice anywhere, and it also appears so after all, that he can and will forgive me because this relationship will never die.

Instincts kick in as my arms have an apparent mind of their own. Overlapping one over the other to gain a sense of passion while also simultaneously feeling a sense of control still within the revolving circumstance. For a moment or two, all sense of worry is eliminated, while a familiar yet distant sensation showers over me. I did feel this same connection with Corduroy and Mother. However, it was never like this before. I can tell I am experiencing the same emotion but perceiving it in an all new way. All of a sudden, the lines anterior to my hands are perfusing with sweat. I began to do that one thing that every basic girl does with their hair for some peculiar reason. Initiating room to breathe, Riley then asks permission to sit. I am exuberant in my response and pat him a seat next to me. Who knew this sweet euphoric reconnection had supernatural abilities at play?

By a swift nod of acknowledgment, Riley starts by unruffling his sleeves. "Why did you run away? D- Did I do something wrong?" By placing my hands onto his and with a trance into those big round hypnotic black eyes of his, I immediately ease his mind with the confession that this was no sort of wrongdoing done on his end. The blame should all be bestowed on me and the birth of a clean slate commences. "No. It was totally justifiable to do everything that you did back there, and I am glad you chased after me. I was just angry and upset at the fact that my mind would play tricks on me to actually convince myself that August's existence actually had the capability to intertwine with our reality. Because of your undying support time after time, there is no question that I am just as important to you as you are to me. Never change Riley. Okay? Especially for me."

He does nothing but continues to cling onto my hands. He embraces me this time around; it is quite nice to receive what you have once given. Speaking of the intent of giving, as a matter of fact, my loyal partner hands me a disproportionate jagged piece of lined paper that reads:

To-Do List!

☑ *Go to work*

☑ *Meet up with Sophia and August*

☐ *Go to pharmacy*

☐ *Ask Sophia about church again*

☐ *Go see dad at work*

"Change of plans Sophia, we are not going to the pharmacy anymore to pick up any more pills. I recently made a stupefying suspicion that if true, which I almost guarantee it is, means you are in mortal danger. You need to speak to my dad right away, Sophia. Please!" I desperately perplex my knight in shining armor as he clearly has no idea what he is talking about. I am perfectly fine. What does he know?

My denial of assistance increases louder with every passing moment. Riley makes no attempt to confirm or deny my suspicions. "Is this a serious matter? Is this an emergency? Riley, just tell me what is going on! I do not need to see Amadeus whatsoever." Hesitant is an incorrect word choice to use, but I am unable to locate a more profound word in its place to saturate an action my friend feels in order to progress the conversation forward. The tips of my mouth begin to expand with an initiation to creep towards my luminescent eyes to form an unnatural smile on my end. Riley responds by doing the same but shows his teeth on his attempt. I try to show him that I am perfectly fine and functional, but in no way does he buy my sorry excuse. Something I did not do instinctively. Although reflecting back now, I should have done that myself to truly convey the emotions felt in the situation. But the past is done and over with. "But how can we? My appointment is not until Friday, three more days until now!" I finally exclaim after releasing a dilemma that had just occurred. I can tell Riley has a plan up his sleeve but has yet to inform me of it. Each of our teeth on our jackets sync with each of the zippers without failure while alongside, the insulation beneath enables us for the weather before us.

Just like his father always does, Riley also holds the door open for me upon exit of the hospital. What a gentleman! Amadeus will be quite pleased to hear that his son knows how to treat a woman with such respect. I wonder if I can manage to slip that bit of information right on in just after my plea for help. If so, the overall picture will not seem so bad. If I succeed, then Amadeus surely will not suspect anything out of the ordinary after myself operating in such an elegant fashion.

The automatic double doors salute us a goodbye, thus marking August as nothing now but a distant memory once we exit the premise. Flurries of snow twinkle in the skylight, surfing off my coat while the majority of them spawn and intertwine with Riley's trimmed afro. I forgot to add the keyword *self*-incorporated within trimmed afro. Not to be rude, think of it as effective criticism; but the reader should see his hair to understand exactly what I mean. Picture the hair follicles crying for constant help as they are all misaligned, and might I add the foreground is atrociously horrendous. Some would say that is being extremely insensitive and rude to the person he is. I call it another distinctive physical attribute to become more identifiable. In an instant, Riley suddenly grabs my hand and rushes forward. "Why are we- Woah!"

"Hurry, Sophia! We gotta ke- kee- keep moving!" Once he states this, his speed intensifies exponentially. It is as if Riley puts a spell around me...excuse me, us, because once he snatches my hand, everybody who would have been impeding our path towards victory voluntarily steps aside for the king and his queen. I glance back one last time at this ever so distant memory begins to melt and watch for a moment as an authorized outsider raises the hospital's unified nation flags mounted on a slightly elevated island at the core of the roundabout.

Just outside the perimeter of Cincinnati Children's Hospital's vicinity lies that bus station I alluded to earlier. It is just along the border of the roundabout, which we just left to be exact. That must be what he is rushing towards! Though we better hurry, my friend. Approaching a public bus paraded with television and other advertisements all over its body, the doors engulf its two final passengers. Our hearts continue to race to the sound of madness, even once we approach Riley's desired destination. I assume Riley feels just as winded and out of shape as me; his breaths are just as heavy as mine when we board the public transport. Riley darts towards my direction and points to the one other open seat across from him with his left hand. "Take this seat. I will b- be ri- right here. Not- not far at all." He says.

Predictable as it may seem for a given circumstance such as this, an inconstant deranged acquaintance reappears. "I will not be sitting next to you?!" I am quick to respond while my so-called acquaintance takes hold of me. It takes on its true form, the form I have only known it to be, the form that my mind perplexes astray beyond belief in this expressive, chaotic, and random phenomenon. Anxiety immediately grabs hold of me and nearly leaves me for dead, tearing at my throat just waiting for me to reduce my self-regulation down to a shrivel of what it is now. Everybody has their demons, and they all come without warning, now I present to you, my adversary.

Why is he not sitting next to me? I cannot sit next to a stranger! I feel comfortable with Riley around me, not somebody who unveils no instantaneous qualities. Not to mention, this forthcoming fellow whose stench reeks of literal garbage with the combination of his filthy, musty, fashion who also needs to be reminded this is the clear definition of dated.

Immediately as I sit down, the man shifts his direction. I do everything in my power to revoke this person. I am sure he is a kind-hearted, respectable man. However, I am not interested in having to learn another name at the moment. I watch my companion as he sits in the seat across from me, also along the aisle. Our conversation officially dies when we individually detect both our comfortable positions. Rather than patiently waiting for our stop with nothing but a questionable multitude of increments of time, my body aches with the reminder of that long-awaited and overdue breakfast. "Cheers to the beginning of the end of my aching tummy." I say in a faint murmur.

A brisk movement of a slightly elevated and precise position of the wrist is all that it took for this plentiful treasure of mine to be unlocked. The flimsy plastic fork inside of the fruit bowl taunts me as I put all my precious patience into an oversized piece of ripe cantaloupe. It is more apparent than ever that the force is not strong with me, pitifully losing an ounce of patience with each repeated jab. If only Master Yoda can assist me in channeling the rage and anger deep within me, that would be deeply appreciated. This one absolute despicable fruit manages to cling onto the utensil alas. I am agile in my motion to devour the juicy goodness and dive in for another assorted fruit chunk.

Authentic and thorough speculation begins and unfolds in the spur of the moment. Believe me when I say this was by no means a planned bus activity. The core of this particular fruit is almost identical to a tree when it is exposed. It's light green color, yet smooth center indicates the heart of the fruit, its radiant soul now exposed and vulnerable. When an elongated tree trunk is sheared, or as it is expressed in a more traditional common sense, unprotected like that... Well, it does not have to be an enormous tree; it can be any size and kind, in fact. Anyway, there are indications and clues to share with the viewer as to how many years old that erect perennial plant is by its rings. Rings on a tree are similar to the insides of this lime green fruit due to its texture and dark seedless appearance.

I am hesitant to ingest such a hideous creation of nature. Just as I am about to do so, the man who I completely forgot who was sitting next to me thankfully interrupts the action in motion. "If you will not eat the kiwi, I sure will." I cannot recall a more immediate motion. "Say no more, you are doing God's work, sir!". The passenger readjusts his plaid newsboy cap and plumps up his overcoat, followed by a formal introduction. He introduces himself as Clarence, and I shake his hand out of respect. I intended to avoid the learning of another name, but since Clarence is not like any other boring stranger on this bus, I figured that there is no harm in knowing him. At this very moment, out of my peripheral view, this is when I could see Riley glance over. The conformation I ever so longed for; Riley is jealous that someone else other than him is talking to me. Although this information was not crucial to me as I already obtained the knowledge that he had feelings for me, but this solidified that clouded fact.

A moderate tone of sarcasm is conveyed within my voice. "Guessing you enjoyed the kiwi...one moment it was hanging by a thread on my fork, the next-. Clarence masticates the last bits of the now mashed solid food. Riley tries his best not to make his spying obvious, but he is a failure when it comes to discretion. A slight clearing of the throat can be heard before the resuming function of his vocal box. "Excuse me, yes. Very delicious, as a matter of fact. Forgive me, but I believe I never got your name, ma'am." I am appalled at my lack of effort in introducing myself. I should be ashamed... "Apologies, my name is Collins. Sophia Collins." My new acquaintance smiles, "It is a pleasure." Is it wrong to identify this person now as an acquaintance? Mrs. Merriam Webster defines the term acquaintance as a person whom one knows but who is not particularly a close friend. Not in the slightest am I doubting or defying Webster, but would it still be considered an acquaintance if I only and truly only see this particular individual soul once in a lifetime? I will let the reader answer this one for the time being. It has been quite a while since they have interacted within the contents of the novel.

More engaged than I have ever been with a stranger before, I find it fascinating to learn the life of someone else other than people within my tight circle. My ears perk up with every different syllable that explodes from his mouth. Speaking of explosions, this might well be the best time to mention the variety of flavors within this nutritious, assorted bowl. Although the plastic bowl includes all the ingredients pre-packaged, I do wish I were able to eat the items in a Tupperware container, a container in which I am already familiar with. A definite factor to take into account for next time. As I am at the moment, pre-occupied with the minuscule amount of food that is left in my bowl. All of a sudden, Riley tugs at my coat. "We are here!" Rising from my seat and offering the rest of the kiwi to my new friend, I can tell he wanted to share one last bit of information with me ... I guess now I will never know what it is. Riley and I thank the bus driver for his services and proceed to enter into my dear friend's father's therapeutic, psychological empire.

Upon bypassing her desk, the front desk receptionist makes a sudden jolt out of her seat, finishing with a mumble and a point of the index finger. Who, might I add, explicitly displays her age by her attire. She makes it blatantly obvious with that inappropriate see-through baby blue and creamy, white, polka dot blouse daunting some galaxy black spectacles. I would bet that you do not need glasses! They just so happened to go along with today's outfit! Almost as if a sudden urge had overwhelmed her and shook her straight to her core, the woman behind the desk immediately reabsorbed her deflected attentive neurons back to her monitor. Guess she kept her mouth shut once she realized who was about to come into view with me.

Riley turns the knob, and it is at this precise moment in time that we both enter through a portal distinguished from the rest of what we were originally accustomed to. Before, reality perceived us as overseers over our very bodies, allowing us to take control of predicaments, we trapped ourselves in. Through the other side, we enter into the world of professionalism—a dimension where errors are frowned upon and where any personal issues become a public matter.

"Dad!" Amadeus shoots his head up after an abrupt interruption with someone who has their back to us. "Riley!" Tailgating my best friend as we both approach his desk, but it does not take long for me to notice those fish again. They remind me of him... of Corduroy. I miss him, and I miss Mother whenever I think of him, and I have been thinking of him a lot lately. I start to track the same fish I once saw so long ago. If not the same one, then undoubtedly similar. The very same aquatic vertebrate that implanted the idea of adopting another member into the family, an addition that could bring an official balance to the family other than C3PO and I. The raccoon butterfly integrates herself into a small school of fish, which obviously didn't give an invitation. She quickly grows tired, and after traveling about halfway across the tank, she veers off from the group, settling in her castle.

Riley gives a hefty tug on the sleeve of my shirt and is successful in pulling me from the tank. Now I stand before the only one who can help me with my dilemma. Amadeus' heir projects his voice above a normal frequency, although not loud enough for it to be classified as a scream. "Sophia needs help, Dad!" He jolts over to me. "Sophia. Tell him." A quick stare at Riley, then Amadeus, finally back to a comfortable yet shameful downward position. "Umm...I... I." Saying this from an inconsiderable muffled orientation, I stay considerably silent for the remainder of our embarrassing discussion, as my eyes metaphorically veer off the overpass to the obsolete bland carpet below. "Riley, I will get to you guys as soon as I am done with this client here. He is the last one before lunch. Just wait outside and-" Amadeus clearly has no understanding of the severity of this, and thankfully, Riley does. "But Dad! This is an emergency! Sophia is in deep trouble. She- She- might die!" Well, I would not go to that length, Riley; but thank you for the dramatic effect.

Amadeus looks at the both of us than at the door that "we" accidentally left open. Why should I be a part of the blame? It was all Riley. I was not an accomplice to his forgetfulness. Oh, he wants us to get out. That is what that signal means; I am not good at signals and signs, there are too many, and most of them have multiple meanings overlapping each other. A very complex form of communication if I do say so myself. "Give us ten more minutes. That is all I am asking of you. Just ten." Riley mumbles something under his breath, followed by my name. Somehow, I just knew he needed me to be on his side at that moment, regardless of who was right in the argument. I follow him out of the room to the waiting area, where we are acknowledged by the same receptionists from just a few minutes earlier.

My partner in crime goes above and beyond the unnecessary and pulls a chair out for me, for I make a conscious effort to rest in the same precise location as last time I was here. An over-exaggerated screech solidifies the fact that we are now present. I would most definitely think at least one individual would perk up from their mundane activity, but to my surprise, apathy consumes the souls confined in their own unique outer shells. One of the chair legs is lifted, so I lean my weight towards that side of the chair; but then the exact happens to the other side. I do not remember sitting in a chair to be this complicated. If I recall correctly, this chair was not like this the last time I was here. I would switch seats to avoid this annoyance, but Riley chose to sit on the left side, which parts him and the seat succeeding me by a small, crowded table with useless celebrity magazines.

I play it cautious not to irk him even more, and, in an attempt to ease his pain; I assume the role of Amadeus and listen to his problems. Although I am unsure of how beneficial this may be considering us both being *lonely*. Never have I heard of an autistic and Down's individual assisting one another in their issues ...perhaps this will be a first. He continues to be distraught about Amadeus not seeing us at Riley's preferred time. "As the time frame might be practical for our schedule Riley, it may not be for your father." The palm of my hand surfaces his masculine arm, and with each individual hair tickling me; this calms him down to some extent. "This is not an immediate matter; we can always spare a couple of minutes." His mouth projects each and every idiosyncrasy his mind feeds him. Most of his comments have to deal with the event that just happened with him and Amadeus. To rectify, *all* of his comments have to do with this particular instance. There is no use going into great detail about what he is confessing to me to then relay it back for the audience's understanding; it consists of mostly the usual tantrum things one obsesses over... no offense Riley.

After some intimate time together with Riley, a door clicks open for me to make direct contact with Amadeus, who is divided between the doorway. The person signals for us to enter, in the mists of taking a sip from his glass. Its repugnant odor from within the glass desensitizes my nasal cavities. A shear quiver escalates throughout the dorsal half of my human body. I never knew he drank. Does he drink often? Another conversation I most certainly have to discuss with my friend. My face portrays it all as Riley attempts to mimic my expression for a laugh to creep out of me just before leading me to the help I never realized I so desperately needed.

"So, what is this all about you two?" Amadeus starts off the discussion by making sure there is enough room for both of us while Riley fetches some water. I brush off some excess crumbs left behind on the dark black leather sofa by what I would only assume as the last patient. By the display of the crumbs, I assume the person was sitting in a crisscrossed position. A small white glass bowl sits at the end of the table containing cashews. "Am I allowed to have some, or is that just for decoration to make the room look livelier?" I ask without deviating from Amadeus' gaze. An open palm pans across the room almost as if he were to say *"go ahead,"* while his parched throat quenches for a thirst.

"Sophia needs help, Dad. We went to the hospital and- and- and- nobody was there." My eyes dash towards Riley just as he places the miniature water bottle on the coaster in front of me. "If you do not mind Riley, this has to deal with mine and August's relationship. *Our* relationship is no longer in jeopardy as you are quite aware. Now I am thankful you were there to help me when I most needed it, but please let me explain my side of the story in more detail to Amadeus. I say this in the sincerest way as I possibly could; I am not mad at you in any way, but please, do not give away spoilers. I am sure Amadeus was curious as to what was troubling us, but now, he knows."

Riley does a quick nod in acknowledgment. As I bite into the first of many cashews, Amadeus takes a sip again. "I lost August this morning." I say. A good amount of the beverage regurgitates back up his esophagus, followed by an alarming rate of coughs. For it, of course, to have it spray in my vicinity. No more than a couple drops actually met my skin, resulting in a yelp from my end. My mouth salivates excessively with every cashew I consume. Patting a napkin firm across his face, Amadeus then sends his heartwarming and appreciated condolences." I- I am so sorry, Sophia. Would you like to talk ab-" A single tear dribbles out of my lacrimal punctum and rolls down my cheek. By suppressing any form of outward physical expression, the doctor takes another sip of his beverage—this time retaining it all, which is an improvement from his last attempt.

Just before Amadeus is about to finish his thought though, Riley makes his presence distinctively known. To be completely honest with you, Riley; I almost forgot you were here. "Stop it! Just stop! Do not feel pity for her, Dad. She is sick. She has a drug addiction! We came here for your help, not to discuss a sorrow story that does not even exist!" Waiting for my turn to talk once again, the void in my stomach slowly begins to become satisfied. All eyes are drawn on me now; I know what I have to say, I just do not know if I have the strength to. "Believe me, I do want to come clean and tell you the truth, but I am just fearful about the repercussions. I do not want you to think anything less of me. I cannot lose you two. This is the longest friendship I have ever had (not including C3PO) and I have no intention of losing this special bond I hold with both of you."

Riley does not say anything, nor does his father. Instead, they assure me that I am loved no matter what. That there are people who are here to help me no matter the circumstance with a time consuming yet long-awaited hug. Accelerating with every passing second, my heart dances to an orchestrated rhythm. It feels as if it were to explode from my chest before I finally make the conscious decision to let go. I hold Riley tight and let his shirt become damp in my tears. One after another, every tear is filled with at least some burden I managed to drag through this life with me. The memories of Mother and Corduroy play on repeat, then is shortly followed by the insecurities and my persistently crippling, delusional, chronic mental health. "Hey, hey, hey, look at me. Sophia. We are always proud of you, and Riley did the right thing by bringing you down here. This is very serious if untreated. Riley, you are a great friend for doing this; it is very apparent that she is very special to you, son, and I am proud of what you have done here today." Amadeus directs his attention to the both of us to initiate an inclusive conversation rather than a personal one on one connection. Finally, removing the water from the coaster, I bring it to my mouth just before my request for help initiates. The tears subside once I take matters into my own hands and wipe away the remainders. Quickly glancing at Riley then back to his father, I take a deep breath and then come to a slow exhale. "So, August is the character in my book as you are well aware, but what I have been purposely disregarding from the information I have told you thus far is the fact that I am taking these pills originally prescribed to Mother to make me focus more on my writing. It gets me more in tune with August and his character. The more I focused on him and his reality, the more I would find myself merging his reality with ours. However, the drug I have been ingesting for so long has manifested to become a part of me. I have tried quitting multiple times but not always as resolutely as I should. I want more Amadeus! I know I do not need more for survival purposes, but I want more in order to stay healthy enough to operate."

A long overdue pause sets the mood and drowns out any sort of tension that was originally present in the room. In a bent over position, Amadeus runs his hand through his own hair, perhaps in an attempt to try and process all of this. This is hard enough to hear for someone like Amadeus who specializes in his particular field, but when you hear it from someone that you know on a deeply personal level and care about them as if they were a child of your own; I can only imagine the heartbreak he must be feeling right about now.

"I hope that is it…" A sigh is then emitted from Amadeus. Covering my head in utter shame, I ask Riley to finish the story for me. Amadeus' son relays the same information he told his father earlier except in more substantial detail. As embarrassed as I am to admit it, my friend explains that I quote-unquote "Traveled to a hospital to communicate with a ghost." After Riley finishes, Amadeus just says one thing, "Oh god!" before going forth to grab a pen and paper from his desk. "What is the drug that you have been taking, Sophia? So, I can provide you with the proper instructions." Instructions! Instructions for what? Well, it is in the best interest, not to ask questions. After all, I should not be questioning at all. If anything, I should be answering those questions that I am being bombarded with.

After all, he is the one with the writing utensil. "Adderall." I utter under my remaining breaths. Never did I imagine this reveal would be a substantial weight lifted off my shoulders. It feels like I am fifteen pounds lighter. Now my arsenal is fully equipped to take on the world. But that comes with an expense, obviously, and a hefty one as a matter of fact. Unbeknownst to me, payment towards the acceptance of one's self to identify there is a problem at play is the first step to a revolution.

Detox Steps

1) Slowly become less dependent upon Adderall

2) Appointments are now two times a week to monitor you -Once on Tuesday and once on Thursday.

3) Distract yourself for fifteen minutes whenever you have a craving

4) Regulate your eating and stay on a consistent sleep schedule

After he sees me glance up, he does not hesitate to ask if he thinks I am capable of doing this. Of course, I am more than capable of committing myself to get better Amadeus; but we both know it will not happen overnight. I nod in acknowledgment then proceed to take a drink of my water. At the same time, Riley does the same, and so does his father. I very much enjoy this list of rules. Although, it sounds easier said than done; we will see how far I can go without breaking.

I cannot stay silent anymore! The anticipation and curiosity are killing me already. I have to know! "What is in that cup of yours? I have seen you sip on it throughout this entire session and this is my first time ever witnessing you drink something while on the job." From the pit of his diaphragm and a slight curvature of the spine, the adult in the room lets out a chuckle. Immediately I turn to Riley in astonishment. "He is chuckling! Why is he chuckling! Nothing about that question I just asked was remotely humorous." The shrug of his shoulder indicates that my partner is just as puzzled as me.

We watch as he rises from his chair and travels to a filing cabinet further beyond his desk anxiously. Although his body is obscuring the majority of the contents inside, I do hear what sounds to be the wrinkling of plastic attract to his hand. "It is tea you two. I always drink this after a hard and long day of work. It prohibits my mind from becoming clouded and from making any poor judgment in some cases." The cabinet closes, there is a slight pause in Amadeus's voice until he rejoins us back at the coffee table. "So, Sophia, do you think you will be able to come off of your drug addiction? It will take some time, but with some hard work and dedication; I have no doubt you will overcome your personal mountain. If you need any help or questions concerning your current predicament, please do not hesitate for a minute to call me, and if for some reason I am not immediately available, call Riley. I am sure he would be more than happy to help you. Let alone talk to you. He talks about you all the time at the dinner table, you know. You are his best friend after all, Sophia." Do I need to say anything? I would like to believe that my facial expression says it all.

To kickstart my treacherous travels, I ask for a sense of guidance one last time before my full-fledged departure. "What if I do not have Adderall anymore? I mean, Riley and I were just about to go to the pharmacy to pick some up, but after realizing this is hurting me, Riley quickly opted out of the idea and brought me straight here instead. As I already briefly mentioned to you too, the medication is under Mother's name, so there is no way of me obtaining any even if I wanted too." Amadeus then asks how many I have left and how often I have been taking them.

Confidently I say no more than 10 and reveal to him that I have been taking them not very often. I continue to tell him that I can go for a week and a half without needing another one. I see your perceptive categorical definition of often is vastly different from mine. A sign of slight relief is present on Amadeus' face. "Phew! I thought your condition was immensely worse. Do not get cocky though; you are neither the best case I have ever seen either. In that case, still follow the guidelines I gave you. But try and keep those few capsules you have as long as possible. I would not say you are addicted to Adderall per se, more so dependent upon it when you feel cluttered and to have a sense of control over your life. Does that sound like that can be a correct assumption?" Snatching what is left of my water and some of the remaining cashews, I am gracious enough to thank Amadeus for seeing me on such short notice. More so, I should be praising Riley for orchestrating this entire meeting without asking any questions and who is reluctant enough to not take no as an answer. I hug Riley goodbye and proceed to head towards the door. Just as I do though, I hear a voice shout out to me one last time. "Sophia! You- You st- still want to go to church with me on- on Sunday? Meet me at my house a- at 11." Suddenly I hear Amadeus whisper something to his son. "10! Meet at 10!" Without deviating from my predetermined path, my heart begins to accelerate, and a smile slowly creeps upon my face. "No setbacks this time. I call the seat next to Riley!"

I arrive back home where I find Dad on the telephone, anxiously rolling back and forth within the confines of his chair inside the kitchen. Papers overlap one another as they are sprawled all across the floor. What does he think this is? A garbage chute!? If you think I spontaneously arrived to magically clean up your mess, you are sadly mistaken, sir. I should have known better to avoid trespassing into such a treacherous land, but I wanted to see how far my luck would last. For your information, I probably would have had better chances of escaping a giant space slug just as Han Solo and Princess Lea did in *The Empire Strikes Back*. Though I digress, walking past Dad, I make sure to make my efforts cautious enough to not step on any of his scattered papers and over to the pantry.

Is it wrong to think this is almost amusing? I imagine the papers as vicious, hungry cobras; just praying for me to accidentally set one of them off. Being very precise in where I step, my left foot advances towards the fruit snacks held in the pantry while my right anxiously waits for an order. I then place my right foot, crossing my left and onto another opening. Just as I do, I begin to lose balance and tumble forward. But not before catching myself on the kitchen table. My palms sweaty and my legs tremble in fear as I take a minute to regain composure, then I proceed to start again.

Planning my route as if my life depends upon it, my legs do a marvel of a job to maneuver me through the minefield. "Dad has his back turned. Advance now!" I manage to somehow muffle under my breath without him breaking concentration. The pantry knob soothes my bitter hands once interacted with. However, it does not open without some excess noise coming from the dated hinges, of course. The slightest movement creates a creaking sound throughout the house. So much for being discreet in my efforts. Dad is quick to turn and put his finger up to his mouth, accompanied by an agitated whisper, but not before re-engaging into his phone call. "Sophia! Yes. Yes, sir. I am still here...It was just my daughter... I know; I have been gone for a while, but you have to understand; This-" I nod and take a hiatus in what I am doing. Dad is on a very important phone call, I presume. He would not be addressing someone as "sir" unless they are of extreme importance or well respected.

With this new intel acquired, I quietly make my way over towards a laptop residing at the kitchen table. Initially, I walk past it without thinking anything out of the ordinary, but upon second glance, my eyes notice something very peculiar. Redirecting my attention back to the laptop, I can visibly see the monitor cast dim in contrast. I start by pressing *F3*, which is to increase the brightness for this specific computer. However, my intellectual plan proves a failure to my disappointment. In my next attempt to resolve this issue, I click on the settings tab while ever so meticulously, trying not to close Dad's excel spreadsheet window. Though I understand why it is called a window, but *why* is it called a window? Yes, I understand that you can open and close it in order to access various functions of a computer, but why is it called a window. Like whoever thought of that name? I find that statement impractical for me to digest. Though I may have actually answered my own question without even meaning to do.

Anywho, just before I am able to click on the settings icon at the bottom left-hand corner of the screen, I take notice of the battery life. Boy, that should have been the first thing I started with. If that had been my first indicator, this all could have been avoided. At one moment, the leaf icon was slightly above the battery icon confined in the perimeter of the toolbar of the screen, and with the blink of an eye, it all vanished, including the rest of the screen. Frantic, I rush to reach the power supply and plug it in the personal computer.

His timing is impeccable if I do say so myself. Wailing his hands and running over to me, he accidentally forgets to put the phone on mute then fixes his error after it is too late. "Hey! No! Sophia. Baby girl, what did you do! Those are all of my expense reports for this quarter...ruined." My eyes are suddenly alert, and an erect posture is presented before Dad; the words tremble at the might of the tyrant's dominion over me. Nothing manages to come out of my mouth except for the carbon dioxide that has been releasing from my mouth from the start of this interaction. I wonder what the reader does when they are in similar predicaments, such as the one that I currently find myself in? I do not want the reader to answer it right away, more so ponder it and prepare for its inevitable arrival.

With the firm announcement of my name for a second time, a trickle creeps its way down a trail to my nose. "I- I- I- I saw that your laptop was out of juice, so I-" Dad is quick to interrupt. "Stop it! Stop it! Stop it!"

I still do not understand how I am the perpetrator here. Although there may be things I am not supposed to comprehend yet due to my still-developing brain, perhaps. "But Dad…" Before I can finish my train of thought, I am abruptly cut off. "Shut up!!" As tears drizzled down my face, Dad instantly knew he went too far with this one. Jolting up the stairs to then collapse onto my bed clenching Threepio, my heart immediately aches with an alien pain.

Amadeus says my superpower has the capability of being controlled and harnessed in the future. I do not want to deny his knowledge, but how long until the future arrives? A day? A year? A millennium? On the brink of death!? No matter how long it takes, C3PO will be with me every step of the way. The one time I actually want this protocol droid to speak, he does not even attempt to. So much for the viewer, knowing you undoubtedly have my back. That was an attempt at sarcasm once again. All of you by now, should be well educated to the point where you are able to differentiate between the assorted dialects of my voice. Threepio is good at detecting when someone is in distress or not. Amadeus and he both possess the same ability to have a deep concern about whatever issue I may have; this very same characteristic of Amadeus' is the reason why I have continued to see him through all these years.

As I conceal myself from the external world, internal is persistent enough to withstand the ravages of time. Like a cassette tape, my mind replays the event that happened moments earlier over and over, exploring the varied scenarios to expect a different outcome. I wonder if Kylo Ren ever had moments where he regretted what he had done to his father? Wonder if his father ever forgave him for what he did? I know I forgive Dad for becoming upset with me. Every relationship cannot be quintessential. See-Threepio is very good at forgiveness. As a matter of fact, I think that is why I fell in love with him and Corduroy so much at a rapid pace. He just had that ambient presence about him. Both of my friends share that special quality, without them ever needing to say a physical word, they show you how much you mean to them both. As I am sharing all that has happened within the last few hours, a form of contact is made with the door leading to my bedroom.

"Sophie, can I come in?" The familiar voice fails to pique my interest. Still buried within the confines of my pillow, my voice makes minimal effort to project outward. "No! Go away!" Blatantly ignoring my demand, the now intruder violates my personal makeshift pillow fortification. I got to admit, it was worth a shot. However, I knew he would never listen to me. I expected this from Dad. I am living under *his* roof, after all. I played no part in the purchase of this house. But if I did, I would have equal authoritative control as him. Until that day comes, I will continue to play and respect his rules.

My attentive listening skills home in as Dad enters the room to only put all of his weight upon the side of my bed as he purposely left his chair at the bottom of the stairs, thus leading to where I reside. Facing the wall away from him, I warn him not to get any closer. This time he respects my wishes and does not advance any closer. But what he does next is something I would not have ever expected for him. He extends his arm outward, thus surfing the area along the minor curvature of my spine. The soothing texture of Dad's hand makes my muscles shrivel. "I am so sorry I yelled at you back there. It is just that I was talking to my boss and-" An initial pause lasts no more than a few milliseconds out of him, but this was different. An exponential increment of time has passed for it to be considered a casual pause anymore. Thinking from a critical thinking standpoint, this is going to prove to be detrimental! The gravity of his weighted excess exhale magnifies my anticipation. "I just found out I lost my job, Sophie."

I roll over to face him almost instantaneously, asking him if my intervention had anything to do with his termination. He shakes his head while he also simultaneously denies my claim. The authoritative character in the room initiates an exit after sharing what he wanted. What fantastic social skills you have there! Looks like I know which side of the family I inherited that from. You are going to end the conversation like that! I need some context, at least an elaboration, something. I am hanging by a thread Dad. Those pristine leather shoes of Dad's interact with the hardwood floor as the ambient noise vibrates the airwaves present in the bedroom. The origin of my mobility does not occur until a set of perfectly orchestrated and aligned syllables intrigue my interest. "I know you have questions, Sophia. I will answer them all over lunch. Skyline okay with you?" You should be well aware that you do not have to ask me twice father when you include a paid lunch in the picture.

Mother never treated me with the luxury of dining out. Every time I would ask her if we can, she would undoubtedly have some excuse as to why we are unable. There were some things about Mother that would just baffle me beyond comprehension, like the fact that she forbade me from ever returning to public school or why she ever thought I deserved Corduroy without any explanation. Although I did not mind getting him one bit. She never gave me a complete answer; I was always taught not to question her permissive nature and to accept the results. Now Mother is not here, and Dad is, so I no longer have to listen to you, Mother. Dad is who I now take orders from.

I do miss Mother with all my heart, but there are just some things that I was never meant to understand, perhaps due to my adolescence. Speculation as to why Mother never bothered to treat me out for dinner could quite possibly be due to the fact that deep down inside the chambers of her most inner self; she may have had insecurities that were so major to her but to us "average" folks, it was minor, unapparent if anything... this could prose as a viable hypothesis.

This paragraph above was merely a transition or filler paragraph, if you will, constructed as a segway to the actual restaurant. Initially, I was thinking about implementing the walk to the restaurant, but nothing interesting transpired over those twenty to thirty minutes. I was kind enough to think of the reader's perspective and evidently opted out of it for time constraint reasons. I am unsure if I mentioned this in the *Prologue,* but apologies if I already happened to do so, but the city of Cincinnati has an ongoing battle against the public on which chili is the best. There are two chains that have been competing with each other for as long as I can recall: Skyline and Gold Star. From an outsider looking in, there is no distinct evidence separating the two, but take it from a veteran who has crossed both sides of the battlefield, the subtle differences can sometimes make or break the last stretch of a battle.

Gold Star Chili is consistent with its flavoring, which is not bad if I may indirectly express my personal input. However, it is much thicker and chunkier than its predecessor, which I find loses its sentimental value. The chunkiness and thickness of the meat, along with the chili itself, distracts me from savoring the flavor because I find myself more often than not, concentrating on constraining it down my esophagus. I usually let it sit in my mouth then patiently wait for my saliva to dissolve it into a form capable enough for my throat to ingest. Forgive me for an extensive and unnecessary explanation as it pertains to my eating habit, but I thought you would be interested. Guess that is something only my protocol droid finds intriguing.

That is the biggest difference that Gold Star has over Skyline, and for that reason alone, I refuse to eat there. Dad and I both do. Did you know that Skyline Chili is predominantly custom to Ohio thus founded in 1949; the same year former president Harry S. Truman was elected for a second and final term. Extensive research was required to regurgitate this information to the reader to emphasize the history of this restaurant. August has entered through this building once before; I remember him telling me so. This was his first experience with the now-famous local chili joint. Mr. Parker, along with his eldest son, ordered the usual fan favorite, and I shall order the same as them if I want to still stay connected with the Parker family.

Dad orders the same as me and proceeds to unknowingly and unironically sit down at the same table where August sat upon his last visit. Against the window on the left side of the restaurant, and Dad agrees to sit closest to the door as that is most preferable by my standards. A waitress approaches us and asks us if she can fetch us anything to drink. I ask for a glass of water, but with the specific instruction for them to hold the ice. Dad orders the same but with ice. I do not care for ice cubes in my drinks. I am always afraid a sliver will slide down my throat unknowingly, and I will suffocate. Anyway, dressed in a navy blue uniform accompanied by the company logo in the upper left and dawning a dark bistro apron; She confirms our requests by developing an enlarged beautiful smile across her face then proceeds to enter behind the counter and into the "*Employees only*" section.

Without wasting a single second, I begin to bombard him with question after question. "So how did you lose your job, Dad? I know you said it was not because of me but are you lying to try and not make me feel bad? If that happens to be the case, you are no longer a trustworthy father. Are you going to get another job? Are you going to get a job here and stay with C3PO and me to form one big happy family?! Then we can be close to Amadeus and Riley! You and Amadeus are able to then rekindle your guys' relationship. That would be wonderful! If you need help with obtaining a job or perhaps maintaining one judging from how your last job went, I can speak to Riley after we are finished here to see if he has a job opportunity for you at the shelter. I can-"

He raises his hands slightly above the table and quickly glances around the room. "Whoa! No one told me I was being interrogated." My hand provides no immediate cover to hide my giggle. "Riley works at a shelter, and you did not bother to share that valuable information with me?" "Daaad." "Okay, okay. I did not lose my job because of you. You are the most important thing to me in the whole wide world, Sophia." I ponder for a bit as he proudly and prophetically proclaims that statement. I do not hesitate to question his loyalty. "More important than Mom?"

Glassy eyes apprehend my appearance as I struggle to watch Dad intently stare into them. Then caressing my hand, he pauses no more than a moment or two. "What! No. You and Mom are my world. I love you, baby girl, and do not ever forget that. Okay? I love you so much, Sophia...and Mom. Just because she is not here with us anymore does not mean I love her any less than you. Come here, honey."

Attracted to his warm embrace, Dad squeezes me tight and vowing to never let me go. If I was able to stop time, I would stay in this precious moment forever. I admit to him that I miss Mother immensely, and he tightens his grip. "I know. I know." He gently whispers into my ear. Indulging myself within this precious moment, sooner than later, I sense Dad gesture and whisper a "Thank you," to our server. Released from his embrace, I am greeted by our meals alongside our beverages once I resume back to my seat. In front of me sits a concoction known as a 3-Way:

•The first layer consists of a mountain of spaghetti, which is then mounted by Skyline's famous chili mounted again with shredded cheddar cheese.

If this fails to give me indigestion, I am unsure of what actually will. Slowly wiping the tears away, I devise the best possible vantage point to strike the food from. Once I consume my first bite is when Dad initiates the long-awaited conversation. "So, I invited you out here to explain the situation to you, and I am a man of my word. I lost my job due to a leave of absence. It was nothing you did, Sophia. I have been away for quite a significant while, as you are well aware. And you know when you have a job, the number one priority besides doing your job is showing up. I ultimately made the sacrifice and ran with the risk of losing my job to stay beside you and your mother's side through all this turmoil that has happened all within the last month or so.-" A nod for acknowledgment as my mouth is currently unable to produce sound. "-There is something else also. Along with me losing my job, I have decided in my best interest that it is best for you to come back to live with me in California."

You know that sensation when you are on the climax of a roller coaster before it plummets, your heart stops, and your throat clenched? Well, that is the best visual description I can provide for this reaction. An experience hopefully, the viewer can definitely relate to in order to grasp the thrill of it. "I- I- I cannot believe what I am hearing! You have no idea how long I have waited to go to California, to see San Francisco" I am now officially able to see my beloved August! Now I can see how he actually is in his natural habitat, no longer being confined to the wires of constant dependability. Although I do have to constantly remind myself now that he no longer exists, the treatment will heal through time. I continue to express my overwhelming gratitude. "Thank you! Oh, thank you, thank you, Dad!" As he quenches his parched throat, his iris enhances his pigment, resulting in dilated pupils. Just before he responds, my appropriate utensils are equipped and ready to tackle another delicious savory bite. "Though it comes with a catch." Dad has never been this hesitant about anything before. It must not be that horrific of a statement. Could it?

"You will not be able to see Amadeus and Riley anymore."
I stand corrected.

A vial act of rage consumes me, accompanied by a pothole of sorrow. "No! I will not accompany you then. Nothing can separate mine and Riley's relationship. It is symbolic and significant, as is the same with Amadeus. Riley is by far the best thing that has ever happened to me! Riley is the first person my age who overrules the norm to see me as a freak like the rest of them. As a matter of fact, he invited me to church this upcoming Sunday with Amadeus. I was pondering whether I should attend or not but judging by the conversation thus far, I would be more than delighted to attend without your presence needed. You have no idea what it is like for me to walk the streets of this city already having the preconceived notion of strangers' magnetic eyes and their jagged, keen, insults tear this delicate, sensitive soul apart! Pardon me, Dad, if my argument does not come across as rational or drastic enough, but I am not ready to go on a plane just to abandon the life I built! No. My friends are here! Riley! Amadeus! Corduroy!"

On the contrary, it is his tears now that flow from the face. Oh, how the tides have turned. "Mother.... The memories of her, the memories of both of them; all of them are dead if I pack up and leave with you. My room is the final physically visible memory I have to remember her by. Although she diligently disproved the construction of my bed and space underneath before I built it, she let me keep the design because she knew in the bigger scheme of things, it would not matter because she realized the unconditional love she had for her daughter Even if the horrendous design was my choice alone….. Her words, not mine." Such a predictable creature that Dad is, wiping his tears as a means to suppress the effect of pity.

Just as I am about to pull away from the residing table, two extended arms invade my personal bubble. Miniscule bumps fairly visible by the human eye begin to form as I am processing our "productive" father/daughter lunch date thus far. His arms, like rustic shackles, begin to loosen their initial grip. "Baby, baby, baby, baby, girl. Oh, my sweet baby girl Sophia, I had no idea. I am so so sorry. I had only given it into my account and did not even bother to consider yours. I am so sorry, Sophia." A period of silence invites itself in as we finish up our entries. Dad finishes just after me, both members of the clean plate club. Never knew you had it in you, Dad, though this changes nothing. I am still increasingly upset with you, and there is nothing in this world that will make me forgive you.

The waiters and waitresses make their final rounds before clocking out for the night crew; one approaches us and dispenses the check at the end of the table in exchange for our plates. Though not the same waitress we had from earlier, she still appeared to do her job just as well as the other one had. Closing a leather booklet containing the check after we contribute our funds, my guardian abruptly rises from his chair with firm possession of his coat only to then initiate a hold of the door for me. "Sophia, what is your favorite animal!?" He shouts. Amadeus tells me it is not in our best judgment to assume things as it is a dreadful act to get one's hopes up for predominantly false records. I think it is safe to say that this instance will not abide by that particular rule.

Dad unlocks the door through the garage and checks for any missed messages. The pressure from the landline speaker radiates down the corridor and all throughout the kitchen and family quarters. I proceed towards the living room after I hang up my coat, I usually do not listen to the automated messages the speaker relays to us, but today was different.

Voicemail: *You have one unheard message. First unheard message.*

Riley: *Hi Sophia, i- i- it's i- it is Riley. I am ju- just calling to tell you ab- about church this Sunday. My Dad and I will come to pick you up at 11 a.m. sharp. So- so be ready.*

Voicemail: *End of message.*

Why are there not enough genuine people, gentlemen, in the world these days? I am lucky even to stumble upon one, let alone be one's inseparable companion. They are an endangered species that are worth preserving. There is no qualitative record of how many we have left on our planet, but it is not abundant. Riley exhibits this endangered element and ensures chivalry by propping open the door for me without question. Amadeus leads us two pews from the altar. He assumes the position furthest away from me as I find an opening against the aisle still next to Riley, like I promised earlier. The research I conducted earlier prior to our arrival has now proven a sense of falsehood. Churches are supposed to have an organ shadowing over its audience upon the second floor. Not only is there an absence of a marvel of an instrument as it reverberates throughout the arena but the spectacular dazzling stained glass window panels that seep rays of light through presenting the Messiah and Virgin Mary overlooking his congregation as well! The defining qualities that represent the very definition of a House of God are lacking. As disappointing as it may be, though, I do find it extremely fascinating that this building once used to be a decaying, vandalized, decrepit clocktower. Coming across old images of what this place once used to be, is haunting—practically something you would find in a *"Blair Witch"* movie.

A dilapidated brick structure with a caved-in roof stood tall, paneled with vulgar images accompanied by obscene derogatory phrases that were infused across the walls ran rampant. I am just glad they got the old clock working again. How else would I know when it is time for the sermon to start or when to leave? Did you know it took them over a year to fully repair the machinery because the city vouched for it to be a "waste of public money?" Obviously, you could not have known that. I was the one doing the research, after all. Another fact that also caught me off guard about this place is that it is supposedly haunted by a nineteenth-century ghost who passed on upon the tower. Legend has it that in 1898, a cowboy was involved in a scuffle at the top of the tower. Approached by three opposing posse members, the altercation became violent quickly, and soon the cowboy found himself falling out of the clocktower, greeting death earlier than he originally expected. Since that catastrophic event, the tower has been left vacant until almost seven decades ago, where now it is repurposed into the very church we find ourselves in today.

You are welcome for the history lesson. Whether you are grateful for it or not, please refrain from answering. My tangent did, in fact, progress longer than the initially intended timestamp if I must admit. Including worship seemed pointless and a waste of paper because it only consisted roughly of fifteen to thirty minutes of finding myself inadvertently glancing at Riley, for I do not feel comfortable singing songs I do not know, nor ever for that matter. Everybody takes their seats once again after worship time and places the book of hymns against the seat in front of them where they initially found them.

"Every decision points your life in the direction you are about to travel." Amadeus spoke those words into me in one of the first meetings I ever had with him, and I still keep that true to me. Wonder if Riley ever got those same words sparked into him? Just as the pastor unveils himself from the drapes barely outside my peripheral vision on the far left of the stage, Riley overlaps his hand with mine. Instantly I begin to quiver with my cheeks becoming a bashful pigment. (whatever color that may be according to science) The time to act is now; it is at this moment that I will discover whether my initial hypothesis can be proven valid or invalid after all of these months! Rotating my hand palm side up now, I patiently wait for the fish to take its bait. In which he does indeed, by interlocking his fingers with mine. Both of us do not look down nor face either other; we just continue to sit in silence as the pastor daunting several tattoos prepares for his message.

The fog has yet to unveil itself; I am unsure if I consider Riley something beyond a devoted friend yet. I still need more time to process my emotions. Certainly, I like Riley as he is my best friend, and I am his undoubtedly. However, with that said, love is different from like, obviously. But which distinct four letters would best describe my feelings towards him? Having an intense debate with Mrs. Merriam Webster about the serenity of these two closely related words; she explains to me that *love* as an emotion being present when *a person develops a strong affection for another arising out of kinship and personal ties or when the connection is deeper on a sexual desire.* When *like* on the contrary, is when *a person feels an attraction or takes pleasure in something.* These definitions sound extremely similar if not identical. But I clearly know the difference. There is no plausible or possible way I can be in love with Riley! August is my one true love. Riley is inadequate to August, inferior if I may. Nothing can separate August Parker from Sophia Collins.

My eyes absorb the enclosed campus one last time before giving the pastor my undivided attention because that would be rude and inconsiderate otherwise. He starts off by greeting the congregation and welcoming any newcomers; that would be me, and immediately wastes no time as he is on a very strict schedule of 45 minutes. "So, I had a lot of back and forth discussions with God this week on what to talk about. Then he whispered one gentle word to me last night right as I was about to go to sleep, *choice.* So, I spent all night revising and rewriting my message all for you guys, so excuse me if I look exhausted. Anyway, let's dive into today's message, shall we? So, I was a quarterback at the University of Cincinnati. Go Bearcats! I was good y'all! Like real good. I aspired to the NFL, and I could have made it. I could have seriously made it if I wanted to, but something changed the trajectory of my life..." We all follow his finger as our heads direct our attention towards the entrance of the building.

"Those doors. Walking through those doors changed my life forever, and it's funny; people ask me if you had a second chance, would you change it? Honestly, no. I wouldn't change it for the world. God brought me to the university but used me in ways I couldn't even imagine. We started this whole thing, only 15 of us and now look at how much it's grown over the past 6 years! Over 400 people are now coming on a weekly attendance! Only God can do that y'all; Like for real. Nothing I do can make you return here week after week. It's Christ who lives in me who can only make miracles happen." Divulging deeper and deeper into the core message for this morning, I cannot help but think of August. I wish he was here to see this fantastic message with me. Well, I guess in a way, he is here with me if he is a figment of my perceptive imagination.

All this talk about Christ and the holy spirit reminds me of August and his religious journey. Finally, reflecting back on it now, it is nothing short of an absolute marvel how the turmoil in our lives can eventually turn anything into a beneficial and grateful experience later down the line. Imagine faith as stages of a flower. It starts off small as a seed then later blooms into something unexplainable through unforeseen events and radiates within the world we live in.

This particular analogy will correspond to August's faith, perhaps. The Parker family grew up in a religious household, attending church only on Sundays and made it so to never to discuss church outside of the confined four-walled building. This is the seed buried in a beautiful garden, surrounded by fertilizer. Remember when I visited August in the hospital? Of course, you do! It was only five days ago. Anyway, he was confessing about that experience being the moment when he felt a burning inside him. Something unexplainable, inexplicable, he said; something similar to a feeling I get on occasion to some extent, yet it was painless. He said it was a drive of overwhelming joy along with a sense of unconditional love. Within that single circumstance, a revolutionary epiphany marinated within August Parker that forever transformed his every sense of reality.

Through the years, I am embarrassed to admit that August's faith had come to a stalemate. No one said it was going to be an easy road August. Life does not always hand you lemons and expects you to make lemonade! You of all people should know that, yet here I am. It takes hard work and dedication to achieve an astronomical goal such as this one. Believe me, August, I know it is scary to take risks; but how will you ever know unless you try.

Throughout time, the unexplainable sensation enlarged. August explained it as if it were a tumor. Although I am quite unsure how he can even compare it to something so detrimental, now if he had experienced one, that analogy would be appropriate. If I am allowed to interject, it is surprisingly offensive to the victims who are actually struggling with that condition, I would imagine. Expansion has two directions; it is able to travel: positively, as seen in August's upcoming case, or negatively as demonstrated with the poorly executed analogy.

In the events of *Episode II: Attack of the Clones,* Anakin Skywalker is commanded by Chancellor Palpatine to safeguard senator Padme Amidala. Anakin then transports Padme to her home planet of Naboo to send her into hiding from assassins hired by the Trade Federation. Throughout their endeavor, the padawan and senator soon fall for each other. I wonder if August feels the same as Anakin did, or is it something completely different? Perhaps the correlation is better compared to the manipulative force and the sensation a Jedi has when they are surrounded by its presence. It is nothing identifiable, but August is certain that he is strong with this force.

Expanding further in his faith in his first year of college, August made the decision to go public with his faith. I am proud of him for taking such a big leap in what he believes in. Personally, you could not get me up on stage no matter the reward. I am not good in front of crowds; I suppose that is why Mother pulled me out of school, that and for me supposedly "acting out" in class. The commencement of baptism is like what I stated before, going public in your faith, and declaring Jesus Christ as Lord and Savior, but the significance travels further beyond that. The body of water that the individual is submerged under for no more than five milliseconds is a sign of purification. Personally, if I had any say in this, I would be more than inclined to immerse the phase transition from a solid to liquid as this demonstrates an excellent alternative method for me to once again reconnect with August for us to become more immersive together. Wish I was there to witness the ceremony. It sounded spectacular. From what I was able to gather from our last official encounter back at the hospital, August walked up on stage and briefly explained to the congregation why baptism is worthy of attention on a personal level. Therefore, commencing a memorable message concluding the gathering just after the baptism.

Passion and peace flood his soul as August now walks a new man. Both of the Parker parents saw something resonate with their son, integrated deep into his soul in the passing months. The eldest son aimlessly wandered about the confines of his church one day after service. After an appropriate increment of time had passed, he eventually was approached by a young bushy thick bearded man who invited him to join his newly established young adults small group. August agreed, of course, and went to the host's house in which he was greeted by the man's girlfriend, who ironically was the co-leader of the group. From August's perspective, the woman seemed to be in her late twenties as well as several of the other people among the vastly diverse group. This was the first instance where August was the youngest individual when it came to any type of group. In school, he was always superior to everyone when discussing age, so you could say August had to adapt to his new surroundings knowing there is a more than likely chance he will not provide brilliant examples.

The notion of memory is due to our increasing in age, we have more capacity to store external experiences or ("examples" in this instance) to then regurgitate them to audiences who specifically are curious or are in dire need of them as they may shed some light on a specific subject in their lives and in turn, those individuals can learn from to then apply it within their own environments. Within minutes of arriving, the session started with a brief introduction.

Over the proximity of an hour, the group discussed how God has shaped them into who they are and why they think He brought them to that specific location tonight. Initially, August believed he was unworthy of sharing a brief synopsis due to inexperience with the Lord.... Could you be more mistaken August! No need to answer as it does not indicate a question mark; merely an observative constructive criticism.

You have yet to experience it, let alone embrace the fact that you were brought here for a reason. This statement not only pertains to August and Riley but the reader just as much. A tap on the shoulder reignites me back into *my* reality. "How do you like it so far?" Riley sporadically asks. "How much longer do we have?" I then replied. Riley peers down at his wrist and whispers, "Ten more minutes" faintly. An honest accident on my part as I only meant to smile, but a chuckle erupts instead. Quickly covering my mouth, then staring at Riley to make him erupt only then in laughter as well. The reader does not know this about Riley, but he does not possess a watch, so I am quite baffled as to why and how he came up with ten minutes. Our diaphragms clinch as we both try and not to create too much of a distraction. Tears secrete out both our eyes, we make minimal effort to control our rude and obscene behavior. Amadeus takes care of that for us, hastily.

A tight grip is then placed upon Riley's arm, leaving him speechless, as it would for me as well. Amadeus turns to both of us and shouts, "I find your lack of faith disturbing!" Maybe "shout" was the incorrect use of the word here. He more so aggressively whispered to drive the point home. Although I have the idea that I would at least fight back with Dad if he ever depicted the same action here. At least he should know never to lay a hand on a woman no matter the circumstances. Applauding Riley for his efforts to resist the urge to fight back. However, Amadeus is right, though; we need to give respect where respect is due. My apologies.

"-And Zacchaeus climbs down from that sycamore tree, and in parting, we all sometimes need to get down from that tree once in a while to see what is truly in front of us or get up for that matter. Everybody's journey is different, and only you can walk it. Just like that girl, I had a mad crush on in middle school, I eventually had to let her go. People of the church, we cannot leave our luggage at the baggage claim going round and round, waiting for someone else to deal with our own personal belongings! Our abandonment, abuse, addiction! It is ultimately up to us to pick up our shattered pieces. God will decide which fruit you can bring into the next season." The pastor thanks the church, and then Amadeus starts, followed by everybody else. The entire church participates in a standing ovation. From a musical standpoint, the instruments grow louder with the ever-increasing applause. Vowing not to be an outcast, I begin to rise from my seat the same as Riley and participate. We continue until the music dies, and the pastor excuses himself from the podium. We gather all our coats and other necessities as I depart my section to the overcrowded and claustrophobic aisle. Such an intriguing message and spiritual belief. Really. A human man who is also simultaneously, God comes down and sacrifices himself for all of humanity as a form of salvation. A way for believers to live spiritually, eternal in heaven once these decrepit bodies waste away. I do see why the Parker's believe in this. Although it is just too convoluted and tortuous for my preferred taste.

Epilogue

Homo sapiens are the few prominent species on the planet who are able to recognize and recall past memories on command. In order to accomplish the task of recognizing information, one has to first indulge themselves within the memory itself. -A vivid image of the memory itself. The act of recognition pertains to indicate selective retention, which is also forgetting certain elements of existence. Formally speaking, recognition, as it pertains to Amadeus' personal field of preferred study, is a form of remembering characterized by a feeling of familiarity when something previous triggers the experienced encounter.

Fed up with the pace at how things are going, I forcefully grab Riley's hand from behind me; at least I hope that was his hand I grasped onto; I push through the crowd and have him hold onto my hand as I fear for separation. Just as we are about to be greeted by the flamboyant, radiant sun, I accidentally bump into these people. Making direct contact with them, a little girl and a boy instantly shout, "You!" If I can explain my next questionable action depicted, I most certainly would for clarification purposes, although I do not have a viable concrete answer for doing so. The upper portion of my body cowers and retreats while my lower extremities contradict my upper portion and propel us forward and outward.

Riley and I eventually post up along the railing once outside the sanctum, watching as the people gather outside to then finish their unsettled conversations and reward themself for enduring the entire service with coffee and a donut. Riley reconfigures his spectacles and adjusts his overcoat. Eye contact with a person is a definite sign to someone that you are intensely engaged in the conversation. I, by no means, want to hinder that from Riley as he refocuses his vision on me. He brushes the collected dust off his coat in which I presume he did not invite onto his coat to start with. Absent of any preconceived notion it was ever going to be apparent to him or me, I quickly ask Riley the question I have been meaning to ask him since the last time Dad mentioned it inside the restaurant. "So, apparently Dad is taking me to the zoo sometime soon Riley, and- and- I was wondering if you would- would- like to go with Dad and me? I will try not to be discouraged if you do not want to accompany me on my upcoming adventure." Looks like the whole reconfiguring your coat there was a complete waste of time, Riley. Waving his arms hysterically, he confirms my suspicion with a warm embrace, followed by a nod of approval.

Emerging from the building finally comes the duo from earlier. Now, where do I know you from? I definitely know you from somewhere, but I can not precisely pinpoint where. Amadeus approaches us from behind and rests his hand on Riley's shoulder. The sister and brother approach us in a non-aggressive fashion. This is quite surprising, judging from the way she blatantly yelled at us just moments earlier in that tranquil environment. "Hi, Mr. Richards!" One of them exclaims. "Hi, you two!" Oh. Right. Now I remember. The girl turns to me while the boy converses with Riley off to the side. "So how is your mom? Did she ever get better?" I am very particular with my formatting of the conveyance of the forthcoming conversation once again, but you already knew that. "Temporarily." She looks at me puzzled as anyone would be after my confined remark. "Temporarily? Care to elaborate…." The young girl states.

"The demons got her. I did everything in my power to preserve her, but ultimately, I was not strong enough. I miss Mother dearly. You would think that I would have at least one regret about the time I spent with her if any at all, but you would be wrong. I will cherish every moment I had with her, even the typical yet occasional mother-daughter bickering."

Crippled by sympathy and sorrow, my recent acquaintance to I have yet to obtain her name, begins to choke on her own aspirations. "I am so sorry. I had no idea." I do thank her for providing some comfort. She then asks if I will be attending church again with Riley next week also. This is an interesting move you portrayed in order to alleviate my pain by switching subjects. Since I am not certain whether I will be back here or not, I ask the girl what does it matter to her. She reveals to me that she would be delighted to sit next to Riley and me, so she is able to form a more secure bond with me. I am not entirely sure what made her think I would approve of her outlandish proclamation, but I shun my head away as a tactic of avoidance to only then find Riley a considerable distance away.

We all struggle with our demons throughout our lives; it is how we cope with them that is the real medication. Before making it extremely apparent, there is an indefinite percentage I will never see these two again, the girl hollers for her brother to come to say goodbye to Riley and me. Amadeus brings the car around to the front of the pavilion and fires up the seat warmers. Regret is a funny thing, we all have some, yet we continue to subconsciously produce more as time advances. I am unsure why I thought this was a clever string of last words to say, clearly, it was not. The younger brother stands beside his sister, and the last thing I manage to say to him is, "Hope you liked those fruit snacks." That is the impression I am going to leave them with! Come on, Sophia! At least it is not as awkward and embarrassing as what Riley did. He does a quick smile towards both of them before leading me to the car. But not an average smile as you would think, the kind that shows no teeth and is an outline of the typical formation. I think the correct term for this is a soft smile. Yes, he did one of those.

"Here, Sophia; we will drop you off, courtesy of us." An eminent voice shouts from the driver's seat and through the passenger window. Propping open the door for me like a true gentleman without missing a beat once again, I slide down to the furthest seat as Riley is soon to mimic my depicted action. "These seats are too warm. A- Ar- Are you o- okay with the temperature, Sophia?"

"Riley, I should tell you something just in case I am unable to see you again." He is hesitant, as anyone would be, but agrees to listen. "-Look, Dad was telling me that there may be a chance this may be one of our last encounters together. You see, Dad wants me to move to California with him, and frankly, I do not want to, but I have no say in it." My friend's eyes begin to secrete tears. However, I tell him that action is unnecessary and quite pitiful. He soon resolves and is stuck with accepting the difficult truth. Trust me, it is not easy for me either, pal.

The church is not too far from home, just about three exits away upon entering the freeway and 5 blocks down from that point, then a left turn on a street in which I embarrassingly always butcher the name, then a mile down that road. Take a right at the light, which leads to my neighborhood. Apologies for not providing the most accurate and precise directions, but I did this in case the reader gets any bright ideas and attempts to find my address. We cannot have any mischievous behavior happening. Dad and I would be extremely upset, as one would assume.

What specifics classifies a freeway different from a highway? From the obvious position, it is just the name, but what are the fundamentals between both structures that make one a freeway and one a highway? I will be sure to ask my intellectual friend Amadeus this perplexing question as it pertains to a wider segway towards greater discussions on our next scheduled appointment.

Thanking Riley and Amadeus for the ride, my shoes make contact with the hardwood flooring within the confines of the house once upon entrance again. Placement is extremely particular in my household. If the reader has yet to grasp that idea, I hang my coat up on the rack aside the door and advance my way up the stairs. However, not before investigating an unbeknownst commotion occurring on the farthest side of the house. Equipping and activating my trench coat, the detective inside of me is incapable of leaving an investigation unsolved. I need to uncover all the clues necessary to find the culprit in the act. No concrete evidence can be detected as I peep around the kitchen, but with just that ten feet distance from the front door to the kitchen, the sound intensifies.

Quiet as can be, I eventually make my way towards the sliding glass door that leads to the backyard. For those of you who are wondering, my backyard is nothing special, and according to visitors: "basic." Consisting of a firepit with outdoor chairs encircle the area on the outer left of the property; followed by an immense luscious green yet overgrown lawn which ironically places Dad at the end of it as he begins to roll the lawnmower attachment on the backend of his wheelchair all through the yard.

The word Sunday is considered a sabbath day, declaring a restful and worship-oriented day devoted to the big guy in the sky. If that may be the only thing I retained from this morning sermon, so be it. The lawnmower spits up shards of grass as it unconventionally drags behind Dad. "Dad! Dad!" The motor gullets shreds of grass in its bagged "stomach." I try once more to avert his attention before I submit to a forfeit and reenter inside for a nice refreshment of freshly squeezed lemonade. Temperament is definitely not a virtue of mine. Most certainly not a strong suit of mine either. Without wanting to strain my voice, I occupy one of the chairs, lining it up precisely, so I am within his peripheral vision at all times.

Apologies for abruptly halting my expedition, but these last few days have been extremely tough. It has been precisely six days, six hours, and fifty-four minutes since the last time I wrote. I bet the reader has been wondering where I have been. To reassure everyone, I have been contemplating on whether I should visit Amadeus. The process of grief operates in stages, working at random. One moment I will be fine, then the next I suddenly break down into a spiral of misery accompanied by tears. There is no mystery as to why I am feeling so dreaded, I dearly miss Mother, and I am afraid I will never see Riley again. I would not say I have been depressed or anything, but I am extremely sad. With that being said, by this point, I may be at the risk of developing clinical depression, according to medical professionals. Dad was supposed to drop me off at both appointments Amadeus had deliberately scheduled for me this week, but I canceled them both at last minute notice.

On the bright side, Riley and I went out to *Graeders* for some of the best ice cream this city has to offer yesterday, in my humble opinion. My accomplice ordered a single scoop of Vanilla on a sugar cone while I got Black Cherry. Let us just discuss Riley's choice of ice cream for a moment here, shall we? Vanilla ice cream is one of those flavors where it is good but not ever loved. Undisputable. At a constant state of consistency, it is by far the most popular of all the ice cream flavors. It is adored and disliked to an equal ratio. The A/D ratio of ice cream I like to call it. It is very peculiar to me as to why Riley's decision to get vanilla shocked me because he is the type of person that lights up the room wherever he may be. He is an unceasing sparkle of joy and compassion with everyone he comes in contact with and is a blessing to be around. So, I just thought he would have picked more of a sporadic color that closely resembles his uniqueness and the spiritual embodiment of this beautiful, wondrous human being. Anyway, enough of my babbling. Who knew a frozen dessert could do such an elegant job to cheer someone up! That is the exact dose of happiness that I needed that day, and I would not have taken that pill with anybody else in the world. Anyway, Dad came up into my room just before writing this and said we are leaving in five minutes. I did not bother to ask the location, whereas I am sure I will find out soon enough. So it is goodbye for now.

Dad removes what appears to be important documents from the passenger seat and places them in the backseat of his truck before I enter. The seat belt resists in complying with my desired motion as I attempt to make myself as safe as possible. Dad does have a tendency at times to drive dangerously...not reckless through. The act of reckless driving is when the driver of the vehicle is accelerating at alarming speeds and swerving in and out of traffic. Drivers of this state are careless and impatient the majority of the time. Perhaps "dangerously" is not the correct term here. After all, people may be getting the wrong idea. To clarify as best as possible, he does not put himself or others in harm's way, but rather makes the car ride more exciting by the excessive music volume and interesting topics we discuss in the car we would not have otherwise. The time it took to go from our current destination to our desired destination took no more than 15 minutes. We would have shaved five minutes off our time, but the perpetual streetlights prolonged our estimated time of arrival. So, striking up a conversation now would not make sense because as we would be to get into the core of the discussion approximately at this moment, we would already be parked and ready to go. There is no sense in wasting oxygen unless a dire circumstance is presented before us.

I appreciate Dad, and that includes all of his spontaneous ways. I can definitely see why Mother fell in love with him in the first place. I mention this because he tells me to close my eyes as a disadvantage for me to uncover our precise location, I presume before we exit the vehicle. I trust he will not let anything terrible occur. I am his daughter, after all. I used to believe stealth was my strong suit, but today I am convinced otherwise. Homing in on my auditory sense, I intently hear and feel a willowed *creek* upon every placement of our feet. As I assume by now, we are fifty percent across the structure when a concerning yelp can be heard coming from my end. The only logical answer to this phenomenal structure is a bridge due to whatever just filed itself into the soul of my shoe. I will soon find out. Before I can catch a clear view of where we are headed, Dad catches me in the act and tells me not to peek. Hopefully, we have only a couple more steps to go because this is starting to get very uncomfortable, very fast. After we cross what I can only assume as a bridge connecting the parking lot to wherever we are now, Dad tells me I can open my eyes. Your idea was cute, but the way you executed it...not so much. I am going to put that event behind us now, and hopefully, we will never speak of it again.

I was correct; it was a bridge we were crossing earlier; guess that explains why there is a splinter inserted into my shoe. I tell Dad to continue to do whatever he was in the process of doing as I am prioritizing my health over the location at this point. Leaning up against a concrete slab, I take off my shoe and release the splice of wood back into its natural habitat. Dad calls me over to the entrance, then proceeds to lead the way through a revolving metal security gate. "Wow! We are at the Cincinnati Zoo! This is the first time I have ever been here. Did you know that, Dad?! Just wait till Amadeus hears about this." I exclaim to Dad as should definitely be nominated for the father of the year award now. I continue on with my train of thought. "Oh. But I asked Riley last week. He said he wanted to come too. He is going to hate me now!" Dad wheels closer to me to assume eye level and puts his hand upon my shoulder. "No, he is not Sophia. Riley will understand. I will tell Amadeus later on and apologize for not bringing Riley. I am sorry, honey. I had no idea you had invited him."

A sigh of shame drapes over me. "You are forgiven." My guardian then resumes back to his original posture. Although that takes little to no effort for him. "With that behind us now and taken care of, let's say we have some fun. What do you say!" I grab the map from a nearby kiosk and plan our route accordingly.

Veering off to the right portion of the park, we soon encounter our first guest. Or perhaps we are the guests in this situation because we are invading *his* home after all. Seeing photographs of these creatures does not do it a bit of justice whatsoever; it is significantly more magnificent in person. I watch in astonishment as those of his tusks are able to mount onto that enormous face of theirs to ward off predators and the trunk. Oh, the trunk is vastly superior to what I originally anticipated. Prior to this current expedition, I thought their only function was to get leaves off of highly elevated trees, but they function as so much more than that, I soon learn after reading the nearby plaque.

Gaining a superior vantage point amongst the crowd as I plunder my way up closer towards the beast, I watch as one of these marvel giants evacuates from a barn-like enclosure. It looks over towards my direction to then greet the people with a calming yet cautious noise. A gargantuan smile is presently endorsed upon my face as I turn back to Dad. He then smiles back and points at the creature. I watch as he heads over to the trough. Excuse me for repeatedly continuing to assume its gender. Its genitalia has not been presented in a manner where I can provide a proper diagnosis. So, *it* heads over to the nearby trough. "Come on, Sophie. Says here, giraffes are up back towards this way." You are right, Dad; we have been here for an exceptional time, and it is time we progress onward into our eventful day. Although it is a good thing we left when we did, we nearly avoided a meteor shower full of water in the nick of time.

Growing up, I never had an opinion on giraffes, I liked the animal, but I also did not hate them. I guess the relationship is mutual. As we get closer to the exhibit, Dad and I experience an assembly of children encircling a zoo employee for a reason we have yet to discover. We patiently wait in line until we get a better understanding of the situation. Turns out, the guests are able to feed carrots to the giraffe. Giraffes do not eat carrots; that is preposterous. Only bunnies and rabbits do. Even so, what do I know? I am not to educate one on an animal's diet. I do not work here. I am merely an observer of the animals. "Excuse me, Miss.? Would you like to feed the giraffe as well?" An employee turns to me as I am suddenly struck by surprise.

Within safe proximity, Dad inches me to advance towards the compassionate giant. My grasp tightens on Threepio inside my pocket as the employee guides my hand up to its mouth. (What! You really thought I would not bring my bestest friend along to experience the thrill of adventure with? He has been on distant planets, survived the rise and fall of The Galactic Empire and The First Order. He can do at least one more mission with me. By the way, he did ask to accompany me after all in my travels.)

Extending the furthest my body allows possible, its extensive neck nears dangerously close to uncomfortable proximity. "It is a safe one. We will not let anything happen to you, sweetie." I am soon reassured as it snatches the carrot by a sliver. The giraffe's herbivores nature inhales the carrot faster than I ever could have expected. After ingesting the carrot, its tongue then extends outward to textualize human flesh I am guessing; thank me for the tasty snack. I do a small yelp and shimmy back to Dad's position, cowering behind his wheelchair, to shield myself from the mammal just in case it decides to potentially switch from its herbivore nature. "Dad, can we venture to the next enclosure, please?

And this time, can I not feed the animals if provoked? I do not want to accidentally lose a finger." He looks up at me and, in a kind manner, obliges to my request happily.

The cheetahs, lions, and hippopotamus were all relatively adjacent to each other, so we saw them all really quick. With that being said, there was not much to look at. We were there for no more than a few minutes at each exhibit, but they were all sleeping. By far, the worst exhibits the park has to offer undoubtedly. If anybody was aching to see these animals, I beg you to come any other day than today and maybe. Just maybe. They will be more eccentric to see the guests. However, if I were to suggest any animal out of these three, I would vote for the hippos.

At least this one was swimming around before it rested, and guess what! They had a special guest as well! Little did Dad and I know, baby hippo Fiona came out of her enclosure for a while. She was adorable! C3PO thought so too; he seems to want to see the baby more than I actually did. I diligently watched while the baby swam with the mom. Swimming in a circular pattern while a zookeeper rewarded them with bits of food behind the glass. My hands collided with each other repeatedly as I urged them to do more swims. We continued to watch the hippos longer than anticipated, and it only led us astray from the entertainment because our gargling stomachs interrupted the session.

Dad soon found a concession stand just outside the cheetah enclosure and ordered two hot dogs for us. We figure we will eat now while we will be able to spectate more animals later to properly manage the limited amount of time we have left here at the zoo. Whenever you get a hot dog or even a hamburger, it would be offensive not to topple it with every condiment available. Dad would disagree, but that is his respected opinion on the matter, not mine. As we finish consuming our food and begin to depart to the next desired exhibit, we come across an escaped animal blocking the sidewalk. Why is no one frantically screaming?! I will only do so unless someone else starts. I do not want to shoo it away as it may become provoked by my depicted action. In desperation, I show Dad, my new acquaintance. As soon as I do so, her gorgeous feathers enchant the circumference around the vicinity.

The peacock pivots its head, magnifying its awesome pattern. I would describe it to the reader, but I honestly believe there are no words too. I feel like if I were to do so, it would by no means do the animal justice. "Woah! Look at your new friend Sophia. What are you going to call him?" In prompt, I stare as Dad just offended my newly acquired acquaintance. "Her. Dad, it is her. Please refrain from calling her a him out of respect, and I was unaware I was supposed to provide a name." My legal guardian is baffled at my response, as would anybody else be, I presume. After reflecting on it, I have come to the realization that I was a bit harsh on Dad. Please forgive me as this was never my intention. "You- You do not have to call him- Apologies, her anything. Just a suggestion that is all." He says while simultaneously extending his hand as his initial thought is for me to latch onto it, I presume. I happily carry out the act of holding Dad's hand as we depart from our newly acquired acquaintance.

Upon approaching the main route, I beg Dad for us to go see the gorillas next; he says that is unethical due to our current location. I disagree, of course. I think it is an absolutely doable and plausible mission to achieve. "This is no discussion; I am going to see the gorillas! It would be wonderful if you could accompany See-Threepio and me, but I understand if you would like to see your animal of choice." We slowly distance ourselves away before I knew Dad finally had to give in to my demand.

"The things I do for you, Sophia Rey!" Whenever someone follows your first name by your middle, that is when you know things are not going according to plan. But on the contrary, I know that if Dad were to get into a heated argument with me, there is always an 87% chance I would always come out victorious. In public places, that is. I know it is not a 100% guarantee, but I will take those odds over Dad's any day. He would rather let me get my way with my misbehaviors if it all out prevents one of my episodes from occurring. I much prefer that option as well; I am not trying to get escorted out before seeing the gorillas. If I was with Mother, I would immediately comply with her. But since Dad is still in the process of understanding my superpower, I can persuade him to almost always give in to my requests. Do I feel bad for him? Do I feel some sort of guilt for taking advantage of him like this? Of course, I do. But I will use this to my advantage for as long as I am capable of doing so. Here, if it makes the reader become more compassionate towards my ruthless demeanor, this will be the last time I will abuse my persuasive power over him. I promise.

Anxious to pass people, my feet begin to accelerate my movement. I hear Dad shout out to me but transmits as cryptic. From a logical standpoint, I know I should wait up for Dad. What if he has something worth saying? But at the moment, I throw all sense of logic out the metaphorical window and continue to race down the narrow asphalt pathway. I am ashamed to admit that I fail to create an exponential distance between my caregiver and me due to a foreign instrument. This newly established barricade is halting traffic, sooner or later, there will be a major accident, and I do not want to be an accomplice of it whatsoever. So out of respect, I advise you to move this obstruction out of the walkway. My frantic gestures implement no reaction… of course. C3PO suggests I should just ask the woman to move to the side. A viable option for a normal person… but he fails to recall that I struggle with intensive social anxiety, and I am anything but normal... So now that option is as good as dead. In an attempt to surpass the obtuse three-wheeled mechanism, my body essentially derails the contraption off the guided path.

After that gentle shove, I cannot recall a single event that transpired within the next five to ten-minute duration. My brain rapidly loses oxygen, resulting in my eyes rolling in the back of my head...so I am told by Dad, who is later confirmed by the onsite medical professionals. He explains to me within the confines of the zoo infirmary that I had a severe episode that caused me to faint beside a woman with a stroller. No amount of brain damage is apparent, which is always a good sign. Though I will have to deal with these skinned knees and bruised arms all throughout the duration of our fully scheduled day. The stroller I do remember. If that was eliminated from the equation, we would not be in this current predicament now, would we? We would already be seeing the gorillas!

As it turns out, I determine this was the most appropriate moment to announce we are now extremely close (13 steps approximately but seven if you include lunges) to my desired enclosure. I am grateful they went with the decision to relocate me from my prior coordinates, after all. Jumping to my feet as time plays a vital factor, I am soon made apparent by my unexpected detour. I grab a cup of water on the way out, and I thank the workers for assisting me in a time of need and also Dad for being by my side when I need him most in this desperate time even though I expose no emotion his way.

When we approach the long-awaited exhibit, an onpour of viewers are distinct in their footsteps nearing my position behind us. "Sophie! Look! The Night Hunters' house. Come on, let's go see them after" invested by my derivative ancestor, my focus obviously relies elsewhere. "No." Puzzled, I would imagine; Dad is late to comprehend my rebuked response. "What do you mean, no!? Young lady, we have seen all of your exhibits so far. I want to at least see one of mine, and that is final!" My denial for approval grows to intensify further as I revoke him from his desired duty. "No." Finally, he pulls a card out of the deck I never thought he would be capable of doing. If Mother were here, she would most definitely have a talk with this stingy character if that type of behavior ever occurred around her. "Okay.

Well, I am going in. You stay here with the gorillas." And just like that...I am now considered an independent.

Gorillas are interesting animals, I do have to admit but not as interesting as I originally expected. Dwelling on the claim I made earlier, these primates are nothing more than unevolved ancestors of homo sapiens. They provide nothing special to the species itself. I can walk on all fours if I concentrate considerably, and Mother used to say I was an excellent climber when I was younger. Why else do you think my room, let alone the bed itself, is a downgraded jungle gym? I quickly grow uninterested in these creatures and stroll through the park with the protocol droid for the first time without someone breathing down my neck!

It is a shame I do not possess the map anymore; I should have confiscated it back from Dad while in recovery. Who needs a map anyway though, there is no better sense of adventure if you are incapable of navigating… am I right? Threepio suggests we continue on the main path for Dad to have a simpler time to locate us later, while I suggest we explore down a nearby secluded path where our feet have not wondered before. To my shock, we did not have to walk very far to encounter the next animal. I like these guys, relatively smaller than I originally presumed, but the intricate color scheme makes up for their size.

Says on this identification sign here this species is called a: Red Panda. "Red Pandas! See-Threepio! That is Riley's favorite animal. I cannot wait to tell him I have officially seen them with my own two eyes and not through a computer screen this time!" Curiosity soon gets the best of me as I am unable to align one puzzle piece with the rest of my metaphorical puzzle. How come they sleep for an extensive period.

The investigation only commences upon my own terms; I have concluded that these animals are nocturnal and crepuscular mammals. For the uneducated ones, nocturnal means that they rest during the day and are active during the night. Crepuscular is practically the same thing but worded fancier and much more sophisticated. Similar to its distant cousin, the panda bear, the red panda species are also bamboo eaters, which I find interesting as that being one of the rare comparisons between the two. Although I have to agree with the giant pandas on this one; the red pandas color scheme is exquisite and makes it difficult for predators to spot them. The orange intertwines with the black so well it is nearly camouflage.

The protocol droid agrees with me; I am glad we are both on the same page here. "I wish Riley was here to create this memory with me. I cannot imagine a world without my best friend involved in it. You do not feel as highly of Riley as I do, do you, Threepio? That is okay. I have learned the hard way that not you are not going to like everybody or vice versa. That is just the way life goes, and that is perfectly fine. You only need one good friend in this life." Amadeus and Corduroy are an addition to my circle of friends, but I would not consider them as close as I am with Riley. I was once extremely close with Corduroy, but we have since drifted apart due to unfortunate circumstances. I would still consider Amadeus, and I close, do not get me wrong. But not as significant as I consider his son to be me.

Epilogue

There is a red panda that See-Threepio is lucky enough to spot who is currently active in proceeding to climb a complex tree with various branches sticking out, leading to a fatal fall for anything of that size. It leaps from one limb to another effortlessly, probably because of its bushy tail providing eloquent equilibrium. According to the informative plaque, Firefox is a nickname of theirs due to their size and orange colors. Guess that explains where the web browser of the same name got its inspiration from. Mr. Panda. That is what I decided to name this character, I know, super original. Anywho, Mr. Panda here props himself up, elongated across a hefty branch enjoying an appetizer before an early dinner. I will let him have the same luxury as I do as I would also not like to be disturbed when I am eating. Until we meet again, little firefox.

Continuing to venture through the zoo further, we come across the polar bears. I was made unaware that the zoo was occupying this specific variant of bear here. How is this animal to survive in such a warm climate compared to its native habitat? C3PO says that it is out of my jurisdiction to answer, let alone ask. I know Threepio, it is called a divergent question. They are unintended to have a directive answer. Amongst the crowd, my eyes fixate on the female bear as she transfers from one of the four elements into another. Now damp and oversaturated, she is reliant only on her ability to stay buoyant. Every muscle works in unison then quickly dissipate, for she submerges under the below-freezing water before my mind can officially absorb the depicted action taking place. Polar bears are accustomed to the frigid temperatures and-

My feet fail to provide equilibrium, thus resulting in a domino effect. The person who was originally in front of me just collided with the person in front of them and so on until the person all the way in the front row faceplants into the glass to where one of the female polar bears is currently getting their cardio in.

Wait! Did the reader believe any of that?! That was an elaborate exaggeration I made up to make the dull transpired event seem elusively interesting. I did bump into the person in front of me, yes, but that is as far as it went.

"Oh, excuse me, Miss… Sophia! What a dandy it is to see you here." A man with a mobile garbage bin and broom enters the area amongst the now disproportionate crowd. My eyes gaze at the man's uniform: A dark green polo shirt representing the place of employment underneath a track jacket of the same design supported by khakis and a baseball cap. "And you are…" He is offended by my answer and therefore filters the time by finishing his interrupted duty as he (from what I can only presume) formulates his next response. "It's Clarence, you know, from the bus the other day." In the most composed manner I have ever managed to ever compile out in public, I kindly ask him to refrain from using literary conjugations as that is a, if not *the* pristine factor in triggering an unwanted episode. Correction, all of them are unwanted though I digress. "Guess you do not bump into familiar faces here often." I respond in a cool and collected manner. My alluding pun results in a crackle from the "untouchable" man as society has heartbreakingly deemed these people to be of a lesser than human status over time.

Tragic does not even come close to a word I would describe Clarence's situation; my deepest sympathy goes outward to you, my friend. "Apologies. You have my most sincere, compassionate affection, sir. I did not recognize you with that uniform on. I never expected someone like you to be working." His appalled expression halts my forthcoming statement from entering into reality. "What are you insinuating, Sophia?! That I am unable to work due to my job status and low salary!" The protocol droid who I have yet to expose signals for a release from a detrimental grip I currently have him in, damaging his circuits and wiring. In an instant, I dart down to see if he is still functional; and then direct my attention back at Clarence. "Uh- Your misinterpretation of my statement is embarrassing, sir." The custodian is vigilant on behalf of me. "-due to this windy climate, I should have specified." A deep sigh initiates in his core and is quick to resolve this minor miscommunication. "Are you here by yourself? You here with the same boy I saw you with on the bus?" Just as I am to admit my current adventure partner, the artificial intellectual droid and I have had, we hear a ring from his radio.

"All units report. We have a code Adam, I repeat, code Adam. The victim was last spotted at the gorilla enclosure daunting a pink beanie, a red turtleneck sweater, with snowflake design leggings and Uggs. Report back if you have seen this young girl, please. The girl's father is frantic."

Clarence suddenly looks up and down at me. "Plan on starting a life of crime early, I see. Take it from someone who has been through the wringer. It is not worth it." The zoo employee grabs my hand and escorts me to a nearby bench, while we patiently wait for Dad to come. Too ashamed to make eye contact, I create distance between us and the bench. "Do you think I am a bad person Clarence?"

He instantly positions himself the same exact way I am (hunched over and staring down into the abyss) after I just perplexed his cognitive organ with such a demoting question. "Whoever said anything about you being a bad person Sophia because I know for a fact I certainly did not. I think you are rebellious, but everybody is at your age. You are a teenager for goodness sake." I thank Clarence for some provided reassurance, and when I finally do look up after some duration, I spot Dad amongst the crowd. He comes over to our location and thanks Clarence for watching over me. I quickly wave my friend goodbye and watch as he soon disappears around the corner and presumably continues what is required of him.

"Why did you leave the enclosure? What did I say about not moving from where you were at!" A pit of rage consumes me, but I reluctantly drown that out. "Never did I confirm or deny your claim. I merely acknowledged the statement. You had no way of enforcing your rule. What you should have done was to ask someone to watch me, in order to provide that sense of a constant enforcer. However, as we all know now, that never occurred." Imbecile!

August was saying his favorite animal was something of a zebra and giraffe mixed. Sounds like a hybrid theory if you ask me. He is delusional beyond the point of no return. The zebras are in no way obscure from my view as I occasionally look past Dad from one of his overdramatic lectures. "Sophia Ray Parker! Do not run off like that ever again! You made Daddy very worried. Maybe I should have had someone watch you. I can no lo-" Hesitant as ever as he finds the right moment to remind himself of his dominance through this minor altercation of ours." Do you hear me, young lady! Are you even retaining any of this!? You listen to me. You may have thought it was the other way around, but oh no. I am the parent, and you are the child. The child is supposed to obey the parent and not the other way around." Dad is firm in the way he presents, and I applaud him for his effort, but I find him quite boring and repetitive if you want my opinion.

As I was saying before, I got rudely interrupted; August Parker identified the species as an okapi; the ones located next to the zebras. I very much enjoy saying the name aloud. The letters roll off the tongue, surprisingly smooth. I should have been respectable to Dad, but I fall short due to my negligence. If I had an opportunity to where I am able to teleport back in time seconds prior to my devious adventure, I would emphasize that he should hire a stranger to keep an eye on me before he does his own thing to see his desired Night Hunters exhibit.

Patient in my efforts, I find a more than pristine opportunity to postpone this little father-daughter discussion of the implications of rules and what could have happened involving my runaway but ultimately did not occur. "Oh, wow! Look at this one, Dad." The child inside of me consumes my being in all that I present to the world for the time being and get as close to the mesmerizing animal as possible without putting myself in harm's way, of course.

The common misconception is perfectly understandable when classifying the okapis to a deranged zebra because of its reminiscent striped markings on the lower extremities. I would have made the same mistake if it was not for Mr. Parker. After further examination, I do have to conclude that both do appear very similar, if not identical, at certain times.

Dad is quick to forgive me for my prior depicted actions; that is one of the many qualities about him that I love. I am proud that he accepts me just the way I am. Most people turn the other direction when confronting a *lonely* individual. Dad is one of the good ones. I turn and face my legal guardian after examining the animal for some time. "Just for you, Dad. I will name him. What do you think of the name Gilbert?"

"He does look like a Gilbert!" He then exclaims though Dad's thumb of approval is all the reassurance I need. The shy native forest dweller cowers at the back end of the enclosure in between two boulders for a sense of shelter from the wicked whirling winds. I do not blame Gilbert one bit; I wish I had that type of luxury right about now. Mesmerized by my new friend, I continue to be in awe of him as I glance to observe Dad doing the same. He then extends his tongue to fetch leaves from safe proximity.

The okapi masticates on leaves for an extended duration. Perhaps their gullets cannot produce enough saliva to disintegrate the excess food, and that is why they resort to leaving it in their mouths for such a long period. This is only a theory, though. I advise you to take everything I am saying about these animals with a grain of salt. Observing this creature for some time now, I can definitely see why this is

August's favorite animal; it resembles him in a lot of ways the more I reflect. They both enjoy isolation, and both are unique in their intricate ways. The okapis and red pandas are going to be my favorite animals after today; they will be interchangeable, of course.... dependent upon what particular mood I am in for that specific day.

It does not take a genius to identify an overstayed welcome when you see one. With a signature swift of the eyes, we send a farewell to Gilbert and then head out the same way we entered from hours before. We travel across the same creaky yet surprisingly sturdy wooden bridge and take all the necessary safety precautions once we enter in the motorized vehicle. Dad and I put his wheelchair in the bed of the truck, and he makes his way back to the driver's seat while I head towards the same seat I was in before. That was a splendid way to perform a Saturday. I do hope we can do this again at some point in the future. The ride home is relatively quiet as it usually is. Luckily, this time we did not hit any lights, so we did get back to the house in record time.

Holding open the car door for me like a real gentleman, I then repay the favor to Dad by holding open the front door; it is the least I could do for him. He thanks me just before I return to my room to reposition C3PO. Placed on the right corner of my desk below the confines of my bed. There he sits, waiting for a change in the typical Cincinnati forecast to take place. Dad initiates the use of Morse code before entering my room. It is his train ticket, if you will, to board the train. For old times' sake, I am guessing. He enters to only then stay stationary in the middle of the room, holding onto my bed for that sense of support until we make the house officially wheelchair accessible. "Sophia, I have done some thinking….." Whenever anyone starts off like that, it usually does not result in any good amount of news.

I advise you to be extremely particular in your wording. " A lot as a matter of fact. About what I said to you about California." A long drawn-out pause is implemented then a sigh before he finds the precise words to expel from his lips.

"I did not come to realize how important Riley and Amadeus mean to you, honey. So, I did some work on the side and found a job here close to the city." Before he can get another word out, my feet are already making way to him. "I am not done yet, Sophie. Hold on, there is more. You are going back to school with Riley! You start back this Monday." The wrap around Dad and the shower of tears does not nearly express what I am currently feeling. I am unsure if anything comes close.

I look at him in a shower of disappointment, for I am only able to focus on the most important factor if all of this news is to be true. "Where will we be staying?" He pivots his head around the room, signifying the only obvious answer. "Here. The court endorsed the property of Mother's half for me. But do not think that this does not come with a price Sophia. Amadeus told me about you and your addiction. *Now* I think I understand why you did not want to go last week to your appointments. I was curious as to why he set up two in a week; presumably, I thought it was an error. Now we know the real truth. This is an extremely serious case of Adderall addiction. Do not take this information lightly. So, your end of the bargain will be for you to attend Amadeus twice a week for as long as it takes for you to become sober." My glossy eyes stay concentrated on Dad's general direction. "I happily oblige."

2,413 miles away lies August's home in California, and I am okay with that. August ultimately found reconciliation; my beloved found someone just like him. Someone with the same condition as him. He knows now that he is not going through the complex thing we call life, isolated anymore. All of this time, I have been searching for someone who is a figment of my twisted reality. I created August Parker to serve as someone who accepts me the way I am without question and who will love me unconditionally because prior to this; I had come to the conclusion that a real-life August Parker simply does not exist. It is too good to be true. Luckily, in the end, I was wrong. An individual with all the same redeeming qualities of August has been present ever since the beginning of myself purchasing Corduroy, but I was always in denial of the real truth. Because sometimes the truth can be a difficult pill to swallow. Everybody has an August out there in the vast universe. You just need to change your perspective.

About the Author

    R. A. Milner was born and raised in Morgan Hill, California. He is currently attending Sonoma State University with a degree in early childhood studies with an emphasis on development.